# DARK SECRETS

SALLY RIGBY

TOP
DRAWER
PRESS

CRIME FICTION BOOKS

# GET ANOTHER BOOK FOR FREE!

To instantly receive the free novella, **The Night Shift**, featuring Whitney when she was a Detective Sergeant, ten years ago, sign up for Sally Rigby's free author newsletter at www.sallyrigby.com

## Chapter 1

Detective Chief Inspector Whitney Walker stood at the entrance to her lounge, watching Tiffany hold her four-week-old daughter in her arms. Ava was Whitney's grand-daughter, and she was the cutest little dot imaginable, with a shock of dark curls. Being a grandmother was weird, especially at her age, but Whitney was enjoying it more than she'd ever believed possible.

She'd booked five weeks off work as soon as soon as Tiffany had gone into labour, knowing that the first few would be the hardest. The labour hadn't been easy, over forty hours, but Tiffany had been amazing, and was taking to motherhood so well. Whitney couldn't be prouder.

Whitney was a single parent too, although she'd had the support of her mum and dad, when she'd given birth at only seventeen. It had totally changed her life, and she'd gone from intending to go to university to shelving those plans and instead going straight into the police force. But she didn't regret it. She had a good career, with a loyal team and a very good friend whom she wouldn't have met otherwise. Dr Georgina Cavendish, a forensic psychologist from Lenchester University who helped them with their more critical cases.

Whitney had loved her time being at home with Tiffany and baby Ava. She'd have put money on her itching to get back to work by now, but she'd barely given work a thought the entire time. And on the handful of times she'd called to check in, there was nothing the team had needed her for. Considering Lenchester was like the murder capital of the country because of the number they had, someone had been looking down on her while she was having some time off.

Damn. Why did she think that? She'd jinxed it. She pushed the thought to the back of her mind and refocused on her family.

Tiffany glanced over at her. 'What is it? Why are you smiling like that?'

'I'm allowed to, aren't I? It's wonderful watching my daughter and granddaughter together.' Her eyes welled up, and she blinked the tears away. Would Ava inherit her emotional gene? Tiffany hadn't. She was made of sterner stuff.

'You're not getting soppy in your old age, are you?' Tiffany asked, grinning.

'You know me. I've always been a heart-on-the-sleeve person.'

'I couldn't have done any of this without your help, Mum. But you already know that don't you?'

'It's been a joint effort so far. When I go back to work it's going to be down to you for a lot of the time.'

'I'll manage. I have to. Providing today isn't an indication of what she's going to be like. I think she's cried more this morning than she has done in her whole four weeks. Hopefully, she's cried herself out because she's now settled.' Tiffany grazed her fingers over the tiny baby's cheek, and her lips turned up into a loving smile.

'How are you finding being a mum?' Whitney realised that she hadn't actually asked Tiffany outright how she was feeling.

'Honestly, it was a massive shock at first. Even having you here all the time, nothing could have prepared me for being responsible for another human being 24/7. I don't feel old enough to look after myself, let alone someone else.'

'It happens to every new mother. Any woman who denies it is kidding themselves. It's something you must experience for yourself. No number of words from anyone else could've prepared you. It's a rite of passage. But look at you now. A natural.'

'Thanks. I had a good role model.'

'Has Lachlan been in touch yet?'

He was Ava's father. They'd met in Australia when Tiffany was out there and they'd both come back to the UK determined to make a go of it when they found out about the baby. But he missed Australia, and they'd split up. He'd returned home, promising to keep in touch.

'I heard from him this morning. He said he couldn't afford the airfare to come over to see us.' Tiffany shrugged. 'It's what I expected. What time's Martin coming round?'

Martin was Tiffany's father, who she'd only recently got to know. For many years, Whitney had denied his exis-tence, saying her pregnancy was the result of a drunken one-night fling. And she'd truly believed that to be the case. Except, when she'd met Martin again over twenty years later at a school reunion, the one and only time either of them had been to one, she'd been shocked to learn that the truth was very different from what she'd told herself. It turned out that he'd wanted to continue seeing her but, in typical teenage style, Whitney had assumed he wouldn't because of what they'd done, and she'd pushed him away.

Martin lived in London now, and they'd started seeing each other again. They were taking it steady because Whitney wasn't ready for a full-on relationship yet. Life was too busy. Martin was a widower and didn't have any children, despite trying. He was beside himself with joy when he'd learnt about Tiffany. He'd waited until she was ready to meet him and, once she'd agreed, they'd become close very quickly. They were so similar in many ways.

As if on cue, the doorbell went.

'Now, by the sounds of things.'

Whitney went to the door and let him in. He kissed her on the cheek and gave her a hug. It felt so right.

'I'm not too early, am I? There was hardly any traffic on the motorway, and it only took me an hour-fifteen from door to door.' They'd arranged to go out for Sunday lunch at a pub in a nearby village.

'Not at all. It's not like we have to put on a show with you. You're part of the family.'

The moment they entered the lounge, he headed straight over to Tiffany and Ava.

'How's my beautiful granddaughter?' he said in a quiet voice.

'I'm about to put her back into her Moses basket. I've fed her, changed her, and she's finally asleep. Hurray. I thought it was never going to happen.'

'What time do you want to leave for lunch?' Martin asked.

'In case you haven't noticed, I'm still in my PJs, so you'll have to give me time to shower and get ready.'

'You take your time, we're not in a hurry.'

'I'm so looking forward to it. This will be the first time I've gone out for a meal since coming home from the hospital. I hope Ava doesn't cry all the time. We won't be popular with the other diners if she does.'

'She's fed, changed, and now sleepy. If she does wake up, we can take it in turns to wheel her pushchair around. Don't worry. I'm sure we won't be the only people there with a young one. We've picked a good day for it. You go get ready, and I'll keep an eye on her,' Whitney said.

'I'm on my way.'

Tiffany had taken two strides towards the door when Whitney's phone rang.

Whitney went over to the sideboard where she'd left it and stared at the screen. 'Crap. It's work. They were under strict instructions not to disturb me unless it was absolutely necessary.'

She glanced at Martin and then Tiffany. She'd gone and jinxed it, just like she thought she would. Bloody typical.

'Answer it, Mum,' Tiffany said.

'Walker. And this better be good,' she snapped, sounding harsher than she'd intended.

'Sorry to bother you, guv, especially on a Sunday and you also being on leave and not wanting to be disturbed, but this is important.'

'It's all right, Brian. Just tell me what's wrong,' she said to Detective Sergeant Chapman, a fairly recent recruit to her team who was turning out to be a valuable asset in more ways than one.

'A family has been found dead at their home in the Westcliffe area. Suspicious circumstances.'

Her fingers tightened around her phone. 'The *whole* family?'

'I don't know if it was all of them. All I've been told is that five people, including children, were found dead, sitting around the dining room table.'

Her stomach plummeted. Children? What on earth had happened?

'Any signs of struggle? Cause of death? Anything?'

Had they been shot, stabbed, or killed in any other obvious way?

'You know everything I do, guv. I've only just put the phone down from the officers who called to let me know.'

Hardly surprising, and she shouldn't have asked, because until the pathologist was there, they wouldn't know.

'You did the right thing calling me. What's the address? I'll meet you there.'

That was the end of her annual leave. She hoped Tiffany wouldn't mind.

'Beech Avenue, number 96.'

That should only take her ten minutes.

'Thanks, I know the area. I'll see you shortly.' She ended the call and turned to Tiffany and Martin, who were both staring in her direction, with resigned expressions on their faces. 'I'm sorry, you two, but I've got to go to work, as you've probably worked out. There's been a death. Several in fact, most likely from the same family and including kids. If I don't go, they might pass the case onto a different team and I can't let that happen.'

Murder cases were always given to her team because of their exemplary reputation for solving them. There were kids involved. She couldn't allow this to go elsewhere.

'That's dreadful, Mum,' Tiffany said, glancing over to the Moses basket.

'Sorry about lunch, I know how much you were looking forward to it.'

'Don't worry, we can still go, if you'd like to, Tiffany?' Martin said.

'Yeah, I'd love to. I've been looking forward to going out for days. I've already planned what I'm going to order.'

Whitney offered a grateful smile in Martin's direction. Thank goodness he was there to take her place.

'Then I'll come back here and stay with you until your mum gets back,' he suggested.

'You can't do that, I might be gone for hours, and you'll need to get back home. You don't want to be driving late in the night,' Whitney said.

'I can certainly stay until early evening, but only if you'd like me to, Tiffany?'

He was so considerate, didn't just take over and assume it would be okay. She approved of the way he sought Tiffany's permission first.

'That's great, thanks, Martin. I'd love to spend the day with you. I knew I had to get used to being on my own soon, it's just come a week ahead of schedule. You go, Mum, and don't worry about us. In fact, we'll think of you while we're tucking into home-made pizza and chips and you're having a sandwich on the fly. If that.' Tiffany smirked.

'Don't remind me. You're not the only one who was looking forward to this outing. Even though I know that's not what you'll be ordering.'

Tiffany was much healthier in her meal choices than Whitney.

'Yeah but saying salad didn't have the same impact.'

'True. Anyway, we'll arrange another time for all of us to go out. Enjoy yourselves and remember, I'm on the end of a phone if you need me for anything.' Whitney wandered over to where Ava was sleeping. 'See you later, little one. Love you.'

'Bye, Mum. Knock 'em dead.' Tiffany's hand shot up

to her mouth. 'Oops, sorry, wrong choice of word. You know what I mean.'

Whitney left home and drove to the scene. She already knew it was going to be a case she'd like George involved with, but the forensic psychologist had gone to London to visit her family. They wanted her assistance with something. It had to be serious for them to demand George's presence. But knowing her friend, she'd want to be informed. After Whitney had been to the scene, she'd decide whether to do so straight way or to wait a while.

# Chapter 2

Whitney drove to the modern, detached house in Beech Avenue, in the Westcliffe area of the city. When she arrived, she parked behind the MGC belonging to Dr Claire Dexter, the pathologist.

Thank goodness it was Claire on duty, and not one of the other pathologists, as this case was going to hit the headlines with force. Brian was standing by the cordon, which went across the drive, talking to one of the uniformed officers who were milling around. She got out of her car and walked over.

'Were you first on the scene?' she asked the police constable who was standing by the rendezvous point, controlling the entry and exit to the house.

'Yes, guv. I was on patrol with Sandy, PC Hall, when we got called out here. The others arrived soon after and are making sure the scene is kept secure.'

'Who's inside?' she asked glancing at the visitors' log in the officer's hand.

'The pathologist arrived ten minutes ago. Forensics haven't turned up yet.'

'Have you looked, Brian?' Whitney asked, turning to her sergeant.

'Not yet, I was waiting for you, guv. As soon as I saw Dr Dexter's car I knew to steer clear.'

'Wise move, I'm pleased to see you're learning fast.' She grinned.

Everyone knew what Claire was like and most were petrified of her. Not Whitney or George. They were too long in the tooth for that.

'Who found the bodies?'

'A friend of one of the deceased children who lives across the street. PC Hall is over there with him. We wanted to make sure he was with his family and kept out of the way.'

'Who was on the scene when you arrived?'

'The boy who found them and his mother. He'd gone back to fetch her and she called from outside the house where they waited for us, as instructed by emergency services.'

'How old is the boy?'

'I'm not sure, but I'd put him as early teens, no older.'

'How much did he tell you?'

'His mother mainly spoke. She said that he'd arranged to go round this morning to call for his friend and went through the side gate to the back door, as he usually did. After no one answered, he went inside as it was unlocked and found the family.'

'The poor kid. We'll go over and question him shortly. If he went inside via the back door, who opened the front?' She nodded towards it.

'I did, guv, to preserve the scene as much as possible. Because the back door was unlocked and the front wasn't I assumed that was the way the killer got in and out.'

'Unless they used a key,' Whitney said.

'Oh …' the officer said.

'Forensics will tell us. You did the right thing. We still have to enter and exit the house.' She turned to Brian. 'Let's go to see Claire.'

They signed the log, and ducked under the cordon tape, heading to the front door.

'Hello,' she called out, walking through the entrance porch into a square hall.

'In here. You can stand by the entrance but no further until I say,' Claire yelled, her voice coming from an open door on the right.

Whitney grinned to herself. Nothing ever changed. It was a comforting thought.

They took a few steps forward until they were standing in the opening to the dining room.

'Good morning, Claire.'

'Is it?' the pathologist said, giving one of her stock answers. She glanced up from behind the camera in her hand and glared at them.

Beneath her white coverall, there peeped out some purple trousers, and in her ears swung a pair of pink elephant earrings.

Claire was well known for her dislike of early call-outs, but this wasn't too bad.

'It could've been worse. You could have been called out ages ago. You were on duty, weren't you?'

'Well, yes, I'm on duty, obviously. That's why I'm here. What a ridiculous question to ask. All I'm saying is on a Sunday morning I don't need to be faced with five deaths to investigate. Any day, for that matter.'

Whitney swallowed hard. *Five*. It was her worst nightmare come true, and she was dreading the fallout once the media got hold of the story.

'May we step closer to take a look?'

'Three steps only. And I don't mean whacking big strides. I don't want this place contaminated,' Claire said.

'At my height, big strides are impossible. And I do know the protocol for these things. I've been in the job long enough.'

She took the three steps, with Brian following her, and surveyed the scene.

Five bodies, a man and woman who appeared to be in their forties, and three children, two boys and a girl, who all looked to be in their early to mid-teens. They were seated around a rectangular dining table, with six chairs, only one of them vacant. The table was covered in a white tablecloth, and on top were plates, each with an untouched meal of lamb shanks in front of them. Two shanks standing upright and crossed. She was too far away to see what else was on the plate. A full glass of red wine in front of each one, including the children. The victims were all upright in their chairs, tied by rope, with their heads lolling to the side.

'What on earth … any idea as to cause of death? I don't see any blood.'

'Seriously, Whitney? You expect me to tell you before I've done a full investigation back at the morgue? You've only just told me you're familiar with protocols and here you are asking for a guess.'

'You might have an idea *off the record*. And it's not like we haven't discussed these things in the past.'

'That was before the latest remit from on high. There have been some serious leaks regarding causes of death at various forces around the country and we've been given strict instructions to keep our thoughts to ourselves.'

'Including to me? You know I'm not going to leak to anyone, and neither would any of my team.'

'It wasn't from Lenchester. These things happened in London and also Newcastle.'

'Okay, so what *are* you going to tell me?'

'There are no overt signs of death, so I suspect it could be some form of drug overdose. And that really is all I'm going to say on the matter.'

'How could they all have been drugged and still be seated at the table? Wouldn't they have been moved post-mortem, or at least post-drugging?'

'If that was the case, I'd say they were placed in these positions after death, for ease of movement,' Brian said.

'It wouldn't be easy to move the father, he's a big man. Claire?'

'Yes?'

'Were they moved before or after death?'

'It's a possibility they were moved post-mortem, but until I can check the lividity, I won't know.'

'It could be a murder-suicide. One of the family drugged all of the food,' Brian suggested.

'But the meals in front of them appear untouched. How would they have been drugged?'

'In their drinks?'

'The glasses are full and don't look as if they've been touched either. Having said that, we can't dismiss anything. From what we can see, though, I'd say that it's leaning towards them being drugged first and then seated at the table.' She glanced at Claire who was glaring at her. 'Obviously, we'll wait for confirmation from you. We need forensics to do their job and then we'll know more.'

'Finally, you accept that making suppositions is a waste of both of our times. Now if you've finished, I need to get on.'

'Before we go, what about approximate times of death?'

'Judging by the rigor, I'd put it at between eight and two, but I'll know more later.'

'Were they all killed at the same time?' Brian asked, craning his neck, and leaning forward. Would Clare complain?

'Which bit of *I'll know later* don't you understand?' Claire snapped.

Whitney turned to Brian and gave him a *shut up* look.

'I still think it could be murder-suicide.' he continued.

'And we won't discount it. Except whoever did it would've tied themselves up after restraining the others? Is that even possible?'

'It's not impossible. I'll know more when I investigate the knots and how each person was restrained,' Claire said.

'We're going to the kitchen. Have you looked there yet?'

'No. The bodies are here. And that's where I'm focusing my efforts. Where's Dr Cavendish, I'd have thought this would be right up her street? The meal, the way the bodies have been left. Definitely one for her.'

'I agree, but George is currently with her parents and unavailable. I'll let her know, though, because she'll want to be a part of the investigation if it's possible.'

Before Whitney and Brian left the dining room, she took a quick look around to see if there were any signs of a disturbance. There were modern paintings on the walls, all of which were hanging straight. On the sideboard were glass ornaments and several photos of the family. One on a skiing trip, one at Disney World, and one which appeared to have been taken at a wedding. These could easily have been displaced if there had been a fight as the room wasn't that big. But there was no evidence that a struggle had taken place. Everything appeared to be in order.

She swallowed the lump in her throat.

14

What the hell had the family done to warrant something so horrendous? Were they targeted or just unlucky to have been chosen?

'This is so sick,' Brian said. 'Those poor kids.'

'Not just the kids. The whole family. Can you imagine if there was another child who wasn't home? They'd be left as an orphan. I hope it was all of them,' Whitney said.

'If there's a missing child they could've been the one to commit the crime.'

'True. We'll know soon enough, though. Let's find the kitchen. I imagine it will be at the back of the house.' They returned to the hall and headed towards an open door at the rear.

The kitchen was ultra-modern with white floor-to-ceiling cupboards and an island in the middle with chrome and leather stools leaning against one side. It looked brand new. Everything was perfect, and again nothing appeared to be out of place. The small sitting room part had two oatmeal-coloured sofas facing one another with a low coffee table in between.

'Was the meal prepared in here? Everything is spotless,' Whitney said, looking around and seeing no signs of cooking having taken place. 'Unless the meal was cooked elsewhere and brought in for them to eat. Or not eat,' she added.

'This is so weird,' Brian said. 'Everything's so tidy. It's like a show home. But they lived here.'

'It makes no sense to me either. You should see my house and kitchen.'

'Mine too,' Brian agreed, nodding.

'I assume that's where the kid who found them came in,' she said nodding towards the open door. 'Unless there's another entrance, but it doesn't look like it. This scene is so bizarre. We could really do with George's input.'

'Yes, guv. But for now you've just got me.'

She glanced at Brian. He was frowning in her direction. Was he resenting that she'd prefer to be with George than him? She hadn't actually said that. He was a good cop, but George brought a different approach and had skills neither she nor Brian had.

She was better company, too, and they'd become firm friends. It was unlikely that would happen between her and Brian. All she knew about him was that he played football, used to work at the Met, and had expensive taste in suits.

'Let's go back to Claire and then head over the road to question the boy who found them.' They returned to the dining room, stopping at the entrance. 'We're going now, Claire. I'll be in touch and will see you at the morgue, hopefully later today or possibly tomorrow.'

The pathologist glanced up.

'Make it tomorrow. Five bodies are going to generate a lot of work before I can even start on the post-mortems. I doubt I'll have time to complete them today, as we've arranged to go out later and it's not something I can get out of.'

The *we* Claire referred to included her husband Ralph, who she'd only recently married, much to everyone's surprise. Whitney had known the pathologist for over ten years, and she'd never known much about her, other than what happened at work. When she had told her and George about the nuptials, you could have knocked them down with a feather. They had yet to meet the man. He had to be something special to cope with Claire and her foibles.

'Somewhere nice?'

'A concert.'

'Who are you seeing?'

'The Lenchester Philharmonic Orchestra. They're performing Vivaldi's 'Four Seasons' at the Opera House.'

'Have fun,' she said, not bothering to ask for further details because Claire would only volunteer information when she decided she wanted to, not when asked.

'I'm sure we will, thank you. Goodbye.' Claire gave her usual dismissive wave, lifted the camera up to her eye and resumed taking photos.

'Let's go,' Whitney said, turning to Brian.

## Chapter 3

Whitney and Brian left the house and crossed the wide road, lined with beech trees, to an identical detached house. Most houses on the Westcliffe estate were similar, having been designed and built by the same developer. Although they were larger than Whitney's semi-detached, she wouldn't want to live in such a characterless area.

'This is going to be a case and a half, guv,' Brian said.

'You're telling me. What on earth happened there? You know what, it's worse somehow than if it was a complete bloodbath. This seemed so calculated.'

'I know what you mean. What sort of sicko would've done it?'

'Whatever *it* is. We'll know more once Claire has done her thing.'

They walked through the open gate up to the front door and rang the bell.

'I still can't get used to the woman,' Brian said, pulling a face.

'Give it time. She grows on you. We've known each other for over ten years, and she's always been the same.

I'll say one thing, you certainly know where you stand with her.'

'Has she always dressed the same?'

Whitney gave a wry smile. 'You think this is bad, you should've seen her when she first started working here. What we see now is tame by comparison. If only I'd thought to take some photos, it——'

She was interrupted by the door being opened by PC Hall.

'Good morning, Sandy,'

'Guv.'

'How's it going in there?'

'Dylan Fletcher, the boy who found the bodies, is quiet and not very responsive. His mother, Mrs Fletcher, is fussing round him and won't leave him alone. In my opinion, he needs time to process what's happened.'

'It's difficult. It's not like they would have dealt with a similar situation before. Is Dylan up to talking to us, do you think?'

'Yes, I think he might be.'

'Good. I'll tread carefully, though. What can you tell me about him, and what else do you know about the situation so far?'

'He's thirteen, but not very mature for his age. If I hadn't known his age, I'd have put him at around eleven. I asked him what he saw and he was able to tell me.'

'Are there any other children in the house?'

'No, he's an only child.'

'Is Mr Fletcher here with his wife and son?'

'No, I haven't seen him. According to Mrs Fletcher, he's out playing golf.'

'Okay, thanks. I'd like you to go back to the crime scene, take a couple of the others and start doing some house-to-house enquiries. Let's hope someone saw something that will assist us.'

'Yes, guv.'

'Before you go, come into the lounge with us and introduce us to Dylan and then arrange for a family liaison officer to come over.'

They followed the officer into the lounge. Whitney tensed at the sight of the boy on the sofa. His eyes were as wide as saucers, staring at her like a rabbit caught in the headlights.

'Mrs Fletcher, this is DCI Walker, and DS Chapman. They'd like to talk to you both about what happened,' PC Hall said to the woman who stood up from being beside the boy and walked towards them.

'Thank you, Sandy. We'll take it from here,' Whitney said.

The officer left the room and Whitney turned to Mrs Fletcher. 'Good morning. We have a few questions to ask you and Dylan.'

'I can't get my head around it. That poor family.' Tears filled her eyes. 'And Dylan finding them, too. It's going to stay with him for the rest of his life. How could it not?'

Whitney could sympathise with how the woman was feeling, but surely she realised that her comments weren't good for Dylan to hear. Yes, of course, it was going to have a massive effect on him, but now wasn't the time to be discussing it. Then again, she'd seen the bodies, too, and was also affected.

Whitney headed over to where the boy was seated and crouched down beside him.

'Hello, Dylan,' she said gently. 'I know this is going to be hard for you, but we need to ask you some questions about what you saw when you went into the Barker house earlier. Is that okay?'

'Yes,' the boy said, nodding.

Whitney sat opposite him and pulled out her notepad from her pocket.

'Can you tell me exactly what happened starting from when you left here and went over to the house? In as much detail as possible, please.'

His fists were clenched in his lap, and he sucked in a loud breath. 'Harvey and I had planned to go to the park to play football today. We'd arranged to meet our friends there.'

'And what time was that?'

'I said I'd call for him at ten so we could walk to the park and meet the others at quarter past.'

'When did you make these arrangements?'

'At school on Friday before we came home. I saw Harvey yesterday morning before we went out shopping, because he was in the garden, and we talked about it again.'

'So, none of your arrangements had been changed?'

'No.'

'Did you check with the other boys that they were still going to meet you?'

'I didn't, but Harvey might have. I don't know.'

'What time did you leave home this morning?'

'I remember hearing the clock in the hall chime as I left, so it was exactly ten. I walked through the gate to the back door of Harvey's house, as I usually do. Mrs Barker always asks visitors to go in that way. They hardly ever use the front door because she says it saves the carpet getting dirty.'

Whitney nodded. 'And then what happened?'

'I knocked a few times, but nobody answered. So I tried the handle, and because the door wasn't locked, I went in. I thought it would be okay. I've done it before, and no one had minded …' His voice drifted off.

'You're doing very well, Dylan. I know this is hard, but let's keep going. Would you like a drink?'

'No, thank you, I've got one.' He picked up an open can of cola from the small table next to the sofa and took a sip.

'What did you do after you walked into the kitchen?' Whitney asked, once he'd finished drinking.

'I called out hello. But there was no reply.'

'And did that concern you?'

'Not really. They might not have heard, and I thought Mrs Barker might still be in bed because she does that on a Sunday sometimes. The same as Keira and Tyler.'

'What about Mr Barker?'

'I wasn't sure about him because he was away a lot and often isn't there.'

'So, thinking back to when you first went into the house, into the kitchen, did you notice anything out of the ordinary?'

She wanted to lead him gently into the time he discovered the bodies, to help the shock of having to relive it.

He frowned, as if mentally examining the scene. 'No. I'm sure it all looked the same as it always does.'

'The kitchen was very clean and tidy. Did you think that to be odd?'

'No. Mrs Barker was very …' He chewed on his bottom lip.

'House-proud,' Mrs Fletcher said, joining in. 'Obsessively so, if you ask me. Not that I want to speak ill of the dead but, seriously, who could live like that day in, day out? I know I couldn't.'

'I understand,' Whitney said. 'What did you do next, Dylan?'

'When I didn't see anyone, I decided to go up to Harvey's bedroom in case he was up there, but on the way I passed the dining room. The door was open, and I could see the back of Mrs Barker. Her head was leaning to the side and looked weird. I walked in to check if everything was okay and that's when I saw them all sitting at the table and …' His words fell away.

Whitney scribbled down her notes, wishing that she didn't have to put the boy through this so soon after it had happened, but time was of the essence in these sorts of cases.

'You're doing really well, Dylan. We've nearly finished. Could you tell me what you did next? Did you touch anything?'

'No. I ran back into the kitchen and out of the house, and then came here to tell Mum.'

Whitney turned to his mother. 'What did you do, Mrs Fletcher?'

'I hurried over to the house with Dylan and left him outside while I went to look. I wanted to check to see if anyone was alive. When I saw all of the bodies, I could see it was too late. I used to be a nurse, that's how I knew they were dead.'

'Then what did you do?'

'I went outside to be with Dylan and phoned 999. They told me to wait for the police to arrive.'

'I understand Mr Fletcher is out playing golf. Did you phone to let him know what had happened?'

'He doesn't take his phone out onto the actual course. None of his friends do. I've left a message for him to come home straight away, but he might go to the bar before checking his phone. I've no idea when he'll be back.'

'What time did he leave this morning?'

'Seven. He goes the same time every week to meet with

23

his friends and play a round. He's usually back by one, in time for lunch.'

'Were you friends with the Barker family?'

'We've known them since we moved here eight years ago.'

'And are there only five of them?'

'Yes. David, Gill, Keira, Harvey, and Tyler.'

That eliminated the theory that one of them could've killed the rest.

'Did you see them socially at all?'

'We'd usually sit together at school events, and sometimes I'd go over for coffee with Gill. Or she'd pop over here. We seldom socialised together in the evenings because we had separate friends.'

'What were they like as people?'

'Nice. Ordinary. You know, like the rest of us around here. Gillian and David were friendly and would always stop for a chat. Gillian would always volunteer to help at any community events. David, too, if he was around. Although his work did take him away a lot.'

'And the children?'

'Well-behaved. They were good kids. I never minded Harvey coming over here. He was always polite and friendly. Like they all were. It's …' She paused for a moment. 'Do you know how they died?'

'The pathologist is there, and she'll make her report to us in due course.'

'She'll have to do a post-mortem on all of them, won't she?'

'That's correct. Have you noticed anyone hanging around the area recently looking suspicious?'

'No. I don't think so. We take neighbourhood watch seriously around here, so even if I haven't seen anything, someone else might have.'

'We're making house-to-house enquiries and should discover if there have been any sightings. If anything comes to mind that you think we should know, please contact me. Here's my card. Dylan, have you seen anyone hanging around here? Or did Harvey mention that he'd seen anything strange going on?'

'No.' He shook his head.

'Mrs Fletcher, what were you doing last night?'

She frowned. 'We had four friends over for dinner. Two couples. Why?'

'We like to check on everyone's whereabouts during investigations like this. Someone may have witnessed something important. What time did your friends arrive?'

'The Andersons were here at half past seven and the Whites ten minutes later. I remember because we laughed about the Andersons being first because they're usually late.'

'What time did they leave?'

'Around midnight, but I can't be totally sure. I'd had a few glasses of wine by then.'

'What were you doing while your parents' friends were here, Dylan?'

'In my bedroom playing video games until I went to bed.'

'Mrs Fletcher, please can you give me the contact details of your friends so we can confirm their timings and to enquire if they saw anything?'

They might also serve as an alibi, but Whitney wouldn't know that until they had Claire's report.

'Yes. Of course.'

Whitney passed over her notebook and the woman wrote down the full names and phone numbers for the two couples.

'We're going now, but we may wish to speak to you

again, Dylan. You've done well. Before we leave, is there anything else you'd like to tell me that I haven't already asked?'

He stared at his mum and then shook his head.

'I'll see you out,' Mrs Fletcher said.

They headed back into the hallway. 'Thank you for your time, Mrs Fletcher.'

'What shall we do now?'

'A family liaison officer will be here soon, and they'll be able to support you. I suggest you look into some counselling for Dylan, as this is likely to affect him for a long time.'

'Yes. Yes, I will.'

'Where to now, guv?' Brian asked once they were outside.

'Back to the station. I'll meet you there.'

She returned to her car and before moving, pulled out her phone. She had to speak to George. This couldn't wait.

## Chapter 4

Dr Georgina Cavendish sat in the drawing room of her parents' home in London pondering the situation the family had found themselves in. Nothing was going to be the same again, and she'd been called back to assist.

Her father had been diagnosed with Parkinson's disease and was no longer able to operate. It had been a huge blow to him, and his patients, as he was a top international cardiac surgeon, courted by heads of state and top celebrities worldwide. He'd also received notice that his court case had been scheduled for six months' time. He'd been charged with tax evasion, along with many other high-profile people. His lawyers were hopeful that he'd avoid a prison sentence, but it wasn't a foregone conclusion. George suspected he'd been told that in order to give him a modicum of hope, although she hoped she was wrong.

She glanced up as her father came into the room. Already his right foot was dragging slightly, and it would soon get worse.

'Oh, there you are,' he said.

'Is there a problem?'

'No. I just wondered what you were doing. Your brother's coming over for dinner tonight for a family conference.'

Her younger brother, also a heart surgeon, was similar to her father in many ways and she would need to bring her *A game*, to quote Whitney, to prevent them from pushing her into a position she didn't wish to be in.

'There's nothing more to discuss. We've been through everything, Father.'

Her parents were deliberately ignoring her advice. It shouldn't be a surprise. It had happened her entire life. Her accomplishments were viewed as second-class when compared with what her parents and brother had achieved. Their attitudes didn't worry her. Ross, her partner, and Whitney were more offended by them than she was.

'Well, I think there is. Considering my prognosis, it would be best for you to move in with your mother and me.'

'There's nothing I can do, Father, as I've already explained.'

'I'm going to be on my own when your mother is working overseas, and we have the mortgage to pay. It's a case of all hands on deck.'

She stared at him. In all her life, he'd never shied away from facing difficulties, but now he was different. This ostrich mentality wouldn't get him anywhere. He had to face his situation.

'You should sell the house and buy something smaller that you can pay for outright.'

He dropped down on the chair opposite her. She'd never seen him so defeated. It was an odd sensation, but he had to deal with this himself.

'I have no desire to move. You could work in London at

one of the universities and contribute to our upkeep. I know the chancellors at all the top places and could arrange something.'

'I'm respected enough in my field not to require an introduction. But it's a moot point, because I'm living with Ross in Lenchester, as you are fully aware.'

'You could both move in here. We have enough room.'

She stifled a groan. She would no more inflict her family on Ross, as she would give up her profession. And that was never going to happen.

'That's neither practical nor possible, Father.'

'What happens when I'm unable to get around? I'll need support.'

'As yet, we don't know your prognosis or how fast it's going to progress.'

'I can no longer operate,' he said, folding his arms.

'But you can still consult. You should consider finding a surgeon who can operate under your guidance. I'm sure there must be someone you've been cultivating for such time as when you retire.'

'No one is ready.'

'Maybe not at the moment, but you must have been tutoring your successor so they can continue your work.'

'Easier said than done,' her father muttered.

Her phone rang, and she pulled it from her pocket. It was Whitney.

'I have to take this call,' she said, glad for a reason to be able to walk away. She left the room and stood in the large, high-ceilinged hall while she answered. 'Hello, Whitney, is everything okay?'

She assumed it wasn't, or the officer wouldn't have contacted her. Her friend was fully aware that George had been summoned to her parents' residence.

'I'm really sorry to bother you when I know you're needed there. How's it all going?'

'It's tricky, but my parents will have to deal with their situation themselves. I can't be there for them all the time, as I've explained.'

'Is that what they want you for? To sort them out. After everything that's gone on between you over the years?'

Even George didn't miss the acute incredulity in Whitney's voice.

'We're having discussions which I hope will soon be resolved. You don't need to hear about my family issues. Why are you calling? Is it important?'

'You could say. I'm not asking for your help, because of the situation you're in. But I'd hate for you to hear about this case in the media and then wonder why you hadn't been informed.' Whitney paused.

George tapped her foot on the ornate Italian floor tiles, waiting for her friend to get to the point. She often had a penchant for the melodramatic.

'I don't have all day, tell me what it is.'

'Sorry. Five deaths all in the same family. It hasn't yet been confirmed that it's murder, but I can't see how it could be anything else. They were all found tied to chairs and seated around the dining room table with an untouched meal in front of them.'

A staged scene. What was the message? Whitney was correct. Her interest was piqued.

'Do you know the cause of death?'

The mode would most certainly be an important factor in determining motive.

'I'm waiting to hear from Claire, but she did suspect that it might be drugs. Until she's had the bodies at the morgue, and she's done her work, she wasn't prepared to commit to an answer.'

'I'm surprised she told you that much.'

'You and me both. But as there weren't any outward signs of death, no blood, or wounds, I think she felt safe in telling me her opinion.'

'Describe the scene to me.'

'Like I said, it's a family of five, two adults and three children, and they were all seated at the table, tied to chairs to keep them from falling.'

'Were there any other family members missing?'

'According to the mother of the boy who found them, the immediate family were all there.'

'Who discovered the bodies?'

'The teenage friend of the middle child. I've just been to see him. In total shock, obviously.'

'I don't doubt. A most disturbing scene to encounter.'

'It's going to be crazy when the news gets out. Five deaths in the same family. It's going to be a media frenzy.'

'In that case, you'll need me back immediately. I'll let my parents know.'

'Are you sure you can up sticks and leave? I thought your parents needed you at home. What is it, by the way, you haven't told me? Unless you're not allowed to.'

She'd forgotten Whitney didn't yet know.

'It hasn't been made public, so this is confidential. My father's been diagnosed with Parkinson's and will be unable to continue with his surgical work.'

'Oh, my goodness. I'm so sorry. Of course, I won't say anything. He must be devastated. How will he cope? I know how important his work is to him.'

George hadn't actually considered how it might affect her father's mental disposition.

'It will take some adjustment, but he has no choice. I hope he has insurance to cover his loss of earnings. It's not something I've had time to discuss. He's also concerned because the date has come through for his court case.'

'Crap. Talk about a double whammy. Is your mum there to help with everything?'

'Yes, but she'll be continuing with her legal work, which takes her all over the world.'

'Is she going to take some time off?'

'I don't believe so. Should she?'

'George, what planet are you on? That's what people in relationships do. I'm sure you'd be there to help Ross, should he need it.'

'This is different. My parents aren't like us.'

'More's the pity, by the sound of it. You should suggest to your mum that she takes some compassionate leave.'

Whitney really didn't understand, but she could hardly blame her. She came from a normal, loving family background.

'They asked me to move back here to assist.'

Voicing it out loud made the idea seem even more ridiculous than it really was.

'So, your mum can continue with her work? What about Ross?'

'He could move here, too.'

'That's bloody stupid. How could he work stuck in the centre of London?'

'They have a basement which he could use for a studio, but they'd have to do something about the lighting.'

'You're talking as if you've decided to go.'

'Not at all, I was answering your query regarding Ross's work.'

'But if you left, that would be the end of us working together.'

'That's exactly why I'm not going,' she said to reassure her.

'You can't be staying because of me because that makes no sense. I know we're friends. Good friends. But even so. I'm not sure I'd make a life decision based on a friendship.'

'There's a whole raft of reasons why I've decided not to go, and that's only one of them,' she clarified, not wanting Whitney to blow it out of proportion.

'I still don't really understand why it's you they need. It's not like they've ever asked you to be at their beck and call in the past. If anything, they've left you to your own devices. Well, apart from when they wanted you there so you could all play happy families for the press when your dad was arrested for the tax evasion. Don't they think about your career at all?'

'My parents aren't good at considering others' needs. My brother and his wife live in London. They will have to help when required. My life and work are in Lenchester.'

'It sounds like you've made a decision. A wise one, at that. When are you proposing to come back?'

'I'll leave later today and will be at the station tomorrow. I'm still on annual leave so it won't affect my work.'

'Wow, I didn't think you'd be coming back that soon. But that's fantastic. I'll see you in the morning.'

George ended the call, a sense of relief washing over her at the thought of leaving the stifling atmosphere of the family home and being back with Whitney and Ross, who understood her and didn't try to force her hand.

Ross would be pleased to see her. She'd call him before breaking the news to her parents.

'Hey, I was just thinking about you. How's it going at Chateau Cavendish?' he asked, answering almost immediately, and using the nickname he'd given to her parents' home following his first visit.

33

'I wanted to let you know that I'll be returning home later today.'

'Cool. How come? I thought you'd decided to stay a little while longer to help your father with the transition.'

'I've had a call from Whitney. There's a case she needs my help on.'

'Oh, that makes sense. Whitney always comes first.'

She bristled. 'What do you mean by that?'

'I'm kidding, George.'

'I didn't realise.'

'You should know me well enough by now. I'm happy you're coming back because I've missed you. It doesn't matter whether it's because of Whitney or not.'

'I'll see you later. I'm looking forward to it, too.' She had missed him, but she wasn't as expressive with her feelings as he was.

'Can't wait.'

She ended the call and returned to the drawing room. Her mother had joined her father.

'I have to return to Lenchester.'

'Why? I thought you were going to be staying for a while,' her mother said, her brow furrowed.

'Some issues have arisen that I need to deal with, and I can't from this distance.'

'Don't tell me it's police work,' her father said, turning his nose up.

How did he know that?

'Yes, it is, Father, and my expertise is required. I also have my university work and Ross to consider.'

'We're your family and we need you.'

What about the times when she'd needed them in the past? Where were they when her best friend had committed suicide at school and George had found her? Or when she'd discovered that she had an issue with blood and was unable to fulfil her dream of following in her father's footsteps and becoming a surgeon. Or when …

*Stop.*

'I've already explained, I'm not in a position to help. You should sell the house and buy something smaller, so you have no mortgage and sufficient money to live on. I assume you have a private pension and insurance for if you can't work, Father.'

She looked at her parents, both staring at her as if she'd asked them to do the unthinkable.

'Yes, I do, but it won't pay anywhere near the same as my surgical work.'

'Then, I repeat, you need to sell this property and adjust your lifestyle. Which you'd have to, anyway, with your illness.'

'That's why we need you here. You're the only one in the family who's lived a more frugal life, so you should be able to guide us.'

'Then listen to me. I will not be moving here. That's not up for negotiation. For the umpteenth time, you should sell the house and buy something small. And when you go out, you don't need to take the best seats when you go to the theatre. Or go to the most expensive restaurants. James is here if you need anything.'

Would her brother be there for them, or was he too concerned with his career? If he was, her parents only had themselves to blame, as they were role models to their children.

'What about when I go overseas, who's going to take care of your father?' her mother asked.

'You thought I was going to come back to look after him to enable you to continue working?'

'You're the one with the least prestigious position.'

'I'm a lecturer at a top university and have an

international reputation. I also assist the police. What you're saying is unfounded. If you're not prepared to give up your position, Mother, then you will have to employ a carer.'

'Do what you want, then,' her father said dismissively.

'I will. Keep in touch and remember what I've said.'

'You're not leaving now, are you?' her mother asked.

'I'm going to pack and will call a taxi to take me to the station after checking the time of the next train.'

Her mother stared at her. 'Thank you for coming here, anyway.'

George blinked away her surprise. Thanks were few and far between in their family. 'I'm always here to advise, but I can't be here all the time. You understand that.'

'Yes, I suppose we do.'

George left and went to her room. It was most odd how the tables had suddenly turned. She would be there for them, but at a distance. She'd go back when the court case was on and she'd help when she could, but she wasn't going to be there when her mother was overseas. They'd have to sort that out for themselves. They could always employ someone to help with her father if he got worse. Her mother earnt more money in a month than most people did in a year.

## Chapter 5

Whitney headed straight for the incident room when she arrived at the station, not even stopping for a coffee. Which she might regret.

'Okay, everyone, eyes towards me. I've just got back from the crime scene, and we need to get cracking. It's—'

'Guv. You're needed in the super's office, pronto. She's already called down twice, wanting to know where you were,' DC Doug Baines called out, interrupting her.

'Why didn't she phone me direct if it was that important?'

'I'm only a lowly DC. She's hardly going to confide in me, is she?' Doug said.

She gave a frustrated sigh. 'Okay, I'll go now. Fingers crossed she won't keep me too long. I'll be back as soon as possible, and we'll get on with the investigation. And, be warned, family life will be at a standstill until this is solved. My gut's telling me this is a big one, and it's seldom wrong.'

'Don't let Dr Cavendish hear you talking about your gut,' Frank, the oldest member of the team, called out.

'She knows me well enough by now.'

Whitney left the office and took the stairs to the floor below where Superintendent Helen Clyde's office was situated. It wasn't like the super to be so demanding. She was actually the best super she'd had. Whitney had butted heads non-stop with Tom Jamieson, Clyde's predecessor. He'd come into the force through the fast-track scheme and had been a pain in the arse from day one. Clyde was different altogether. Although Whitney hadn't enquired about her rise to the dizzy heights of superintendent. She hadn't wanted to in case she didn't like the answer.

Clyde's office door was closed when she arrived, instead of being in its usual half-open position. Did she have someone with her? Should she go and come back later? Doug had said she had to go straight away, so she'd better knock and find out. She gave a double tap on the frosted glass and waited.

'Come in,' Clyde called out.

'Morning, ma'am,' Whitney said, as she entered the room and looked across at the super's desk, which was empty.

Where was she? Her eyes were diverted to a shadow by the window. Crap. Chief Superintendent Grant Douglas stood there. Or *Dickhead Douglas* as she referred to him. She couldn't stand the man, and the feeling was mutual. He'd single-handedly tried to derail her career from the moment she'd joined the Lenchester police force when he was a sergeant.

And all because she'd rejected his advances and his pathetic little male ego couldn't take the embarrassment, or her threats to make him suffer should he ever try again. Which he hadn't.

He'd only recently returned to Lenchester from the Met, following a promotion. It was like someone was testing her. The good thing was, Clyde knew about their altercations and was a buffer between the two of them. Although Clyde wouldn't admit it, Whitney sensed that she didn't have much time for Dickhead, either.

'Come on in, Whitney. We need to speak to you about these latest deaths,' said the super, who was standing to the left of Douglas.

'Yes, ma'am. I've just got back from the scene and will allocate tasks to the team once I get back to the incident room. We need to get onto it pronto before the media finds out.'

'Absolutely. We won't keep you long.'

What was going on?

'Yes, ma'am.'

The super gestured for her to sit at the round table used for meetings. It was large enough to seat ten, so it gave Whitney the space to sit as far away from Douglas as possible. And why was he here? There was no need for his involvement.

When he'd returned to Lenchester, she'd contemplated looking for a post with another force, but it wouldn't have worked. She needed to remain in the city to be close to her mum and brother who lived in residential care homes, and now to be with Tiffany and the baby. Plus, why should she be pushed out of the place she loved working because of a wanker like him?

Whitney had hoped that with the super between them she wouldn't have to see much of him. So, what was he doing there?

Douglas sat next to the super, his arms folded and his narrowed eyes focused on Whitney. If he thought he was intimidating her, then he had another think coming. He was a pathetic twat.

'We have an issue with this case,' the super said.

Whitney frowned. 'Already? What issue?'

The case had literally come to light a couple of hours ago. How could there already be a problem? It made no sense. Surely there hadn't been a leak.

'What I'm about to tell you must be kept out of the media. It will only muddy the waters, and we don't want it to be even more of a circus than it's already destined to be. Five deaths all in the same family, in such bizarre circumstances will have the press camping outside our door 24/7.'

'Do you understand? Because if it does get out, I'm holding you personally responsible. Make sure every member of your team knows,' Douglas said.

'Yes, sir,' Whitney replied just about managing to refrain from rolling her eyes. 'But I do need to know what it is we're dealing with.'

She could do without all the cloak and dagger stuff.

'The victims are cousins of Chief Superintendent Douglas's wife,' the super said, lowering her voice, as if there was someone else in the room.

Whoa. She hadn't expected that.

'I'm very sorry to hear that, sir. Please send my condolences to your wife.'

Her mind was a mass of thoughts, not least that until the case was solved, he'd be like a thorn in her side.

'Thank you, Walker. It's obviously a very distressing time.'

'May I ask how your wife already knows, as details of the deaths haven't yet been released?'

'I happened to be here at the station when the news came in. As soon as I discovered the address, I realised who it was. I went straight home to break the news to my wife and then returned to work. Obviously, having a connection, I can't be seen to be involved in the operation, but I do expect to be kept informed throughout.'

Which meant he was going to be on her back the whole time. And how come he was here on a Sunday?

'I know this is going to be a very difficult time, but I would like to interview your wife to get some background on the family.'

'I expected that. What do you know so far about their deaths?'

'The bodies were found seated around the dining table, tied with rope to the chairs. An untouched meal was placed in front of each of them.'

Douglas paled. 'Do we have causes of death?'

'I'm waiting for confirmation from the pathologist. We discussed it at the scene, and she suspected it to be drug-related, but wouldn't commit herself.'

'Is Dr Dexter still the pathologist?'

'Yes.'

'At least we have the best, even if she's downright rude and infuriating.'

Whitney tensed. She didn't like anyone else speaking ill of Claire in that way, even if it was true. It was like with family. *You* can criticise, but just let anyone else have a go.

'Dr Dexter is one of the best pathologists in the country. We're lucky to have her.'

'Did I say otherwise, Walker? No. What's more important is to find out the cause, and if it was from drugs, who administered them, and why?'

'Yes, sir. Would it be possible to interview Mrs Douglas this afternoon?'

She sensed he didn't want his wife involved, but even he would realise that it was impossible for her not to be.

'I can give you any background information you might need,' he said, looking at the super and not her.

'Sorry, sir, but that's not an option. Mrs Douglas will

have useful information for us, especially as time is of the essence, as you yourself pointed out.'

'I'd rather not bring her to the station. I suggest that we make an appointment for you to interview her at home.'

'I'd rather she came in to see us. Travelling to your home and back will take unnecessary time from my day.'

Whitney glanced at the super. She'd have to sort this one out because there was no way he'd listen to anything she said.

'Walker—'

'Sir, with due respect,' the super interrupted. 'DCI Walker is the senior investigating officer on this case, and we should leave these decisions to her,'

Yes. Whitney refrained from punching the air at getting one over on him.

'Okay, I'll bring my wife in later. We'll interview her in here, Helen. I don't want her sitting in one of the interview rooms, she's too distraught. I'll observe.'

Damn, just what she didn't need. But at least it was better than him giving background information and making decisions regarding what was important, and what wasn't.

'Thank you, sir. I think that's going to be best and will help us with our enquiry. Is that all, ma'am? I need to get back to the team.'

She couldn't get out of there quick enough. And could just imagine the team's response when she told them about Dickhead's wife being involved.

'Yes, thank you, Whitney. I'll let you know when Mrs Douglas is here,' the super said.

Whitney returned to the incident room, went over to the board, picked up a marker pen and wrote Mrs Douglas's name up there.

'Attention everyone. I've been to the see the super

and we have something else added into the mix. The dead family were cousins of Chief Superintendent Douglas's wife. I don't know whether it's the husband or the wife she's related to, but I'm interviewing her this afternoon and will find out all I can about their relationship.'

'Bloody hell, what are the odds on that happening? I suppose that means he'll be sticking his nose in the whole time,' Frank said.

Whitney glanced over at Brian, who knew Douglas from when they both worked at the Met, and they both now were part of the Lenchester police football team. Was he going to take offence at any comments against the man?

'We'll deal with it, Frank. Whatever he does has to be done on the quiet, or it could be construed as a conflict of interest. Let's hope the super acts as the intermediary. But we do need to be on our toes on this one because every move we make is going to be scrutinised, and questions asked. But we've dealt with his interference before, and we can do it again.'

She hoped. She had to put a positive spin on it because the team looked to her for a response.

'Can I book annual leave?' Frank said.

'He won't be bothering you,' Doug said. 'I doubt he even knows who you are.'

'He knows me, all right. Remember, I've been here a long time and was around before he even made sergeant. He was a twat then, too.'

'Frank.' Whitney glared at him. She didn't want any of this getting back to Dickhead.

'Sorry, guv. He was a lovely man before, and also now.' Frank gave a cheesy grin, and everyone laughed, Brian included.

She should learn to trust Brian more. He'd already

proved himself several times. It was just he liked Dickhead, and she couldn't understand anyone who did.

'Right. Fun time over. We need to focus. I spoke to the mother of the teenager, Dylan Fletcher, who found the family. The husband was out at golf and couldn't be contacted. The family needs investigating. They claim to have an alibi, but it needs checking out. Frank, you can deal with this, I'll text their details. Also find out which officers did a house-to-house this morning to see if any statements need following up. Collate all the information and let me have it later.'

'Yes, guv.'

'Ellie, I want you to look into the Barker family finances. You know the drill. See if there's anything suspicious.'

'Yes, guv.'

'Meena, I want you to check the social media presence of all the children and find out who their friends were. Brian, find out if Mr and Mrs Fletcher worked, and where. We'll need to speak to their colleagues. Doug, you can investigate the couple's family, friends, and their social media presence. I'm going to be interviewing Mrs Douglas this afternoon in the super's office. Oh, and FYI, the chief super has warned that there'll be trouble if it leaks that his wife is related to the victims.'

'He can't hold us responsible for that,' Meena said, an incredulous tone to her voice.

'You don't know *Dick* ... I mean, Douglas,' Frank said.

'I'm beginning to get an idea,' Meena said.

'Don't worry, it will be me who's in trouble,' Whitney said, giving a wry smile. 'But I can't be held responsible for anyone outside of this team and I'm sure the super will stick up for me if it does get out. Assuming that it isn't one of you lot.'

'You know us better than that, guv,' Doug said.

'I do. And you should know me well enough to know that I was joking. Right, let's get on with it. If we can solve this case within the week not only will the drinks be on me, but I'll treat us all to a meal.'

And she wasn't being altruistic. This was one case she wanted rid of as soon as possible.

## Chapter 6

Whitney pulled a brush through her tangled curls, which she'd forgotten to put up when she'd left unexpectedly for work and was now regretting, and smeared on some lip gloss, before returning to the super's office to interview Mrs Douglas.

She'd never met the woman but had often wondered who'd want to be married to someone like him. Unless he had a different side to him when out of work that no one in the force ever saw. But she seriously doubted it. Leopards and spots and all that.

Were they married when he'd come onto her all those years ago? She wouldn't be at all surprised.

When she arrived at the office she knocked on the door.

'Come in,' Douglas called.

Great. Did him answering mean the super wasn't taking part? She sucked in a breath and entered the room. The super *was* there. Thank goodness. It must have been Douglas showing off to his wife that he's in charge. Typical.

The three of them were seated at the table. Douglas, with the usual pompous expression on his face, was facing her, and to his right was the super. To his left was, who Whitney assumed, Mrs Douglas, a petite, elegant, well-dressed woman who looked to be in her early fifties with short sleek silver hair tucked behind her ears. Her eyes were red and swollen from crying.

If Whitney had conjured up a picture in her mind of what Dickhead's wife looked like, it certainly wasn't this. Without even hearing her speak, it was obvious she was way too classy for him.

'Sir. Ma'am,' she said, looking first at Douglas and then the super. She then turned to the other woman. 'Hello, Mrs Douglas.'

'Call me Belinda,' the woman said, giving a warm, genuine smile, which took Whitney by surprise. She'd expected a cold reception, especially if Dickhead had warned his wife about her.

'Sit down, Walker, and we'll get started,' Douglas said.

'Are we all going to be in here?' she asked.

Hadn't they already discussed that he couldn't be openly involved? Or did he think this didn't count?

'We'll stay in the background while you speak to Mrs Douglas,' the super said.

Whitney forced back a scowl. How was she meant to probe and ask difficult questions in this company? Or were they paying lip service to the interview?

She dragged her chair until she was facing Mrs Douglas, keeping the other two out of her eyesight, as much as possible.

'Thank you for coming in to see me, Belinda, at such a difficult time. I'm very sorry for your loss. It must have been a huge shock to learn what had happened to the family.'

'Yes.' Tears filled the woman's eyes, and she blinked them away. 'Who would do something like that to such a lovely family? Grant can't understand either, can you?'

*Grant?* Oh … Douglas.

'No,' he said, giving a sharp shake of his head.

'Who was your cousin, the chief super didn't say?' she asked, quick to move away from including him in the interview.

Knowing Douglas, he was waiting for the chance to take part. Well, he wouldn't get it from her.

'David was my first cousin. His mother and my mother were sisters. They were brought up in Lenchester and were very close until they both got married and started their own families and then moved to different parts of the country. It meant they couldn't keep in touch as much as they'd like. It was before the internet. That's changed everything,' Mrs Douglas said, a wistful tone in her voice.

'Yet, both you and David both ended up back here in the same town.'

'Yes, it's funny how these things turn out. I worked in London after university until meeting Grant and then moved here to be with him. I'm not sure why David came here. Most likely it was work, too.'

'What sort of relationship did you have with David?'

'He was younger than me by quite a few years. Nine or ten, I'm not sure exactly. My mother was the older sister and had me at a young age. David's mother didn't have him until she was older. He was an only child, but not spoilt. We would see each other at family gatherings when growing up, and also when we had our own families we'd get together occasionally.'

Whitney scribbled in her notebook.

'What can you tell me about David and the rest of his family?'

'I know this might sound ridiculous, but they really were perfect. Like you see on the washing powder commercials.'

No way. That doesn't happen. All it meant was they were clever at hiding whatever went on in their relationships.

'Could you give me a little more detail?'

'Obviously, I didn't see what went on behind closed doors, but there was never a time when I thought there were issues in the family.'

'Would you have been able to tell?'

'We're family, and if any cracks showed it would be with us. But there was nothing. David worked hard and was always there to support his family. He was so good with the children. I never once heard him raise his voice to them.'

'There must have been times when they tried his patience. All children do that.'

'I'm sure there was, but because he was often away on business, he made sure not to neglect them. They always came first.'

'Did Gillian ever complain that he was away so much?'

'No. She seemed to take it in her stride. There wasn't ever a time when he didn't travel for work. When he was away, she took care of the family. The children were now all teenagers and didn't need so much looking after, but more ferrying around to various clubs and activities. You know what it's like at that age.'

'Yes, I remember those times. Would you say you were close with Gillian?'

'We always got on well when we saw each other. We'd often stand in the kitchen at family get-togethers, doing the washing up or helping out.'

'When we went to her house, the kitchen was spotless. It was like visiting a show home.'

'Gillian prided herself on keeping everything clean and tidy. I was always amazed whenever we were there. So different from our house.'

Whitney stole a quick glance in Douglas's direction. His lips were set in a firm line. Was he annoyed that his wife had mentioned the state of their house?

'When were you last there?'

'Just over a year ago, I believe. Gillian hosted a party for my aunt's eightieth birthday. She died six months later.'

'Did they hold the funeral in Lenchester?'

'No. It was in Norfolk. We weren't able to attend as we were away in America at the time.'

'Do you know who their friends were?'

'No, I don't, sorry.'

'Can you think of any reason why someone would want to harm the family?'

'Nothing springs to mind. I keep asking myself, what could they have done to warrant this? Unless it was a random attack, and it could've been anyone. Do you think that's the case?'

'That's what we're investigating. It's early days, and we don't have enough information yet to draw any conclusions.'

'Is that it, Walker? I'm sure there can't be anything else you need to know. My wife has had enough for the day.'

Belinda turned to Douglas. 'It's okay, dear. I'm more than happy to continue. This is important.'

It might be okay for her, but Whitney wasn't foolish enough to believe that it would be okay with him, and he'd make his feelings known once his wife had left.

'I won't be much longer, Mrs Douglas. I know you can't think of any reason why anyone would want to harm the family right now, but do you know of anything in David or Gillian's past which might have come back to haunt them?'

Mrs Douglas bit down on the bottom lip and thought for a moment. 'No. I'm sorry there's nothing.'

'And their children? Were there any issues with them?'

'Not that I know of, but we didn't live in each other's pockets, as I've already explained.'

'When was the last time you saw the family?'

'You've already asked that, and my wife told you it was at David's mother's birthday party.'

'That answer was in respect of when your wife was last at the Barker house, sir. I wondered if she'd seen them other than at that time,' Whitney said, forcing her voice to stay calm, when in fact she wanted to smack him.

'Actually, we did see them at my parents' diamond wedding anniversary party last year. All the family were at the celebration.'

'Including David?'

'Yes, he was there, too.'

'What about Gillian's family, do you mix with them at all?'

'No, because she came from down south. I don't know her family at all, only to nod to if we ever saw them at parties.'

'Do your children go to the same school as the Barkers?'

'My children have left home now, and we lived in London when they were at school.'

'Okay, well, thank you very much for your help. I'll give you my card and if anything comes to mind, anything at all, please contact me.' Whitney pulled her card from her pocket and held it out.

'There's no need for that, Walker. If Mrs Douglas remembers anything she can tell me, and I'll let you know.'

'Yes, sir,' Whitney said, returning the card to her pocket.

'I'm sorry I couldn't have been more help, but just catch whoever did this.'

'You've been a great help and given us some insight into the family,' Whitney said.

'You know, they were a lovely family. I ...' Belinda's voice broke, and she pulled a tissue from her sleeve and dabbed her eyes.

'That's it. Interview over,' Douglas said, standing up and going over to stand behind his wife.

Whitney picked up her folders from the table. 'Thank you, Mrs Douglas. It was very good of you to come in. I'll leave you to it then, sir. Ma'am.'

She left the office and returned upstairs replaying the interview in her mind. She hadn't got much out of Mrs Douglas other than they were an almost perfect family. That in itself was worth investigating. As was the fact the husband worked hard and was often away from home. How much time did he spend at home? And what was he doing when he wasn't there? Answers she hoped would help with the investigation.

# Chapter 7

George knocked on the door that went directly into Whitney's office, but there was no answer, so she carried on down the corridor until reaching the incident room. She was hit by the usual frenzy of activity when they were working on a case. The clicking of computer keys. Voices on the phone. Discussions between colleagues.

She immediately relaxed. It was good to be back in familiar surroundings and away from the absurdity of what was happening with her parents. Of course, she'd been upset about her father having to face such a debilitating illness. Who wouldn't be? But the fact they'd assumed she could drop everything to be with them showed how out of touch they were with her life. Seeing Ross last night and now being at the station with Whitney and the team confirmed that this was where she belonged. She would help her parents, when possible, but she had no intention of leaving Lenchester and the life she'd built for herself.

Whitney was towards the back of the room, staring at the large whiteboard, which had five photographs along the top. The deceased, George assumed. She headed over to the DCI, passing other members of the team who were seated at their desks working, either on the phone or staring at their computer screens.

'Hi George,' the officer said once she was close.

'Good morning.'

'Are you okay? You're looking harassed.'

'The last few days with my family have been difficult, but I'm happy to be back.'

She hoped her friend wasn't going to press her for more details, because she had no desire to talk about it. She needed distracting. Maybe she'd elaborate more once she was back into the swing of her life in Lenchester.

'You've arrived at the right time because I was about to feedback to the team about my interview with Mrs Douglas yesterday. They weren't all here by the time I'd finished which is why I'm doing it now. And, by the way, that's Douglas as in Chief Superintendent Douglas's wife. Who would believe it?'

'What's she to do with the case?'

'She's David Barker's cousin. I was stunned when I found out, because you know what that means.'

George grimaced. Whitney was going to have to watch her step throughout the investigation. She'd witnessed the chief superintendent's dislike of her friend and the way he tried to derail her. It wasn't in Whitney's imagination. If there was any time when Whitney needed her help, then now was it.

'The chief superintendent will be keeping an eye on the case?'

'And that's an understatement. I had to interview Mrs Douglas in the super's office, with her *and* Dickhead watching. As I'm sure you can imagine, it wasn't an easy situation to deal with.'

'Nothing that you can't handle, I'm sure,' she said, wanting to reassure her.

'I can, but the additional pressure isn't something I'm looking forward to.'

'But he can't be involved in the actual case because of his link with the family, can he?'

'You're right, he can't. And he's mentioned that. He's also told me he wants to be informed of what's going on. So, I'll leave you to draw your own conclusions on that. Although, I will say that his wife seemed okay. God knows what she sees in him, that's for sure.'

'Maybe he's different when away from the office.'

'That would entail a total personality transplant, so I doubt it very much. Right, now you're here, let's get cracking. Listen up, team.' Whitney turned from George to face the rest of them. 'Let's catch up with where we've all got to. I'll start. According to the chief super's wife, Mrs Douglas, who's David Barker's cousin, they were the perfect family.'

'Well, that's a red flag for a start,' called out Frank.

'My sentiments exactly. She was very complimentary about her cousin and said although he worked hard and was often away on business, he was very supportive of his family. Mrs Douglas could think of no reason why anyone would want to harm them, although she did mention that they didn't see much of each other. They'd meet mainly at family gatherings. It's not much, but it's a start.'

'And was *Dick* …' Frank paused and looked across at Brian. 'I mean, the chief super. Was he at the interview?'

'He was, Frank.'

'Would she have told you more if she was on her own, do you think, guv?'

'Difficult to say, but I don't believe so. I think she told

me all she knew. The rest of you, what do you have from your research. Ellie?'

'I've done a preliminary investigation into David and Gillian's financial history and, so far, there doesn't appear to be anything dodgy going on. They had a joint account, and both of their salaries went into it. Their spending patterns were normal for a family. Food, bills, clothes, a few luxury items. And there were no recent irregularities, either. I'll keep on digging.'

'Thanks, Ellie. Frank, have you got anything else to report?'

'I checked out the alibi for the Fletchers and it was confirmed by both sets of friends that they didn't leave the house until midnight. I'm still waiting to hear back from uniform regarding which neighbours were spoken to and what they said.'

'Okay, keep on going. Anybody got anything else, Brian?'

'David worked for Hutt Consulting in Birmingham and Gillian, I'm not sure of yet.'

'She worked at Lenchester Physio, according to the bank deposits,' Ellie said.

'Thanks, I'll contact them for details,' Brian said.

'Anything else? Meena? Doug?' Whitney asked, staring ahead at the two officers.

'The children all have social media accounts, and I'm looking into their posts and who they're friends with.' Meena said.

'Parents also have accounts, but hardly ever post. I'm in the process of digging deeper,' Doug added.

'George and I are heading to the crime scene and then to the morgue. Call me if anything comes up.' Whitney turned to her. 'Is that okay? Do you have time?'

'I'm with you for the day.'

'Excellent. That's what I was hoping. I'll pop back to my office to grab my bag.'

George followed her and after going through Whitney's office they made their way down towards the car.

'You're handling Chief Superintendent Douglas's involvement very well,' George said.

'What choice do I have? I couldn't let my annoyance show to the rest of the team. They must focus one hundred per cent on finding our killer and not my feelings. But seriously, I can't believe I've got to put up with him. It's going to be a nightmare. You remember what he was like with the train murders? This will be the same, I'm sure of it. You should have seen him yesterday, the way he was staring at me. It was like he was willing me to fail, so he could appoint another team to do the investigation.'

'Don't let him see he's rattling you, because he'll thrive on it. Act like he's simply another person. I know you don't like me saying this, but you have to compartmentalise. It's the only way in this instance.'

'Easy for you to say, being on the outside. Thank goodness for the super being our go-between. I know she's got my back.'

'Why didn't you interview his wife on your own? I'd have thought that would've been a given.'

'Because he wouldn't let me. First, he wanted to interview his wife himself, but luckily the super intervened. It's incentive enough to get this case solved as quickly as possible. That way I won't have him threatening me with traffic duty if it isn't solved to his satisfaction.'

'The main thing is you're aware of what he's like and can adjust your behaviour accordingly. Providing you don't let it get to you.'

'Which is where you come in. I'm relying on you to sort me out when I start losing it.'

'All you need to do is keep out of your own way.'

'Whatever that's meant to mean.'

'That you—'

'I know what it means, I was being facetious.'

'Oh.'

They reached George's Porsche Cayenne, which she'd parked at the rear of the station car park, out of the way of other cars.

'We're going to 96 Beech Avenue, it's in Westcliffe.'

'Thanks.' She keyed the address into the satnav and then drove out of the station car park, in the direction of the crime scene.

'While we're on the way, you can give me an update on what's going on with your parents.'

Did she want to have the conversation? The trouble with Whitney was she would try to get it out of her, and considering she already knew a large part of it, having her input might confirm that she'd made the right decision. Except, when had she ever needed that sort of assistance? She'd clearly been hanging around with the officer for too long.

'They're struggling to cope with my father's prognosis, especially as he already has tremors. The fact he's no longer operating means his career in that sphere has come to an end.'

'But surely there must be something he can do, even if it's not actually performing operations himself.'

'My thoughts exactly, but all he's managing to do is wallow in self-pity, which is most unlike him.'

'That's a natural response. You must know that. Especially for someone like him who's so respected and important.'

'Once he begins to accept his situation I'm sure he'll be able to undertake some sort of work. There'll be plenty of people who will want to employ him. That's if he'll take their offers.'

'Could he do academic work like you?'

George doubted he'd lower his standards sufficiently to do that. His view, not hers.

'It's an option but knowing him, it isn't something he'd consider. Remember the adage … *those who can, do. Those who can't, teach.*'

'That's nonsense. Why doesn't he retire? I bet he's got loads of money stashed away.'

'I hadn't realised you'd seen his bank account.' George turned her head and saw the shocked expression on Whitney's face, following her sarcastic comment.

She didn't normally speak like that. Clearly, the situation with her parents had affected her more than she'd imagined.

'Sorry, I didn't mean it. I was being flippant. Of course, I don't know how much money your folks have.'

'I should apologise, too. There was no need for my response. Put it down to the stressful situation I've found myself in.'

'Apology accepted. Beech Avenue is the next left, and the victims' house is third on the right.'

George parked on the street, under one of the tall, wide-spreading green beech trees lining the road, and they headed over to the entrance which had a cordon across it and an officer on duty.

'It looks like forensics are still here. That's Jenny's car,' Whitney said, nodding at the white Honda Accord parked on the other side of the road.

They went up to the officer on duty, signed in, and then headed up the tarmac drive to the front door, which was open. As they got close, Jenny was on her way out, pulling off her protective clothing.

'Morning, Whitney. George,' Jenny said.

'I didn't expect to see you still here,' Whitney said.

'We finished yesterday, but I left my torch upstairs, so I came back to collect it.'

'Anything to report so far?'

'We did a full sweep of the house, and there was nothing out of the ordinary. Plenty of fingerprints, which we assume will be from members of the family. The only anomaly was the kitchen.'

'Anomaly?' Whitney asked.

'No prints anywhere. It had been wiped down to within an inch of its life. Every piece of cutlery. Every piece of crockery. Every cooking implement. Every surface. All spotless.'

'When I looked yesterday, I thought that someone in the family was excessively house-proud and we've since learnt that Mrs Barker was. But this doesn't sound like that. Even the most house-proud person would leave some prints. Especially if there are prints in other places. What about the bathroom, that would be comparable with the kitchen if someone was a germophobe?'

'The bathrooms appeared clean to the naked eye but, in fact, had many prints, like every other room in the house. They were what I call superficially clean, by which I mean if you peep behind the toilet or along the top of the tiles, there are places which haven't seen a cloth for a long time.'

'In which case, the kitchen could have been cleaned by the killer. Why? Did they cook the meal left in front of the victims?'

'Sorry, I can't help you with that. I've got to go because

I'm expected back at work. We're short-staffed and the work is piling up,' Jenny said.

The forensics officer left, and they headed into the house. George followed Whitney into the dining room and pulled on the pair of disposable gloves the officer had given her.

'This is it,' Whitney said gesturing at the crime scene. 'They were all found seated around the table. David Barker was at the head, at the far end. Gillian Barker was opposite. The two boys sat next to one another to the left of their mother, and the daughter sat on the right, with an empty space beside her.'

'And they were all tied to their chairs with a meal on the table?'

'Yes. We'll go to the morgue next to speak to Claire for an update. Have you any observations to make? Brian wondered whether it was a murder-suicide, but I can't see it myself because of how they were all left.'

'There would seem little point in tying oneself up unless it was to ensure they wouldn't be found guilty. But why do that, if they're all dead, anyway?'

'I know, right? That's why I discounted it.'

'Unless it was to implicate someone else.'

'How likely would that be?'

'In my opinion, not very. But we shouldn't discount it. Having said that, assuming there was a killer, and it wasn't done by one of the victims, then two thoughts immediately come to mind regarding how the killer operated. First, they could have been seated at the empty space, and so would have been in the house already and not be suspected. Or they came in through the door, and the father would have been the first one to have seen them. The father would need to be dealt with first, as he would be the most likely to fight to save the family. Maybe the killer had a weapon. Something to ensure they had control.'

'That makes sense.'

'You mentioned the victims had a meal in front of them. What about the empty space, was there a meal there, too? Was it set with cutlery, in the same way as the others?'

'Possibly, but I can't be certain because Claire wouldn't let us get close enough to have a proper look. She would've taken the meals and utensils to analyse, we'll ask when we see her.'

'What was the meal?'

'Lamb shanks.'

'But none of the food was touched?'

'Not that we could see.'

'If there was a place setting in the spare seat, it would indicate that someone either was there or had been invited. Even if place mats are left out on a table, it would be unusual for cutlery and glassware to be.'

'Yes. But who? And were they the killer? That's what we'd need to find out.'

'Let's have a look in the kitchen. I'm interested to see it,' George said.

Whitney led the way.

'See what she means about it being spotless, you could eat your dinner off the floor. Even yours isn't this clean and tidy,' Whitney said. 'No offence.'

George headed over to the wall where there was a calendar, ignoring Whitney's comments. It was full of entries which she read.

'Whitney, I've got something. On Saturday's date there's the name Corey written, but it's been crossed out. This could be the sixth person they were expecting for dinner. And, if so, who cancelled and why?'

Whitney came over and joined her.

'Well spotted. I'll take this with us. There's powder residue on it, so it's been dusted for prints. But why didn't Colin or Jenny bring it in? Maybe they didn't spot the entry.' She pulled out an evidence bag from her pocket and dropped the calendar into it.

'Jenny did explain how backed up forensics are. Perhaps they missed it,' George said.

'I'll give Ellie a call and get her to track this Corey down.'

George continued looking around the kitchen while Whitney spoke to the officer. She pulled open drawers, opened cupboards, and looked on all the surfaces, but didn't discover anything of interest, or that appeared to be out of the ordinary.

'There's nothing else of note here,' she said once Whitney had ended her call with Ellie. 'I've examined everywhere, and nothing is standing out. It's only the calendar that might be of some use.'

'Okay, we'll go to the morgue and find out what Claire has for us.'

They left the house and returned to the car.

'How's Tiffany and the baby?' George asked as they were driving towards the hospital. She hadn't yet asked about them, which was remiss of her.

'Would you like come round later to see them?'

'I saw them when Ava was first born.'

'That doesn't mean you can't see them again. Why don't you have dinner with us tonight? Tiffany would love to see you.'

George was partial to the company of Whitney and her daughter and, despite not being at all maternal, when she'd met the baby and held her, she did experience a wave of affection for the child.

'Thank you, that would be delightful. I'll text Ross and let him know I'll be late.'

'Would he like to come, too?'

'Ordinarily, I'm sure he'd love to, but he's working to a very tight deadline on a recent commission.'

'Okay, we'll arrange it for another time. Now put your foot down and get us there quickly. We've got a lot to do.'

## Chapter 8

Whitney pushed open the double doors to the morgue and immediately turned right to go into the small area where Claire and the other pathologists had their office. It was a tiny space, devoid of any personal touches, and each of the three desks had a computer screen on them. As they got closer, they heard Claire in a one-sided conversation, indicating she was on the phone.

The pathologist glanced at them and held her hand up, gesturing for them to stay where they were and not come in, so they stepped back into the larger entrance area.

Whitney couldn't hear what Claire was saying because her voice was low and a different tone from normal. None of the abrasiveness that was her trademark. Was she talking to Ralph, the husband they'd yet to meet? He was also a pathologist, and that's about all Claire had told them. The pathologist kept her social and work lives separate. Except for when she'd joined George and Whitney for a post-wedding celebratory drink and the rare occasion after work they'd got together at the local pub.

Whitney looked at George, who had a distant expression on her face. She was probably worried about the issues with her parents. Talk about a turnaround. They'd never had time for George, and now suddenly they needed her and expected her to jump. They couldn't be more different from her own parents if they'd tried. For all their money, and fancy house and lifestyle, Whitney wouldn't want to be part of George's family for anything on Earth.

'What's wrong?' George asked, catching her staring.

'Oh, nothing. Just thinking about life,' she said dismissively, not wishing to share her musings.

'Enter.' Claire's voice boomed out.

They walked into the office and the pathologist stood, coming over to greet them.

Today's outfit was a horizontally striped blue and red dress, which came to just above her knee, complete with purple ribbed tights and a pair of red shoes with a bow. In her ears were the largest gold ball studs that she'd ever seen.

Whitney forced back a smile. She should be used to Claire's attire by now, but it still made her laugh. She'd give anything to meet the pathologist's husband and discuss fashion with him. They might not have been introduced, but she'd googled him and at least knew what he looked like, which was very conservative in comparison to Claire.

'Good morning,' George said.

'And good morning to you both, too,' Claire responded.

'You sound happy today,' Whitney dared to venture.

'Actually, I am. I was just speaking to my husband, and he's booked a holiday for us in Iceland so we can see the Northern Lights. I'm looking forward to it immensely.'

'Oh, that's going to be cold,' Whitney said, a shiver running through her at the thought.

'It's a place I've always intended to visit. I'll be very interested to hear from you what it's like,' George said.

Whitney would much prefer a holiday in the sun. Somewhere in Europe would be perfect. She couldn't even remember the last time she went somewhere hot.

'The same for me. Ralph booked it as a surprise for my birthday,' Claire said.

'It's your birthday today?' Whitney asked, amazed at how much the pathologist was sharing. She was acting so out of character.

'No. It's for the future.'

'When is your birthday?'

'It's nothing to do with you as we don't exchange cards or gifts.'

That was more like it. Whitney was beginning to worry that Claire had morphed into a whole new person.

'Well, make sure you've got plenty of warm clothes to take with you because you're going to need them,' Whitney said.

'That's a given. I'm planning a shopping trip very soon.'

'Where do you buy your clothes?' Whitney had always been curious but hadn't ever plucked up the courage to ask. This seemed the perfect opportunity to find out.

'There are several special places I go to, and don't even think about asking where they are. I'm not sharing their names and locations with you. I don't want you to start replicating my wardrobe.'

'I'd never do that. You have my word. You have your own style, which is nothing like mine,' Whitney said, pushing back the bubble of laughter that was threatening to come out of her mouth.

'That's enough of this chit-chat. I'm assuming you're here about the bodies discovered yesterday,' Claire said abruptly, signalling that the conversation was over and they were back in work mode.

Whitney breathed a sigh of relief. She'd couldn't have remained serious if they had to discuss clothes a moment longer. Even if she was still none the wiser as to where Claire shopped. Had it amused George as much? She doubted it. Knowing George, she'd think Whitney was mean for finding it funny. Perhaps she was a little, but she'd never share her views with anyone else.

'I'm hoping you've got something useful for us. This case is tricky in more ways than one.'

'I see,' Claire said.

'Don't you want to know why?'

'If it's relevant to the post-mortem.'

The pathologist was very like George in some respects. It could be frustrating, to say the least.

'It probably isn't, but I'm going to tell you anyway. Chief Superintendent Douglas's wife was a cousin of David Barker, which means he's going to be on our case the whole time.'

'He's the chap you don't like, if I recall correctly,' Claire said.

'It's a bit more than that, Claire. I don't dislike people for no reason. We have history, and he's been a thorn in my side since I joined the force.'

'In that case, you'd better come with me, and I'll share what I have so far.' Claire pulled on her white coat, and they followed her into the morgue area. 'I haven't got all the bodies out as we don't have sufficient tables. I'll show you some of my findings and talk you through the rest.'

'Perfect,' Whitney said.

'There were some differences between the victims, which is interesting. We'll start with David Barker, who is over here.'

They followed Claire to the far side of the room where the body was laid out on the table. Claire pulled back the white sheet, revealing the Y-shaped incision from where she'd completed the post-mortem.

'Do you know yet how they were killed?' Whitney asked, anxious to discover if they were drugged.

'I've sent their bloods off to toxicology, but from my investigation I believe that they were injected with an over-dose of a sedative. After examining each victim's cardio-vascular systems and their coronary arteries, without exception their aortas and aortic branches were enlarged. Also, the veins inside their lungs were swollen from haem-orrhaging. This indicates they were given an overdose of an anaesthetic, like midazolam. Toxicology will confirm my conclusions.'

'I thought you said there were differences, but this implies they were all killed in the same manner,' Whitney said.

'Stop being impatient, I'm getting to that.'

'Sorry. Please continue.'

'That's what I'm trying to do.' Claire glared at her. 'Yes, they all received the sedative overdose, but not in exactly the same way. And that's where the differences lie. Can you see the bruising around the needle site on this victim?' She pointed to the side of David Barker's neck.

'Yes,' Whitney said nodding, as she leant forward to look at the purple discolouration on the victim's skin.

'It presents as a random, ill-conceived action, with several attempts to inject into the vein. Because of this, in my opinion, David Barker was sedated first. When I exam-ined the other victims, it became apparent that they were injected in a more careful manner, in the deltoid muscle of their upper arm, and not the neck. There was also far less bruising around each of the entry points. I'll show you on this body.'

Claire moved to the table next to her, where one of the young boys was laid out.

Nausea washed over Whitney. She could face most things, but not the death of a child. 'Sick bastard,' she muttered.

'Are you okay?' George asked.

'I'm fine. Seeing a child like this just gets to me.'

'We have to learn to suppress our feelings,' Claire said, the kindness in her voice surprising Whitney and throwing her off balance.

'I'm trying. Show us this entry point.'

The pathologist used the end of a pen to highlight a tiny spot on the arm. 'It was here, but hardly visible,'

Whitney couldn't see anything.

'It would make sense for the attacker to go for David Barker first because with his build and strength he would most likely be the greatest threat. Once he'd been disabled, the others wouldn't have tried to do anything. The killer would have stabbed him with the needle in the easiest place. Necks are usually on show,' George said.

'Yes, they were my exact conclusions, too,' Claire said.

'We need to consider whether the killer had a weapon, because simply wielding a syringe surely wouldn't be enough to stop an altercation.'

'That's for you to discover,' Claire said.

'Is there anything else that differs between the victims?' Whitney asked.

'Yes, there is. There are traces of duct tape around the mouth of Gillian Barker and not on anyone else.'

'So she had tape on her mouth for part of the time and then it was removed,' George said.

'That's correct.'

'Post-mortem?'

'Yes. There was no sign of inflammation from it being removed.'

'Did you see the tape anywhere at the scene?' Whitney asked.

'No,' Claire said.

'Was it used to stop her from screaming, do you think?' Whitney asked.

'Why do you continue to ask questions like this? At the risk of repeating myself, that's for you to find out, not me. My role here is to explain what was found, not do your investigative work for you.'

'Don't tell me you don't try to draw any conclusions, because I don't believe you,' Whitney said.

'Not when there are so many bodies to deal with.'

'Were there any marks on the bodies which would indicate a physical assault?' George asked.

'No. From my investigation, there were no signs of struggle. I would also suggest that one of the children was given the job to tie everyone to their chair.'

'Which child?' Whitney asked.

'The girl. Keira Barker. There are rope fibres under her fingernails that are consistent with her having contact with it.'

'Couldn't they have got there from being tied up and trying to wriggle free?' Whitney asked.

'I don't believe so. The way each of them had been tied, it wouldn't have been possible for those fibres to have got there. Also, she was tied by a different person from the others, as evidenced by the different knot used on her. A basic square knot, or reef knot as you might know it, was used on the rest of the family. On Keira, it was a taut line knot, the type used to secure a tent.'

'So, our killer goes camping,' Whitney said. 'I'm not

asking you, just musing,' she added, before Claire could have another go at her for inappropriate questioning.

'What can you tell us about the rope used on the victims?' George asked.

'It was a blue sisal rope, with an eight-by-ten-millimetre twist. Very common and available in most DIY stores, so it's unlikely we'll be able to trace where it was bought.'

'So, they weren't drugged first and then put into position, like we thought they might have been when we first viewed the crime scene.'

'Lividity centred on the victims' buttocks and backs, which is consistent with them dying in situ. Also, there were no signs of movement on any of the bodies from being dragged into position, which is what I'd have expected if they were placed there later. It is my opinion that they were seated, tied up and then drugged, except for David Barker who was drugged before being tied.'

'Could this have been a murder-suicide by the daughter?' Whitney asked.

'Unlikely.'

'Is that a definite no?' Whitney asked.

'In my professional opinion it was not a murder-suicide as none of the forensic evidence points to it. Is that good enough?'

'Perfect, thank you, Claire. What about food? There was a plate left in front of them which none of them had eaten, but had they had anything to eat at all?'

'Yes. All of them. When I examined the stomach contents, there was some undigested food, and some of it in the small intestine. My analysis concluded they'd eaten a meal of spaghetti bolognaise no earlier than three hours before they died.'

'Had they been drinking?'

'Toxicology will confirm whether alcohol is present, and if so, the quantity.'

'How many meals were set around the table?' George asked.

'Six. There was a meal set for the empty space. I've taken samples from each of the plates, and the wine in the glasses, and sent them away for analysis. I'll let you know when the report comes back.'

'Other than the lamb shanks, what else was on the plate?' George asked.

'The shanks were served on a bed of lentils in a sauce with a portion of sliced leeks on the side.'

'Interesting choice.'

'Have you established time of death?' Whitney asked.

'Between 10 p.m. and midnight for all five of them.'

'It's all very neat and tidy. Definitely a well-thought-out plan, carried out by someone who was able to enter the house, either from being invited or through a door that was left unlocked. And all they had to do was disable David Barker first. Like you said, George, a weapon would most likely have been involved. Probably a gun. You've given us plenty to work with, Claire, and hopefully will ensure Douglas keeps off my back.'

'If that's everything, I'm busy, so you can go,' the pathologist said.

'We're off. Thanks, Claire. Please let me know as soon as the toxicology reports come back.'

# Chapter 9

George returned with Whitney to the station and after dropping their bags off in her office, they headed into the incident room, where the team were working. Whitney made a beeline for the whiteboard and wrote down several of the details Claire had given them. She then turned to face her officers.

'Attention, everyone. George and I have been to see Dr Dexter and received an update on the victims. She's waiting for confirmation from toxicology regarding substances in the blood. However, she believes they all died from an overdose of a drug that's used as an anaesthetic. Most likely midazolam.' Whitney pointed to where she'd written the word on the board.

'Is it widely available?' Frank asked.

'It's used by doctors, dentists, surgeons, vets. Anyone with a medical connection could access some. And even if they don't have this connection, there's also the black market, where I'm sure it would be readily available,' George said. 'So, in answer to your question, yes it is.'

'That's not much of a lead, then,' Frank said, his voice despondent.

'On its own, no it isn't. But it will be added into the mix. Dr Dexter also examined their stomach contents. The family had eaten their last meal of spaghetti bolognaise no more than three hours prior to being killed. The lamb shank meal left in front of each of them was most likely a message. So, too, is the fact there were six meals left on the table,' Whitney said.

'Do you believe the scene was staged?' Doug said.

'Yes, that's our view. George, what can you tell us about that?'

George hadn't had the time to mull over exactly what implications the staging of the scene had, but she could give a broad opinion. She didn't like making categoric statements until she'd given it sufficient consideration in case she gave the team incorrect information which sent them in the wrong direction.

'It could mean several things. First, that the killer saw themselves as part of the family and wanted to be acknowledged as such. Alternatively, someone in the family might have rejected the killer in the past, and the staging was to send the message that rejection had consequences. We'll know more once further evidence comes to light. I have nothing more to add at this stage.'

'Thanks, George. That's still useful. We should look to see if David or Gill are responsible for hiring and firing within their businesses, or if either of them had an affair that turned sour. Also, were the children dating or could they have rejected someone at school.'

'Would you say the killer was male or female?' Doug asked.

'Good question. I don't wish to assume at this stage, but

I'm leaning towards them being male. Even with a weapon, it would have taken some strength to have injected David Barker in the neck while still wielding it, because he wasn't a small man and he might have taken the chance to tackle a woman. But I may be wrong as we don't know the circumstances, so it would be foolish to exclude anyone,' George said.

'Agreed,' Whitney said, nodding. 'Another point Dr Dexter brought to our attention is that Gillian Barker had duct tape placed across her mouth, which was removed post-mortem, and no one else did.'

'Was it to stop her from shouting out?' Frank suggested.

'It's possible, but why her and not the others?' Whitney said. 'George, any thoughts?'

'She was a mother witnessing an attack on her children, so it could be to silence her. Until we know the motive, I wouldn't want to speculate, though.'

'And why remove it once she was dead?'

'The scene was staged. Having her gagged might not have fitted in with what the scene represented.'

'I see. The post-mortems also highlighted that it was Keira, the daughter, who restrained the family. She, in turn, was most likely tied up by the killer who used a different knot Whether selecting Keira was intentional or random, at this point we don't know. But we need to be mindful of it.'

'That could fit, if the murders are linked to Keira's ex-boyfriend Ellie discovered,' Brian said.

Whitney frowned. 'She had an ex-boyfriend? When did we find out about him?'

'I identified him only minutes before you came back, guv, and I told Brian. I think that Corey, the name written on the calendar, is Corey Hudson. Until recently, he was Keira's boyfriend. They'd been in a relationship for a long time but according to their social media accounts, it ended several weeks ago, and within a few days she'd started seeing someone else. Corey took it badly.'

'Hence the reason he was invited for a meal, and then his name was crossed out. How would that fit with your theories, George?'

'If Keira had ended their relationship, then he would feel rejected. But why murder the entire family?' She cupped her elbow with one hand while tapping her lip with her other. 'It doesn't sit right.'

'Unless he'd totally lost the plot,' Frank said.

'Yes, his mental health may have been badly affected, and that could have led to him committing an otherwise unfathomable act. I'd need to see him and analyse his actions and reactions before making further assumptions.'

'We'll get the young man in for an interview, and you'll be able to observe his behaviour. How old is he, Ellie?'

'He's seventeen and still at school.'

'Does he go to the same school as Keira and her brothers?'

'No, he's at Kingsford. The all-boys school on the outskirts of Lenchester.'

'We'll need at least one of his parents in as well when we interview him, as he's only seventeen. Brian, sort that out, please. I want him here as soon as possible, preferably within the hour. Ellie will give you the contact details.'

'Yes, guv.'

'Frank, anything yet from the house-to-house enquiries on Sunday morning?'

'Yes, I've seen the statements and, according to one of the neighbours, a young man was seen hanging around and watching the house on more than one occasion. I don't have any details other than that.'

'Could it be Corey Hudson? Do we have a photo of him?' Whitney asked.

'Yes, guv, I have one,' Ellie said.

'Frank, take a copy and visit the neighbour who mentioned it to confirm if it's him. Also, find out how often, when and where he stood when they saw him. Call on the other neighbours to see if they noticed anyone hanging around and show them the photo, too.'

'Yes, guv.'

'Ellie, is there anything else you can tell us about Corey Hudson from his social media posts?'

'When he was going out with Keira, he posted often, usually photos of the two of them together. He was always smiling, and his posts were funny and typical of a teenager. After they finished, he hardly posted at all and, if he did, it was memes and nothing personal.'

'Teenage break-ups can be the most devastating, especially as hormones are running riot at that age. But was he disturbed enough to murder Keira and the rest of her family?'

'There have been instances in the past when unrequited love has led to murder, so it's certainly possible,' George said.

'Ellie, I want you to continue digging. Pay attention to Corey and Keira's friends, see if there's anything that suggests he might have been involved.'

'Will do, guv.'

'Has anything come back from forensics yet?'

'Yes, guv, an interim report came from them half an hour ago,' Brian said. 'A set of size ten footprints were found in the back garden, and close by several cigarette butts were discovered.'

Whitney's eyes lit up, as they always did when evidence built up.

'Find out the shoe size of each victim, so they can be excluded. Dr Dexter will furnish you with the information.'

'If the footprints belong to Corey Hudson, that ties in with him hanging around the area. From memory, the garden was large enough for him to sneak in without being seen. We'll get his shoe size when he's here for the interview,' Brian said.

'Yes. I'd also like someone to check out both David and Gillian's background. So far, we know that David was an only child, and his mother died six months ago. Is his father still alive, and if so, where is he? As for Gillian, all I ascertained from Belinda Douglas is that she comes from somewhere down south. Doug, find out what you can.'

'Yes, guv.'

'Good. I'm going to see the super and give her an update on where we are. Fingers crossed the chief super isn't in there with her.'

## Chapter 10

George stared at the board in the incident room. There were individual photos of each victim, with their name written underneath, and also one of the family at the murder scene, all seated around the table with the plateful of food in front of them. It was most definitely staged, as they'd discussed. But why? What did it signify? And was it something a rejected boyfriend would do?

'Here you are,' Whitney said, stood beside her.

'You weren't long with Superintendent Clyde.'

'No, she had a meeting to go to, so I gave her a quick update. You were staring intently at the board. Have you had any thoughts?'

'Observe the manner in which the meals were placed in front of each victim. All in an identical way to one another, even down to the width between the cutlery and plates. It's as if a tape measure was used.' She pointed to a photo of the family.

'I hadn't noticed that before. What do you think it means?'

'Our killer was verging on the obsessional. This was

also evident in the way the kitchen was so meticulously cleaned after the meal was prepared.'

'Assuming that it was prepared there, and not brought in.'

'That had crossed my mind. But if it was brought in, then there would have been no need to undertake such a thorough clean. Also, did the killer use food already in the house, or bring the ingredients with them? If the latter, then is there anything significant about it being lamb?'

'That the killer lived on a farm?'

'What?' George said, frowning.

'Sorry, I was being stupid. But seriously, how many teenage boys do you know who can not only cook like that, but are also obsessively clean, and know the significance of food?'

'I wouldn't discount it. Do we know whether the crockery used belonged to the Barkers? Was it part of a larger dinner service?'

'We don't.' Whitney turned away from George. 'Brian. Have you been in touch with Dr Dexter yet?'

'Yes, guv. I've got shoes sizes for the victims, and none of the family wears a size ten.'

'Good. Doug?'

'Yes, guv?'

'Contact Dr Dexter and ask her for a description of the plates the meal was placed on. We want to check whether they belonged to the family, or if the killer brought them in. Then go to the house and take a look at all of their crockery.'

'Will do.'

'Thanks.'

'While you're there, check the contents of the fridge, freezer, and the pantry. That might assist us in discovering who bought the ingredients for the meal. In particular, check for tinned or dry lentils, and vegetables,' George said. She glanced at Whitney, to check if she'd usurped her authority by giving Doug an order.

'Good idea. Also, look for any wine they have, and what it is,' Whitney said.

'We'll need to find out where the daughter's bedroom was, because if it overlooked the back garden and it was the ex-boyfriend, that would make sense as to why he stood in that position,' George said.

'We'll ask him when he arrives,' Whitney said.

'Guv, Corey Hudson and his father are here,' Brian called out.

'Perfect timing. Brian, you're with me, and George is going to observe.'

They took the lift to the ground floor and headed through the double doors into the corridor where ten interview rooms were situated.

'They're in room eight,' Brian said.

George left them when they reached the observation area, and once in there she stood by the two-way mirror and scrutinised the young man. He appeared to be a typical teenage boy. His dark blond hair was cut into a crew cut and was slightly longer on top. He wore a faded moss-green coloured hoodie, which was zipped up, and beneath it the neckline from his navy T-shirt was showing. His head was lowered, and his hands tightly clasped together in his lap. His father was seated beside him, staring ahead with his arms folded.

Whitney entered the room holding a folder, which she placed on the table. She sat opposite the boy and Brian opposite the father. Whitney leant across and pressed the button on the recording equipment.

'Interview on Monday, June 7. Those present Detective

Chief Inspector Walker, Detective Sergeant Chapman, and, please state your names for the tape.'

'Julian Hudson,' the father said.

'Corey Hudson.'

The boy looked up. His eyes were red and swollen. He didn't have the appearance, or demeanour, of someone who'd committed the murders in such a calculating manner.

'Mr Hudson, you're here as an appropriate adult and are not to speak unless a question is directed at you, or if you believe Corey is uncomfortable with any of the questioning.'

'I understand.'

'Thank you for coming in to see us, Corey. We're here to discuss the deaths of the Barker family. When did you find out about it?'

'My dad told me.'

'How did you learn of it, Mr Hudson?'

'My neighbour had seen in on the news, and he informed me.'

'Corey, how did you feel after you learnt about the deaths?' Whitney asked.

'That's a ridiculous question to ask. How do you think he felt?'

'Mr Hudson, please allow Corey to answer. The question wasn't directed at you.'

'I didn't believe it. I kept thinking it wasn't true. Why did it happen?' His eyes filled with tears.

Whitney slid over the box of tissues on the table and the boy reached for one and wiped his eyes.

'That's what we're investigating. We understand that you went out with Keira until recently, when she broke up with you.'

'Yes. We were together for two years.'

'Which was ridiculous at their age. Quite frankly, my wife and I were happy when it was over, and Corey could concentrate on his studies. We're hoping he'll get into Oxford University, Worcester College, where I went,' Mr Hudson said.

'Ask Mr Hudson a few more questions about this. I want to gauge his reactions,' George said into the mic.

Whitney gave a tiny nod. 'Mr Hudson, you clearly didn't condone the relationship between Corey and Keira.'

'That's right.'

'How did you make your feelings known?'

'We didn't initially, as we thought it wouldn't last. Recently, when Corey mentioned he was thinking of applying to Lenchester University so he could be close to Keira, that's when we made our feelings clear.'

'Ask him if he had anything to do with Keira ending it with Corey?' George said, a thought forming in her mind.

'Were you instrumental in the break-up at all, Mr Hudson?'

'No. Of course I wasn't.'

'He's lying, his blink rate slowed right down.'

'Are you sure about this?' Whitney asked.

'Dad?' Corey said, turning to his father.

'Okay. I might have been. I spoke to Keira a few weeks ago and explained how she was ruining your future. I did it for you, Corey.'

'What did Keira say?'

'She told me that things weren't good between them, and she'd been thinking of ending it.'

'That's a lie. She said that because she'd always been scared of you. It was all your fault.'

'I'm sorry. I did what I thought was best. But this has nothing to do with what happened to the family.' Mr Hudson looked from his son to Whitney.

'Go back to questioning Corey,' George said.

'Corey, did you take the break-up badly?'

'It was the worst time of my life.' He stared down at his lap.

'Do you know Keira's new boyfriend?'

'Yes, he goes to my school.'

'Did you confront him when you discovered they were dating?'

'Maybe,' he muttered.

'What did you do?'

'I said if he didn't end it he'd be sorry, and so would she.'

'What did you mean by that?' Whitney asked, leaning forward slightly.

'Nothing. It was a threat to get him to finish with her. I wasn't going to do anything.'

'Is it right that since Keira ended the relationship you've spent time hanging around where she lives watching her house?'

His cheeks flushed. 'Yes.'

'Were you there on Saturday?'

Corey looked at his father, who was staring back at him, his eyes wide. 'Yes.'

'What time were you there?'

He shrugged. 'I don't remember.'

'Morning, afternoon, or evening?'

'Evening.'

'How did you get there?'

'I drove.'

'You have your own car?'

'No, I used my mum's.'

'Where did you park?'

'Two streets away in Lime Grove, in case Keira or one of the family noticed the car.'

'What time did you leave the Barkers?'

'I don't remember. Maybe nine. It was almost dark, and curtains had been drawn so I couldn't see inside.'

That was before the time Claire had said they'd died. If he was telling the truth, which George couldn't be certain of.

'Where abouts did you stand while watching the house?'

'In the street on the opposite side of the road, next to one of the trees.'

'What's your shoe size?' Brian asked.

He turned to Brian. 'Ten. Why?'

'Do you smoke?'

Corey took a sideways glance at his father, and bit down on his bottom lip. 'Sometimes.'

'I didn't know—'

'Mr Hudson, this isn't the time to discuss Corey's smoking habits,' Whitney interrupted.

'Sorry,' he muttered, continuing to stare at his son.

'Corey, if you were watching Keira's house from across the road, can you explain why, under a tree in the back garden, there was a size ten footprint, and several cigarette ends?' Brian said.

'Um …'

'Was that you?'

He nodded. 'Yes.'

'How do you know it was from Saturday and not from another time?' Mr Hudson asked.

'Because it was raining on Friday and any footprint would've been washed away,' Whitney said.

'Why were you there?' Brian asked.

'I can see Keira's bedroom from the back garden.'

'So, I take it that wasn't the first time you spied on her.'

'No.' He hung his head.

'What if someone had seen you?'

'I couldn't be seen from the house.'

'Were you able to see into the downstairs rooms?' Whitney asked.

'Only the kitchen.'

'And you say you left around nine? Did you drive straight home?'

'Yes.'

'How long did that take?'

'Fifteen minutes.'

'Can you vouch for your son being home by nine-fifteen, Mr Hudson?' The man drummed his fingers on the table, not making eye contact with Whitney. 'Mr Hudson?'

'The rest of the family wasn't there. We'd gone to a party and didn't get back until eleven. Corey was watching the television when we arrived home.'

'Dad,' Corey said, scowling at him.

'Where were you at ten, Corey?' Whitney asked.

'Home.'

'Are you sure you weren't still at the house? Did you try to get inside to see Keira?'

'No.'

'You'd been invited to dinner that evening, hadn't you? It was on the calendar.'

'Yes. We had finished, so I didn't go.'

'Instead you watched the house. Were you waiting to see if the new boyfriend turned up?'

'Yes. But he didn't.'

'Was there anyone other than family there?'

'Not that I saw.'

'So, it was just you. Are you sure you left at nine?' Whitney pushed.

'I don't think my son should be speaking any more. Not without a solicitor present. Are you charging him?'

'We'll be holding him in custody and will interview him again once your solicitor arrives. In the meantime, we'll be requesting a search warrant for your house. One of my officers will escort you to the custody suite.'

After Corey and his father were taken away, George went out into the corridor to meet Whitney and Brian.

'There's something Corey isn't telling us,' George said.

'Yes, I thought that, too. Why did you want me to question the dad, did you suspect him of being involved?'

'It was the proud tone when he was discussing Corey going to Oxford. I wanted to gauge his involvement. From what I witnessed, it's unlikely to be any more than what he told you.'

'Okay. I'll arrange for the warrant, and then we'll search the house.'

## Chapter 11

The search warrant had come through in record time, thanks to the super, although it was most likely Dickhead who'd expedited it. Either way, Whitney was grateful they didn't have to wait long, especially as once Hudson's solicitor had arrived, they would need to reinterview him.

Whitney took George, Meena, and Doug to the Hudson house in Maidenwell, a pretty village ten minutes out of Lenchester. The Hudson house was a semi-detached, Georgian, red-brick double-fronted property with a separate garage to one side.

She rang the bell, and a woman in her forties with short, dark, wavy hair answered.

'Mrs Hudson?'

'Yes. Are you the police? My husband called to say you were coming.'

'Yes, I'm DCI Walker and these are members of my team. We have a search warrant for your house.' Whitney held out the document for her to see but, like most people, she only gave it a cursory glance.

'I don't understand why you think my son could be

responsible for those dreadful murders. He's such a gentle boy.'

'Corey has admitted to being at the scene on the evening the deaths occurred, and we need to eliminate him from our enquiries. I understand you were away at a family gathering on the Saturday.'

'Yes. We were at the Majestic Hotel in Milton Keynes for my sister's silver wedding anniversary party.'

'Please can you give me details of someone you were with, so we can confirm this?' Whitney handed over her notebook and pen.

'Don't you believe that's where we were?'

'It's standard procedure to ask everyone we come in contact with, to eliminate them from our enquiries.'

Mrs Hudson took the pad, wrote down a number, and handed it back to Whitney. 'This is for my sister. She'll be able to vouch for us.'

'What time did you arrive home?'

'Around eleven I think.'

'Why didn't Corey go with you?'

'He had homework to do, so we allowed him to stay here. We only took our twelve-year-old daughter, Charlotte, with us.'

'Corey said he used your car to drive over to the Barker house. We need to examine it, and I've arranged for our vehicle recovery operator to remove it and take it to our premises.'

'My car? But I need it. I have a dentist appointment tomorrow. How long will you have it for?'

'That depends on what we find. I can't give you a definite time for when it will be returned to you. Is your car the white BMW on the drive?'

'Yes, that's it.'

'Does Corey often use it?'

'If I don't need it, I'll let him borrow it. We're buying him his own car for his eighteenth birthday.'

'We'll need the key.'

'It's in my handbag. I'll get it for you.'

Whitney followed the woman into the kitchen, where she stopped at the island. Mrs Hudson opened the large black tote bag on there, pulled out the key and handed it to Whitney.

'Your husband told us that neither of you were happy with the relationship between Corey and Keira.'

'That was more him, to be honest. Julian is obsessed with Corey going to Oxford, to his old college, and he thought that Keira was going to stop it from happening.'

'Were you aware he spoke to Keira a few weeks ago, to warn her off?'

She nodded. 'He informed me what he'd done afterwards, and I told him off for interfering.'

'You didn't mind so much about Corey and Keira?'

'She was a lovely girl, always polite and considerate. But I believed they were too young to be so serious. It turned out to be a one-sided relationship. Keira wasn't so into Corey as he was her, because she told Julian that it was almost over.'

'How did you feel when it ended?'

'It upset me to see how distressed Corey was by the break-up, and I wanted to take the hurt away. I'm his mother. It's how we are with our children. I hoped that eventually, with our support, he'd get over it.'

'When your husband phoned, did he mention that Corey had been watching Keira from the garden of her house?'

'Yes, he told me, but I'm sure it was only because he was so upset.' She ran her fingers through her hair. 'He wouldn't have done anything to harm the family. I know my son.'

'Do you think he might have been watching Keira on a regular basis?'

'I …' She looked at Whitney, a helpless expression on her face. 'I want to say no. But I'm not sure.'

Whitney couldn't put the woman through any more.

'I know this is hard and thank you for your honesty. Is there anywhere you can wait while my officers are here?'

'I could go next door to Sandra's. I saw her arrive home a little while ago and I'm sure she won't mind me being there. How long will you be?'

'Hopefully, no more than an hour. We'll let you know when we're leaving. Which bedroom belongs to Corey?'

'His room is the second on the left.'

Whitney escorted Mrs Hudson to the front door and watched while she walked down the drive and then to the neighbour's house. She waited until the door was answered and the woman went inside.

Whitney turned to the team, who'd been standing on the drive.

'Right. George and I will search upstairs, and you two down,' she said to Meena and Doug.

Whitney handed George some disposable gloves, and they headed straight for Corey's bedroom. It was a square room with a large bay window overlooking the garden, which was full of bright flowers and shrubs.

'This room is exceptionally tidy,' George said. 'Look at his bookcase. The books are all in author alphabetical order. And everything on his desk is set out neatly.'

'I agree. It's not what you'd expect for a teenage boy. Or girl, for that matter. I don't believe it's down to Mrs Hudson. The rest of the house isn't overly neat and tidy.'

'It's most certainly in keeping with the murder scene.'

'Do you now believe he did it?'

'As I mentioned earlier, he was definitely hiding something. But what concerns me is whether he was sophisticated enough to orchestrate the crime scene. For me, it was carried out by someone more mature. But we've only seen him in a state of grief from the deaths.'

'He didn't come across as particularly mature. In which case, could he have done it with another person?'

'That doesn't seem likely if the daughter had been instructed to tie everyone up. Unless she was made to do it for another reason but, again, I'm not convinced.'

'You're right.' Whitney walked over to the wardrobe and opened it. 'Everything in here is regimented, too. Hang on … what's this.' She crouched down and retrieved a rectangular shoebox. She placed it on the bed and took off the lid.

The box was full of items relating to Keira. There were photos, letters, and concert, train, and bus tickets.

'A memory box,' George said, peering over Whitney's shoulder.

'Yes, but I think it's more than that. Look at these photos. These are from a Polaroid camera by the looks of it.' She held them up so George could see. 'These are of Keira with another boy, presumably the latest boyfriend, and they've been taken discreetly. And look at this, there are pen slashes across the boy's face. According to the automatic date the camera leaves on the photo, these are less than a week old.'

'He'd been following her. It's not surprising as we know he'd watched the house.'

'I'd say stalking. Some of these photos are taken from behind and from the side. And look at the ones where he's zoomed in so close to Keira that her face fills the photo.

This is the work of someone who was clearly obsessed with the girl and hated the boy.'

'I agree, he has an abnormal infatuation with Keira.'

'As far as we're aware the new boyfriend hasn't been harmed. You'd have thought Corey would've done something to him, too, if he was responsible for the deaths.'

'It's a puzzle. If he is the murderer, then what's his motive? And, as you stated, why is the new boyfriend unharmed? Assuming he is.'

'We'll find out soon enough. Have you seen any devices around here?'

'There's a laptop on the desk.'

'We'll take that with us.' Whitney pulled out a large evidence bag. 'And his box of *goodies*. We'll reinterview him once we get back, providing his solicitor is there. We also need to speak to this new boyfriend of Keira's, to find out if he'd been threatened by Corey. Let's take a quick look around the rest of the upstairs. I suspect there won't be anything, but we still need to check.'

They checked the daughter's room, which was the opposite to Corey's and a total mess, then went into the parents' room and the spare room, which was set up as a study. Again, they found nothing of interest.

'We now have confirmation that his room is the only tidy one,' George said.

'I'm changing my mind about Corey. I know you think he's not mature enough to have orchestrated the crime, but remember he's planning to go to Oxford, so he's very clever. The evidence is all pointing at him.'

'Perhaps, but we need to keep an open mind.'

When they returned downstairs, Meena and Doug were in the dining room looking through the cupboards in the sideboard.

'Found anything?' Whitney asked.

'No, guv,' Doug said.

'We've taken some items from Corey's bedroom and we're heading back to the station to reinterview him. Finish up here and wait for Mrs Hudson's car to be collected. After that, go next door and let her know you're about to leave. Fingers crossed this leads to an arrest so Dickhead won't bother us.'

Meena giggled, and Whitney glanced at her. 'You didn't hear that from me.'

'No, guv.'

They left the house and went back to George's car.

'You really should be careful what you say in front of the team regarding the Chief Superintendent,' George said, once they were driving away.

'They know what he's like. They've witnessed it for themselves.'

'Your old team know the history, but not the new members.'

George was right, but sometimes it was hard not to let her feelings be known.

'They're not so new now, and Meena has settled in very well. It's like she's always been a part of the team.'

'Yes, but you are a Detective Chief Inspector and should know better.'

'Will you stop having a go at me? You're right, and I promise to try better. Okay?'

'I'm only doing it to help. I'd hate to see you in trouble for insubordination.'

'I know you are, and I really appreciate your concern. But for now, my mind is focused on reinterviewing Corey Hudson. How amazing would it be if we could solve this case in a day?' She grinned at George.

'That's hardly likely,' her friend said, frowning.

'Are you jinxing it again?'

'No, I'm not. There's no such thing, and for someone of your intelligence to believe there is astounds me.'

'You're jinxing. Thank you very much.'

'You're ridiculous,' George said, as they drove away from the house.

## Chapter 12

'Get this laptop sent off to Mac in forensics, please,' Whitney said to Ellie when they arrived back in the incident room. 'Tell him it's urgent. Work your magic on the man. We also need the name of Keira's latest boyfriend, and his contact details. After you've done that, please could you copy some of the photos in this box for me, together with some of the items. I'm particularly interested in the photos taken of Keira Barker from behind or when she was with a boy. Not Corey Hudson.'

'Yes, guv. I'm onto it.'

Whitney turned to George. 'Let's grab a coffee before we reinterview Hudson. If I don't get a caffeine fix soon, I won't be responsible for my craziness. I could do with something to eat as well.'

George was happy to agree. Whitney without caffeine wasn't pleasant for anyone.

'Okay, then after the interview I have to go to the university. I want to collect some research papers my secretary's printing for me so I can do some work at home. I much prefer working from hard copies. I'll meet you back at your house later, unless you need me for anything before then,' George said.

She was embarking on an exciting project looking into qualitative profiling of forensic psychologists applying for employment in young offender institutions in Europe, and she'd hoped to spend time working on it. Her interview schedule was planned, but before embarking on any, she needed to complete a literature review on what was already out there, to help her frame her own research questions.

The plan was to present her paper at an international conference in Brussels next year, providing she wasn't too distracted by her father's situation, and house-hunting with Ross.

She'd finally agreed to look for a somewhere they could live together permanently, rather than continue with their current arrangement which was they stayed at hers in Lenchester during the week and his at the weekend. He lived nearly an hour away, and she had to admit the travelling was becoming tedious. Once they'd found somewhere suitable, which had a separate space large enough for Ross to use as a studio for his sculpting, they would each sell their own property.

'I thought the students had finished and you were on annual leave?'

'They have, and I am. But I still like to work.'

Although George had permission from her departmental head to work with Whitney on important cases, it still caused friction with some of her colleagues. If it wasn't for her high research profile in the field, she doubted she'd still be allowed to assist the police.

'Okay. I won't need you after we speak to Hudson again.'

'Thank you.'

They took the lift to the ground floor and headed to

the canteen. They'd no sooner sat down with their coffee and cake when Whitney's phone rang.

'For goodness' sake, you don't get a moment's peace around here.' Whitney picked up her phone. 'Walker.' She nodded. 'Okay, thanks.' She ended the call. 'Corey Hudson's solicitor has arrived. He'll need some time with his client, so there's no rush. We'll finish up here and then collect Brian. I want to take copies of the evidence found in his *memory box* with us. The boy has a lot of questions to answer.'

After finishing, they headed back to the incident room.

'Guv, I've got the name of Keira's new boyfriend. It's Zak Lyle,' Ellie said as they passed by her desk.

'He's still alive then?'

'As far as I know.'

'Good. Frank, I want you to interview him. Ellie has his details. You can speak to him at his home.'

'I've only just got back from seeing the neighbour. Can I grab something to eat first?' Frank said.

'Make it quick. Did they confirm that Hudson was the person they'd seen hanging around?'

'Yes. I also spoke to some other residents, but none of them had seen him.'

'When you speak to Zak Lyle, find out if he thought they were being followed by Hudson, and if he'd been threatened by him.'

'Yes, guv.'

When they reached the interview room, George slipped into the observation area again, and took another look at the suspect. His father was no longer with him and instead he was alone with the solicitor.

'Interview resumed, Mr Hudson is replaced by …' Whitney nodded towards the solicitor.

'Malcolm Templeton, solicitor for Corey Hudson.'

'Corey, we've searched your house, and what do you think we found in your wardrobe?'

A look of panic crossed his face. 'I don't know.'

'I believe you do.' Whitney pulled out some sheets of paper from the folder she'd placed on the table. 'There was a box full of items relating to Keira Barker. These are copies of some items we found.' She slid the papers over to him and he pulled them close, staring down at the images.

'There's nothing wrong with me keeping mementoes of our time together.'

'No, but what about these?' Whitney slid over another sheet of paper, with photos of Keira and her new boyfriend.

He reached for it. 'Um …'

'These were taken secretly. You were following them.'

'There's nothing wrong with that, either.' He kept his head down, avoiding looking directly at Whitney.

'You were angry with Keira for ending it with you and then going out with Zak Lyle, so you decided to do something about it.'

He turned to his solicitor, who leant in and whispered something to him.

'I've got nothing else to say,' Corey muttered.

'That's up to you, but you're not helping yourself. We *know* you were outside the house on the night of the murders. We *know* that you have no alibi for at least part of the time when they took place. We *know* you were stalking Keira Barker. How do you think that looks, from our perspective?'

He pressed his fists to the side of his head. 'I didn't do it. I didn't. I swear on my whole family's life. I loved Keira. I never wanted to harm her. Why don't you believe me?'

'My client's very upset. I want you to stop the interview,' the solicitor said.

'The interview will end when I say so, and that won't be until Corey answers our questions.'

'Corey?' the solicitor said.

'I'm okay,' Corey said, quietly, bringing his hands down to his lap and sitting still.

'When you were stalking Keira, did—'

'I wasn't stalking her,' Corey interrupted Whitney.

'Okay. When you were *following* Keira and *watching* the Barker house, did you see anything unusual? Was there anyone acting suspiciously?'

'No.'

'On Saturday night when you were hiding in the back garden, you told us that you could see Keira's bedroom and also the kitchen. What exactly did you observe?'

'I watched Keira in her bedroom for some of the time. She was sitting on the window seat on her phone. I saw her again when she went into the kitchen to help her mum with the dinner.'

'You'd been invited for dinner that evening, as we'd discussed earlier. What time would the meal have been?'

'Mealtime was always seven in the evening and Mrs Barker would get cross if anyone was late. Eating dinner together was a family thing, so they could all talk about their day. A bit weird really.'

'What do you mean by *weird*?' Whitney asked.

'You know, like you see on the telly. But it's not real. I don't know anyone else who does it.'

'Is it correct that you can't see the dining room from the back garden?'

'Yes.'

'So why did you stay until nine, if you couldn't see anything?'

'I was waiting until after they'd finished to see what Keira did.'

'And did you see her again?'

'No.'

'Did you see any of the family?'

'Mrs Barker came into the kitchen to get the dessert at around eight, I think, and after that I didn't see anyone. But I stayed a bit longer just in case.'

'Did dinner often go on for a long time?'

'It depended on whether Mr Barker was there. If he was, then they would stay at the table for ages talking. Sometimes until after nine.'

'When we looked in your bedroom it was tidy, and all your books were in order. Have you always been like that?'

'I don't know. Maybe.' He shrugged.

'Your parents aren't like that. Does it annoy you?'

'No.'

'He's lying,' George said in her ear.

'I don't believe you. It must be annoying if you're obsessive about tidiness.'

'That makes me sound weird. I'm not obsessive.' He folded his arms tightly across his chest.

'If you say so. Do you enjoy cooking?' Whitney asked.

'Yes.'

'That's unusual for a young man of your age. What's your signature dish?' She might be rubbish in the kitchen, but Whitney loved watching all the cookery shows on the telly. They always talked about having a *signature dish* on there.

'I don't have one.'

'When was the last time you cooked a meal?'

'I made Sunday lunch for my family two weeks ago. We had roast lamb, mashed potatoes, and parsnips.'

Lamb? Coincidence?

'Do you know of anyone who might have had a grudge against the family?' Whitney asked.

'No, how would I know something like that?'

He glanced upwards, a tiny frown on his face.

'Give him a few seconds, Whitney, he's thought of something,' George said to her.

'Actually …' He paused. 'It looked like they were a perfect family, but they weren't.'

'Can you be more specific?' Whitney said.

'You know, people always thought they were this awesome family. Keira and her brothers did well at school. Keira and Harvey especially were popular with other kids and were just … you know … Cool. Mr and Mrs Barker both had good jobs. But I can tell you there was definitely something going on with Mr Barker.'

Whitney leant forward, her senses on full alert. 'What do you mean *going on?*'

'There was this one time when I was there and I heard him on the phone. He was in the garden, and I was on my way out to pick up my hat that Keira had thrown out of her bedroom window in fun. I heard him and then stood by the door, not wanting to go outside until he'd finished. Some of the things he was saying made it sound like he was talking to another woman.'

'Can you remember what he said?'

'Yeah. That he missed her and blowing kisses down the phone and all that crap. It was disgusting. A man of his age.'

'How do you know he wasn't speaking to his wife?'

'Because she was in the kitchen cooking. It wasn't her.'

Was he telling the truth or trying to send them on a wild goose chase, to take the pressure off of him? If it was true, they'd found a chink in the family. If David Barker was seeing someone else, that could be a motive to harm the family.

'How long ago was this?'

'I'm not sure exactly, but maybe three months.'

'And what did you do after you heard him? Did you mention it to Keira?'

'I went straight to her room and told her, but she didn't believe me. She said I hadn't heard it right. But I did. I know it.'

'Did you talk about it again with her?'

'No. I didn't want to upset her.'

'Do you think Keira ended your relationship because of what you said about her dad?'

'No. Or she would have done it straight away, wouldn't she?'

'But even if David Barker wasn't who he seemed, it doesn't change the fact that you were at the scene on the night the family were murdered, and you have no alibi.'

'I didn't do it.' He turned to his solicitor. 'Why won't they believe me?'

'Because you have a motive,' Brian said.

'Motive? That's stupid. I loved Keira. Why would I want her dead? And why kill the rest of her family? You just want to pin it on someone. But you're wrong.' A single tear rolled down his cheek, and he brushed it away with the back of his hand.

'I don't believe you're going to get any more out of him. His expression is closed. You need to give him some time,' George said.

'My client has nothing more to tell you. May he leave?' the solicitor asked, just after George had spoken.

The interview would finish, but she wasn't going to release him yet. He was the only suspect they had.

'He's going to remain in custody. We have thirty-six hours before we have to charge him.'

'But there's nothing to charge me with. That's what I keep telling you.' Corey banged the table with his fist.

'That's what we're investigating now. You're our prime suspect. You were at the scene of the crime and have an issue with one of the family members. What would you do if you were in our position?'

'But …' The solicitor rested his hand on Corey's arm, and he stopped talking.

The young man was returned to custody and George met Whitney in the corridor.

'Did you believe him about David Barker on the phone?' Whitney asked.

'He didn't show any signs of lying.'

'That's great. Now we've got something to work with.'

'I'll see you later, back at your house,' she said.

'Looking forward to it. We'll grab a takeaway, and you can see the baby. I've already texted Tiffany and she can't wait to see you.'

# Chapter 13

Whitney walked into her office and hung her jacket on the back of the door. As she sat at her desk, she spotted a pink sticky note in the middle of her computer screen. The super wanted to see her as soon as she was back for an update. Why? She'd only been to see her a few hours ago. Should she pretend not to have seen it and instead grab a much-needed coffee and go into the incident room to see how the team was doing?

Except, it would have been one of them who'd taken the message and she didn't want the super accusing them of not passing it on. Not least because Dickhead was so closely involved, and he could've been the one to demand her presence.

She gave a loud groan and then left her office, going to the next level, where her boss was situated. The door was slightly ajar, so she knocked and stuck her head around.

'You wanted to see me, ma'am.'

'Yes, Whitney. Come on in and sit down. I'll contact the chief super because he wanted to be included in your update.' She gestured to the seat in front of her desk.

'There isn't much more to tell you following my earlier briefing. Why don't I give you the latest, and you can pass it on to him without me having to be here?' It seemed a perfect solution to her because it meant she could keep out of his way and get on with her job, which is what he wanted her to do.

'No, Whitney, that won't be possible. The chief super asked to be kept informed, and he specifically wanted you to be here,' Clyde replied, giving a dry smile. She picked up the phone. 'DCI Walker is here, sir.' She replaced the phone on the desk. 'He'll be along in a minute.'

His office was only three doors down so it shouldn't take that long, or was he pretending to be busy? Considering he was all about image, she wouldn't put it past him.

'Yes, ma'am,' Whitney said, forcing a smile.

'Is there any more to report since our meeting earlier?'

'Yes, ma'am. We now have someone in custody, but I'll explain all that when … um … the chief super arrives.'

She pressed her lips together, only just stopping herself from referring to him as *Dickhead*. Clyde might be on her side, but that would be pushing it too far. Not only that, her attitude was ridiculous. George was right. She really needed to stop dwelling on her dislike for the man because the only person she was damaging was herself, and she'd end up getting into trouble. He'd love to be able to demote her. She could imagine the look on his face if …

The door opened and Douglas strode in like he owned the place.

'Walker. Tell me everything that's happened so far.' He stood next to Whitney's chair and stared at her, his arms folded. That said it all.

'Let's sit at the table, shall we, it's much easier to discuss that way,' the super said, as she walked around her desk.

Whitney immediately rose and joined them.

Douglas positioned himself right next to the super, rather than spreading out. Was it an intimidation tactic designed to show it was the two of them against her? If it was, it wasn't working.

'Over to you, Whitney,' the super said.

'We have someone in custody.'

Douglas exchanged a glance with the super. 'Excellent work, Walker. Who is it?'

Praise from him? That couldn't be right. No doubt the digs would follow.

'The ex-boyfriend of Keira. His name is Corey Hudson. Do you know him? They went out together for a couple of years until she finished with him recently.'

'Can't say as I do, but then we didn't see them very often. I don't even remember how old Keira was when we last saw them.'

'If you recall, sir, Mrs Douglas mentioned that you were with the family at her parents' wedding anniversary celebration last year,' Whitney said.

'Of course, so I would have seen her then.' He paused a moment. 'From memory, Keira wasn't with a boyfriend, but I'll check with my wife to make sure I'm correct. And he did all this. It's unthinkable.' He shook his head.

'He'd been stalking Keira since she ended their relationship a few weeks ago. He was in the garden of the family home on Saturday night watching them, in particular Keira.'

'In the garden? Well, it's large enough not to be spotted, if you're in the right place, I suppose.'

'Yes, sir. He positioned himself under one of the large trees situated along the boundary, on the right.'

'And he admitted all this?' Douglas asked, leaning forward slightly, a frown on his face.

'He did after we informed him that his size ten footprints were found in the garden, and also that a neighbour had identified him as hanging around the area staring at the house. But he's denied the murders, saying that he'd already left the house and gone home. He doesn't have an alibi because there was no one at home to vouch for him at the time the murders took place.'

'Have you charged him?'

'Not yet, because we don't have sufficient evidence.'

'What's the hold-up? Get the evidence,' Douglas snapped, back to his usual self.

'It's not so clear-cut. The boy is only seventeen and, as Dr Cavendish pointed out, the way the scene was staged, required a degree of intelligence that we're not convinced he has.'

'So, he was working with someone else, then.' Douglas stared at her like she was stupid.

'That is another thing we've considered. But … if that was the case, then why was Keira the one to tie up the rest of the family, and not his partner?'

Douglas stared at her for a few seconds. 'Let me get this straight. You have a boy in custody who was most likely there at the time of the crime, but you believe didn't actually do it. So, basically, you've misled me. You haven't got very far at all, have you?' He glared at her.

'We are making progress, sir, which is what I'm updating you on. I didn't claim to have solved the case.' She paused, catching sight of a warning look from the super. 'We do have another line of enquiry.'

'Which is?' Douglas growled.

'We've been led to believe that David Barker was having an affair and that the family wasn't as *perfect* as we thought.' She accentuated the word perfect by doing quote marks with her fingers.

'I see.'

'Can you help with this?'

'I can't shed light on there being an affair ... I'll admit that sometimes I had detected some undertones between David and Gillian.'

What the ... Why the hell hadn't he disclosed this to them before? Surely, not out of loyalty to the family. Even he wouldn't be such an idiot.

'Why didn't you say anything when we were discussing the family yesterday?' she demanded.

'I didn't believe it was relevant, because I had nothing concrete to tell you. A gut feeling is hardly evidence, is it?'

Whitney glanced at the super, who gave an almost imperceptible roll of her eyes. She could seriously swing for the man. He was a chief superintendent, for goodness' sake. But she'd get nothing from him unless she calmed herself down a bit. She could let off steam later when he was out of sight.

'True, but please could you tell me a little more about these *undertones?*'

Had he realised how much he'd annoyed her? Probably not, knowing him.

'Occasionally, David seemed secretive when I'd asked his about job and what was happening in his life.'

'Could you be more explicit?'

'Not really. I'd ask a question, and he'd deflect it. Like I said, it was nothing you could put your finger on, and I hadn't even thought about it until now.'

'Did your wife have the same *feelings?*' She clenched her fists in her lap to stop from doing the quote thing again.

'We didn't discuss it. I'll ask her this evening and report back to you in the morning.'

'Perhaps we should interview her again, sir,' Whitney suggested. There was no *perhaps* about it. They definitely should, if he'd let her.

'That's not necessary.'

'But, sir—'

'I said, it is not necessary.' His tone was icy, and she wasn't prepared to challenge him.

Would the super? She should. Maybe she'd do it once Whitney had left the room.

'Yes, sir.'

'What are you going to do with the boy in custody?'

'We've got thirty-six hours, as you know, and we haven't totally discounted his involvement, so we'll keep him here.'

'Do we have confirmation on cause of death yet?'

'I'm waiting to hear back from the pathologist, and I'll update the super when it comes through.'

'Make sure you do. If this boy isn't guilty, which seems possible, then the killer is still out there. That's not acceptable. I want them found without delay.'

'This is only day two and we're already making progress, sir.'

'Not fast enough for my liking. This case should be top priority and every member of your team should be giving it their full attention. I don't expect anyone to have a day off until this is solved. All overtime will be authorized by me. Don't make me regret allowing this case to remain with you.' He stood and then marched out of the room.

'Don't say anything, Whitney,' the super said, shaking her head.

'No, ma'am, I won't. At least you get to witness what he's like where I'm concerned and can see that I'm not exaggerating.'

'I know, but my advice is for you to ignore it and prove you're the right team for the job. Keep up the good work. I'm happy with the way the investigation is progressing. We'll speak again tomorrow.'

## Chapter 14

'Come in,' Whitney said to George while she stood on the doorstep holding the bottle of white wine she'd bought from the supermarket on her way there.

'Am I early? I wasn't sure what time you were expecting me.'

'Don't be daft. Any time is fine, you know that. It's not like you haven't been here hundreds of times before. Martin should arrive soon, and he's bringing a takeaway from that lovely new Thai restaurant in town. I told him to make sure to bring enough for you.'

She'd met Martin several times before and had found him most agreeable. Ross had enjoyed his company, too. But she didn't like to intrude on this family occasion. Whitney didn't have the chance to spend a lot of time with him, and now the baby was there, too, having her there might be too much.

'Are you sure you still want me, I don't wish to be in the way.'

'The more the merrier. Tiffany's really looking forward

to seeing you, and I know you want to see Ava. You won't believe how much she's grown already.'

George walked into the house and closed the door behind her. 'I'll put this in the fridge.' Wine had to be at the correct temperature to enjoy it, and the journey from the supermarket to Whitney's house had increased it. Fifteen to twenty minutes should be plenty of time.

'Help yourself. You know where everything is, we're in the lounge.'

She placed the wine in the fridge and headed into the lounge. Tiffany looked up and smiled, a contented look on her face. George had never entertained the idea of having children. It wasn't on her agenda. But seeing the happiness shine out of Tiffany, had she been wrong? At only thirty-seven she was certainly young enough to consider children, but did she want the upheaval in her life? Ross had once told her he'd always imagined having a family, but other than that, they hadn't discussed it.

'Hey, George. Look at Ava, she's twice the size since you last saw her.'

George headed over to the sofa and sat next to Tiffany, staring at the tiny bundle in her arms. 'She's still very small.'

'What do you expect at just over four weeks,' Whitney said, laughing.

'Bigger, as you'd said how much she'd grown,' she admitted.

'Would you like to hold her?' Tiffany moved Ava closer to George.

'I'm not sure she's ready for that,' Whitney said.

'Of course, I am,' George said, not wanting to admit that the thought of it was unnerving. She'd never held a baby before.

Tiffany passed over Ava, who was wrapped in a pink

blanket. 'Hold her in the crook of your arm and keep her head supported.'

George stared at the child's tiny face. Maybe she should consider … no … she wasn't going to go there. 'She's beautiful.'

'Beautiful and perfect. I feel so lucky. There's something I want to ask you, George,' Tiffany said, turning to face her.

To babysit? No, she had Whitney for that. Unless they wanted to go somewhere together. She could do it. Ross would help. Both of his older sisters had children, five between them.

'What is it?'

'I'm not having Ava christened because it's hypocritical, as I'm not religious. But that doesn't mean there won't be any godparents. I need to make sure there's someone who could be Ava's guardian if anything happens to me or Mum. Will you do it, please?'

She hadn't been expecting that. It was a huge task for anyone to undertake, let alone someone with her total lack of experience in childcare.

'Um … I don't know anything about children,' George said, staring down at Ava, panic coursing through her veins.

'Nor did I before giving birth, but I learnt. And will still be learning throughout her life. Look, it's not likely to happen, but in case it does, we want to know that you'll be there for her. We know you'll take good care of Ava. You are the best person by miles. Say yes. Please say yes.'

She was stunned into silence. A guardian to Ava. Could she take on that responsibility? She'd taken on other responsibilities during her life without there being an issue. But for another human being. What would Ross say?

Should she discuss it with him before deciding? No. It

was her decision, and she knew he'd go along with it. How could she say no? Tiffany and Whitney were so special to her, and now Ava.

'I'm extremely honoured to have been asked and would be privileged to accept.'

'See, Mum. I told you she wouldn't say no,' Tiffany said, a smug expression on her face.

'Did you think I would?' George asked, looking up at Whitney, who was leaning against the sideboard staring at them.

'I knew you've never wanted children and assumed you'd say no to Tiffany's request. Then again the pair of you do have a special relationship.'

Whitney was correct about their connection. George had been instrumental in locating Tiffany's whereabouts after she'd been kidnapped by a pair of psychotic twins. She would've been dead if it hadn't been for her discovery.

'Yes, we do,' George agreed.

'But now you've said yes, I'm thrilled to bits. You'll be perfect. I know you won't let any harm come to Ava, and you'll do your best to make sure she has a wonderful life. Which is all we could ask.'

Her lips turned up into a smile. She'd received many accolades in her life, but this was right at the top.

'As she will, with both of you. Nothing's going to happen. And before you say anything about jinxing, that's ridiculous,' she warned, locking eyes with Whitney.

'I wouldn't say that when we're talking about Ava. Now that's sorted, it's time for a celebration.' The doorbell rang. 'It sounds like Martin's arrived. Good, I'm hungry.' Whitney left the room.

'Can I give Ava back to you, Tiffany?'

'Yes, it's time she went down.'

'Here you are.' She gingerly passed the baby back.

'Thanks for agreeing to be Ava's guardian. There's no one else I would trust with my baby apart from you.'

'I promise she won't want for anything if ever the situation arises.'

'Was Mum right about you not wanting children of your own?'

It wouldn't be fair to tell the young mother that George's experience of growing up in a family wasn't one she'd wish to replicate.

'It's not something I've considered.'

'It's not too late, you know. Lots of women don't even start having children until they're in their forties, and you're nowhere near that.'

'I'm too busy with my career, helping the police, and being with Ross. We've decided to sell both of our houses and buy something together.'

'Where are you looking?'

'Close to Lenchester because of my work. It needs to be large enough for Ross to have a studio. We're thinking one of the villages, rather than in the city itself.'

'Make sure you have a spare room for visitors, so Ava can come to see you. Me, too.' Tiffany grinned.

'You'll be welcome any time you care to visit.'

'If you do decide to have children, they'll be able to play with Ava.'

'It's not on my agenda.'

Tiffany was typically idealistic, as kids often were at that age. It was amazing that even though she was only fourteen years younger than George, it seemed an enormous difference.

'That's what you say now, but you never know.' Tiffany grinned.

'I do know.'

Before they could continue the conversation, Whitney and Martin walked in. Excellent timing.

'I hope you're hungry because Martin has brought enough food to last a week.'

'I wasn't sure what you all liked, so I have a selection. Take these, Whitney, I want to see my gorgeous grand-daughter.' He handed Whitney the three large brown paper bags that he'd been holding and walked over to the sofa.

'Hello, Martin. How are you?' George asked, standing as he came over.

'Great, thanks. You?'

'Very well.'

'Would you like to take Ava?' Tiffany asked.

'You bet I would.' He leant down and took the child from Tiffany. 'She's so beautiful, isn't she? Just like her mother.'

'Yeah, all right, Martin. No need to get all sloppy,' Tiffany said, laughing. 'I'll put Ava down to rest while we're eating.' She took the baby from Martin and laid her in the Moses basket.

'Come on, let's eat before it gets cold. We'll go into the kitchen so we can spread the food out on the table,' Whitney said.

The lids were taken off the boxes, and everyone helped themselves.

'This is so delicious,' Tiffany said. 'We'll have to go here again, Mum.'

'Definitely,' Whitney agreed.

'Martin, George has agreed to be Ava's guardian if anything happens to me and Mum,' Tiffany said.

The smile on Martin's face froze. He wasn't happy. Were they seeking his approval?

'But I'm her grandfather. Surely I should be down as her registered guardian.'

'George lives here in Lenchester, and if anything happened to us, we'd want Ava's life to be disrupted as little possible. Also, it's not easy to bring up a child on your own, speaking from experience,' Whitney said.

'I could manage, if you'd let me. Nothing against you, George, but you're not related.'

'It's all hypothetical. Nothing's going to happen to us,' Whitney said, waving her hand dismissively.

'I understand why you'd want to be involved in Ava's life. But if it came to it, we could do it together,' George suggested.

'Yes, that's a good idea. Anyway, let's not talk about this now as nothing's going to happen to me or Mum. It's just something we wanted to put in place, for our peace of mind,' Tiffany said.

'I second that,' Whitney said, holding up a glass and then taking a large swallow.

'Don't overindulge on the wine. We've got a lot of work to do with the case,' George said.

'Spoilsport,' Whitney said. 'Although you're right. I feel guilty enough for coming home early.'

'Six o'clock isn't early when you left for work at six this morning. You've got to get some rest,' Tiffany said.

'You know that, and I know that. But try telling it to Dickhead, because he thinks we should be there 24/7.'

'Dickhead?' Martin said, frowning.

'One of my bosses. I've known him for years and he hates me.'

'I think hate is too strong a word,' George said.

'What would you say, then?'

'If you want my opinion, I'd say he's envious of your

ability, and feels threatened by you. He always has done. He's simply using his position to protect himself.'

'Even if that's true, he's still a dickhead. But that aside, this will be my only drink this evening, because I need to get up early to make a start. I've asked the team to be there by seven-thirty tomorrow morning.'

'I've got a research committee meeting at work tomorrow morning and a department meeting in the afternoon, so won't be able to make it in,' George said.

'Does that mean your annual leave is now over?'

'These meetings were arranged after I booked it. I've cancelled it just for tomorrow.'

'That seems a bit unfair to you. What if you'd gone on holiday somewhere?'

'I haven't, so it's a moot point. I don't mind going in. I'd rather be there than not, to make sure my views are heard regarding any decisions.'

'That makes sense. What about Wednesday?'

'I'm back on leave then. I'll see you first thing.'

## Chapter 15

By seven-fifteen everyone had arrived, and Whitney called the team to attention. 'I appreciate you all being here early because we've got a lot to do. It's already nearly forty-eight hours since the Barker family bodies were found, and I want an update on where we are. As we are all *very* aware, we're under intense scrutiny and our every move is being monitored.'

'Providing they don't start spying on me in the loo, then that's okay,' Frank said, giving a loud belly laugh.

'Not too much curry again? Haven't you learnt by now that it doesn't agree with you? Remind me to give you a wide berth, and use the toilets on the next floor,' Doug said, screwing up his nose.

'Seriously? You're starting already, when you know we have so much to do? I have no desire to hear about anyone's bowel movements. Now, or at any other time,' Whitney said, unable to suppress the grin on her lips.

'Don't blame me, it's him,' Frank said, jabbing a finger in Doug's direction.

'You started it,' Doug said.

'Enough,' Whitney said, holding up both hands. 'Let's get on. I'll start. Following the interview with Corey Hudson, I spoke to Chief Superintendent Douglas about David Barker possibly having had an affair. He didn't know but did say that he'd been acting secretively the last time they'd met.'

'Why didn't he tell you this before?' Frank asked.

'Your guess is as good as mine. I asked to interview his wife again, and he refused. He's going to speak to her and let us know if she has anything further to add. It's not ideal, but my hands were tied and as long as we get some answers it shouldn't matter.'

'If you say so,' Frank said.

'Yes, I do. Where are we on the finances, Ellie?' She turned to face the officer.

'I might have something for you later. I'm currently undertaking several lines of enquiry.'

'That sounds mysterious,' Frank said.

'I want to be sure of my facts before making accusations,' Ellie said.

'That's fine. There's no point in telling us bits and pieces as you go. Just remember that we need to move on this as soon as possible, so work quickly.'

She wasn't sure why she'd said that, because the speed with which Ellie could work was mind-boggling.

'I know, guv. Leave it with me,' Ellie said.

'Where did the kids go to school?'

'Eden Vale Secondary, guv,' Meena said.

'Were they all at the same school?'

'Yes. Tyler was in year nine, Harvey in year ten, and Keira in year twelve.'

'Good. It makes it easier when we go to visit if they were all at the one place. Do we have further details about the parents' workplaces? Brian, you were looking into that, weren't you? What did you find?'

'Gillian Barker worked part-time as a physiotherapist at Lenchester Physio and David Barker was a senior technology consultant at Hutt Consulting which is based in Birmingham. His work involved travelling around the country visiting clients and providing technical support. He spent a lot of time away from home,' Brian said.

'Thanks. What do we know about the extended families of David and Gillian? Other than David was an only child, and his mother is dead, which Belinda Douglas told me.'

'David Barker's father is still alive, but he's got dementia and is in a nursing home in Bath. He's been in there for three years. Other than that, David's closest living relative was an aunt on his mother's side,' Doug said.

'That's Belinda Douglas's mother. What about Gillian's family?'

'She had a younger sister, Penny Burn, who still lives in Poole, where the family moved to in the nineties, as do her elderly parents. The police down there informed the family of the deaths. Penny is coming to view the bodies and formally identify them later today.'

'Okay. You can coordinate that. You'll need to speak to Dr Dexter to let her know when you'll be there.'

'Yes, guv.'

'When you're with the sister, find out what you can about the family and if she knows of any reason for them to be targeted.'

'Will do, guv.'

'What else did you find on social media, Meena?'

'Out of the three of them, Keira, posted the most. There are lots of photos of her with her friends, also of her with Corey Hudson. She'd recently been posting photos of herself with her new boyfriend. There was nothing out of the ordinary on her account that I could see. Harvey's posts were mainly him with his friends at school or playing football. Usual teen boy stuff. The youngest, Tyler, had a social media account but seldom posted.'

'Okay, now we have some background, Brian and I will go to the school to speak to the children's teachers and classmates. We'll see if there's anything they can add to what we already know. Then we'll head to Gillian's work-place because it's close. We'll need to visit David's work-place, too. Because it's in Birmingham that might have to wait until tomorrow. Frank, did you speak to Zak Lyle?'

'Yes, guv. He wasn't aware of Hudson following him and Keira. At school, Hudson had ignored him, but not threatened him or caused any aggravation. Hardly surprising, because Lyle's a lot bigger.'

'I want you and Doug to go back to Beech Avenue and scour the area for any security cameras. We're looking for any footage that can corroborate the time Hudson said he left. I know there's no CCTV in the vicinity, but Meena, check footage leading to the Westcliffe area to see if there's anything unusual.'

'Yes, guv.'

'Okay, everyone knows what they're doing. Come on, Brian, let's go. We'll take your car.'

'No Dr Cavendish today?' Brian said as they were on their way to the car park.

'She's at work.'

'Which is why I'm going with you.'

Despite being on the team for over six months, Whitney still wasn't quite sure what he meant with comments like that. Was he stating a fact, or feeling second best?

'Not necessarily. Is it an issue?'

'Merely an observation.'

She still wasn't sure what that meant, but she didn't have time to ruminate over it. They had a job to do.

'Once we get to Eden Vale, we'll arrange to interview the teachers first, and then we'll speak to the pupils. If there was anything untoward going on, it might have affected their schoolwork. Also, speaking to the children's friends should give us a better picture of the family. If there were issues, the kids might have confided in their close friends.'

'If they're at school today. They might have stayed at home because of the shock.'

'Maybe, but my guess is they'd rather be at school with their friends so they can comfort each other. That tends to be what happens.'

'True,' Brian said, nodding.

# Chapter 16

They drove in silence towards the school, allowing Whitney time to think about the previous night. Martin had clearly been upset when they'd asked George to be a guardian to Ava should anything happen. Was he justified? She got that he'd want to be in their lives, but he'd hardly been around long enough to be considered suitable for being Ava's guardian. Plus, his situation was far from practical. He lived alone in London. George was the perfect choice. She lived close by. She had Ross. And she had an unbreakable bond with Tiffany, after saving her life.

It was all hypothetical, anyway. Nothing was going to happen to her or Tiffany.

'We'll see the head teacher to arrange meeting with the form teachers,' she said when they pulled into the school car park and found an empty space close to the front entrance.

They walked through the entrance and turned left, following the directional signs to the school office. They walked over to the woman seated behind a desk which had a *School Secretary* nameplate on it.

She held out her warrant card. 'I'm DCI Walker and this is DS Chapman. We're here about the Barker children. We'd like to speak to the head, please.'

'We're all devastated. They were such lovely children.' The woman's eyes filled with tears, and she pulled out a tissue from the box on her desk and wiped her eyes. 'I'll let Dr Johnson know you're here. She's been expecting your visit.'

'Thank you.'

The woman left her desk and headed over to a closed door to the right. She knocked and walked in without waiting for a response, closing the door behind her. Whitney could hear voices but couldn't make out the words.

After a few minutes, the door opened and a tall woman in her fifties, with wavy grey hair, wearing a navy trouser suit and pale-blue blouse, came out. The school secretary followed and skirted behind her and returned to her desk.

'I'm Deirdre Johnson, the head teacher. Please come on through and take a seat.' She gestured for them to go through into the office and once in there Whitney and Brian sat on the low chairs surrounding a coffee table.

'It must be very difficult for everyone here at the school,' Whitney said, once the head teacher had joined them.

'It's yet to sink in properly for most of us. Staff and students alike. We have counsellors ready for any of the pupils who might require it, although so far not many have taken up the offer. It's early days though. After discussing with the senior management team, we decided to continue with lessons, as usual, to give the children a sense of normality, although in a more relaxed manner. The whole atmosphere in the school is one of shock and disbelief, and

I don't expect it to change for a while yet. Not while it's the focal point in the media.'

'I agree, and the media won't leave it alone until we have found the killer. While we're here, we'd like to interview the form teachers of Keira, Harvey, and Tyler, and then any of their friends who are in school. If we could do so in here that would help. It's private, comfortable, and out of the way.'

'Yes, here would be the best place for you to talk freely to them. I'll arrange for the form teachers to see you straight away and they'll let you know who their friends are. Do you want me to sit in on the interviews?'

'It would help if you were here while we speak to their teachers. You may be able to give us some information. We'd like to speak to the children alone in case they feel intimidated with you present.'

'That seems the most appropriate course of action. Would you like some coffee while I arrange for the teachers to come here? It might take a while to find them and have someone sit in their class while they leave it.'

'That would be lovely, thank you,' Whitney said.

'Did you go to this school?' Brian asked once Dr Johnson had left.

'No, I went to North Lenchester Academy on the other side of the city. This school wasn't around when I was young. It was built when the city expanded.'

'Is that where you started singing? I've heard you're awesome.'

'Who told you that?'

'Frank. He said you sing in a choir, and they've been to watch your concerts.'

'I'm a member of the local Rock Choir, but I miss more rehearsals than I attend. Perks of the job. But—'

The school secretary came in carrying a tray with two

mugs of coffee and a plate of biscuits which she placed on the table and then left.

Brian handed Whitney a mug, and she sniffed before placing it on a coaster on the coffee table. She helped herself to a biscuit, and they waited for Dr Johnson to return.

'You were saying,' Brian said.

'Only that I belong to the choir, but it's hard because of the job.'

'When's your next concert? I'd love to watch.'

Whitney glanced at him. Was he being serious?

'We usually do three a year. Most likely August, and if not, definitely one at Christmas. I'll let you know, but don't feel obliged to watch.'

'If the rest of the team go then I'd like to be with them.'

'Okay, that would be great.' If he was trying to be more involved then she wasn't going to stand in the way.

After a further ten minutes, the door opened and the head walked in, followed by two men and one woman.

'This is Anne Parkinson, Keira's form teacher. Bill Asher, who was Harvey's and Eric Robinson, who was Tyler's,' Dr Johnson said, nodding at each of her staff in turn.

They all sat around the table and stared directly at Whitney.

'I'm DCI Walker, and this is DS Chapman. We're very sorry for your loss. It must have been a shock for you all and your students.'

'I couldn't believe it when I saw it on the news,' Anne Parkinson said, the oldest of the three teachers, her eyes filling with tears, which she blinked away.

'We'd like to speak to the children's closest friends. But before we do that, what can you tell us about each of them? If we could start with Keira.' Whitney scribbled some notes while focusing on Anne Parkinson.

'Keira was an excellent student and planning to go to university to study languages. She was popular and a delight to have in the class. She was close friends with two other girls, Phoebe Tindall, and Isobel Norman. The three of them were inseparable at school.'

'Are Phoebe and Isobel in school today?'

'Yes. I've spoken to them privately and said that if it gets too much to find me. They said they'd rather be here together and with the rest of their class, than at home. I think it's for the best.'

'I agree. We know that Keira recently finished with her boyfriend, Corey Hudson, and started dating Zak Lyle. Neither boy was from this school. Do you know anything about that?' Whitney asked.

'No, sorry. I don't. Keira didn't ever confide in me regarding her boyfriends. Why would she?' Anne Parkinson said with a small shrug.

'Is there anything that you can think of concerning Keira that I should know?'

'Nothing other than what I've told you. I'm sorry.'

'That's fine. What about Harvey?' Whitney asked, turning to Bill Asher, a short, stocky man in his forties, who was leaning forward in his chair his fists clenched.

'It's such a tragedy. Harvey was a lively and popular boy. He hung around in a gang of four or five boys in the class. He wasn't the best behaved, and at times pushed the boundaries, but it was harmless pranks and nothing serious. I liked him. He certainly wasn't academic, like his sister, but he was good at sport and was on the football and cricket teams. I understand that Dylan Fletcher found the bodies.'

'Who told you this?' Whitney asked. They hadn't released any of the details to the media.

'He did this morning, when he came back to school.'

'How's he coping?'

'Trying to act all manly about it in front of his peers, but when we were alone, I could see how much it had affected him. I've spoken to him at length about having counselling. I hope he goes.'

'We suggested it to his parents. What can you tell us about Tyler?' She turned to face Eric Robinson, the youngest of the three teachers, and dressed more casually in chinos and an open shirt.

'Tyler was a loner and would mainly hang out with Rex Smith. Both of them were hard workers, and appeared content with their own company, or just being with each other. I rarely saw them with any other students in the class.'

'Did Tyler appear unhappy? Was he bullied or teased by others in the class?'

'No. Tyler's peers accepted that he preferred to be on the periphery rather than the centre of attention. His older brother and sister were hard acts to follow, for different reasons. Whether that had any bearing on his behaviour in school, I can't say.'

'Was he academic or sporty?'

'He achieved good marks because of his diligence and no doubt would have gone on to higher education. He didn't show any interest in sport, other than during designated PE time.'

'We'd like to speak to their closest friends if you could bring them here. Before that, did any of you notice anything out of the ordinary at school over recent weeks? Anything which gave you cause for concern. Someone hanging around who looked suspicious. The Barker children acting differently from normal. Any deviation whatsoever in their behaviour and routine.'

The teachers exchanged glances with each other and then all shook their heads.

'Thank you. If you could find the children and ask them to come to the office, please. Also find Mrs Allen and ask her to join them. She's our pastoral care teacher,' Dr Johnson said, turning to Whitney.

'Are you speaking to all of them at the same time?' Bill asked.

'Yes, it will be less intimidating for them. They've had enough to deal with already, without having the worry of speaking to the police,' Whitney said.

Dr Johnson opened the door for the teachers to leave and returned to sit opposite Whitney.

'Before the students arrive, there's something that I've remembered. I don't know if it's relevant. A few months ago, I saw Keira with her friends outside during the lunch break. She appeared upset and was crying.'

'Did you ask her what was wrong?' Whitney asked.

'Yes, and she told me it was nothing. I didn't pursue it as her friends were taking care of her. At that age, young people are full of hormones and get emotional over things that we'd consider not to be huge in the grand scheme of things. It most likely has nothing to do with the deaths, but I thought you should know.'

'Thank you. I'll keep the girls back after we've interviewed the students and ask for further details. That way, they might open up more.'

There was a knock at the door, and it opened immediately. The school secretary ushered the seven students into the room and they were followed by an older woman.

Once the students were seated, Dr Johnson introduced

each of them, including Mrs Allen, who was seated in the corner observing.

'I'll leave you to it,' the head said to Whitney, on her way out.

Whitney turned to the students, who sat in silence staring directly at her, every one of their faces ashen.

'I'm Detective Chief Inspector Walker and this is Detective Sergeant Chapman. We're here because of what happened to Keira, Harvey, and Tyler. We understand from your teachers that you were all close friends with one of them and we're very sorry for your loss. We're going to find whoever did this, and we need your help to identify anyone who might have been involved. Is there anything you can tell us? Anything at all that might help with our enquiries?'

The students stared at them. None of them speaking. Had she gone in too broad? Maybe she should be more direct.

'Rex, how was Tyler when you last saw him?'

'Okay,' the youngster replied, keeping his head lowered.

'When was this?'

'At school on Friday.'

'Did you arrange to meet over the weekend?'

'No.'

'Did he tell you what he'd got planned on Saturday and Sunday?'

'No, we didn't talk about it.'

The teacher had told them about Tyler and his friend being loners, but she hadn't realised quite how much. Were his parents concerned? She'd have been.

'Thank you, that's very helpful. What about Harvey?' she asked, turning to his four friends.

'We'd all arranged to play football on Sunday morning.

I don't know what he did on Saturday,' one of them said.

'He went shopping with Mrs Barker on Saturday because he wanted to buy some clothes for cricket camp in the summer holidays,' Dylan said, his face pale and drawn.

'Thank you. Can you think of anything that Harvey was concerned about?'

'His report. He talked about it all the time because his dad said if he didn't improve from last time he might not be able to go to camp. But it was too late to do anything about it,' Dylan said.

'And was it going to be better than his previous one?' Brian asked.

'I don't know. None of us have really good reports. But they're not totally bad,' Dylan said, shrugging.

'Does anyone have anything else to tell us about Harvey and Tyler?' Whitney asked.

The kids all shook their heads and muttered 'no.'

'Thank you for your help. If any of you think of something that might help us, Dr Johnson has my card, and she'll contact me. You can all go, except Phoebe and Isobel. We'd like to talk to you alone.'

Whitney went to the door and opened it so they could leave. Dr Johnson was standing by the secretary's desk, and she headed over to them.

'Come with me, boys. We'll go to the hall, and you can sit for a while before returning to class.' Dr Johnson gave a slight nod in Whitney's direction.

Whitney returned to the head's office. Phoebe's knuckles were white as she held onto her skirt and Isobel stared blankly ahead.

'It's all right. You're not in any trouble. There are a few things we'd like to go over with you in private without the boys being here,' Whitney said, to reassure them.

Both girls visibly relaxed a little.

'Okay,' Phoebe said, while Isobel nodded.

'We've been informed that several months ago, Keira was upset about something, and she was seen crying at school. Can you tell me what that was about?'

The girls exchanged a glance, uncertainty in their eyes.

'Um …' Phoebe said, biting down on her bottom lip.

'You're not going to get into any trouble, and it might help us catch the person who did this awful thing if you tell us whatever you know.'

Whitney waited. Again they looked at each other. Isobel gave a nod, and Phoebe did the same. Good. It appeared that they were going to tell her.

'Keira found out something about her dad,' Phoebe said.

Whitney went on full alert. A lead? Or was she just repeating what Corey had told her, even though she didn't admit to him that she believed it?

'What was it exactly?'

'Her dad was having an affair.'

Nothing new there.

'How did she find out?'

'Corey, who she was seeing at the time, told her.'

Whitney's shoulders sagged. It was the same as Corey had told them. Not that it wasn't a lead, because it appeared most likely true. But Whitney had been hoping for more.

'And she believed him?'

Whitney didn't want to let on that they already had this information.

'Not at first. She thought Corey had got it wrong. She said her dad would never do anything like that.'

'What happened to change her mind?'

'Even though she didn't believe Corey, she couldn't stop thinking about it. She talked about it all the time. We decided she should get hold of her dad's phone when he was asleep. He always kept it downstairs at night so he wouldn't get disturbed.'

'Wasn't it locked?'

'She guessed that his pin was the same as the one he used for his credit card. It's what all old people do.'

Whitney shifted in her seat. It was exactly what she did, too.

'I'm assuming she found something on his phone.'

'Yes, he'd been texting a woman.'

'Did you see these texts?'

'No. Keira told us about them.'

'Did she tell you the woman's name?'

'No. She just called her *the bitch*,' Isobel said.

'Did she mention knowing her? Could it have been a family friend or a colleague?'

'I don't think she knew her,' Phoebe said.

'Did Keira say anything to her mum or dad about what she knew?'

'No. She didn't want to in case it caused her parents to split up.'

'So, the only people who knew what she'd found were the two of you,' Whitney confirmed.

'Yes. And we swore to keep it a secret.'

'Why didn't she tell Corey that he was right about what he'd heard?'

'She was thinking about ending it with him by then and didn't trust him not to tell anyone. He could be very possessive and difficult.'

'Did she think he might threaten to tell her mum and force her to stay with him?' Whitney asked, not wanting to assume, but that seemed to be it.

'Yeah,' Phoebe said.

'Was there anything else going on with Keira that we

should know about? Her relationship with Zak, for example?'

'That wasn't serious. She liked him and enjoyed having fun. After Corey that's all she wanted. She was upset about her dad but had decided to stop thinking about it because nothing at home had changed.'

'We appreciate your honesty. You can go now. Remember to contact me through Dr Johnson if there's anything else you want to discuss.'

They left, along with Mrs Allen, and Brian turned to her. 'Now we're getting somewhere.'

'We need to get hold of David Barker's phone. Let's call into Gillian Barker's work, and then we'll go back to the station.'

## Chapter 17

'Lenchester Physio's on Compton Street. Do you know where that is?' Whitney asked Brian when they returned to his car.

'No, but my satnav does.' He keyed in the address.

The clinic was a twenty-minute drive and was situated in a modern, white, single-storey building with a car park behind it. They entered through the door at the rear and followed the signs along the wide corridor to the reception.

Whitney held out her warrant card, so the woman behind the desk could see it. 'I'm DCI Walker from Lenchester CID and this is DS Chapman. We'd like to speak to the person in charge, please.'

'Is this about Gillian?' the woman asked, her voice breaking.

'Yes, it is.'

Tears filled her eyes. 'What happened to them is so awful. I can't stop thinking about it. Why would someone do that to such a lovely family?'

'That's what we're investigating. Who's in charge here?' Whitney repeated, gently.

'Our head physiotherapist, Kate Simons. I'll ask her to come out to see you, she's in her office.' She picked up the phone. 'The police are here to see you about Gill.' She replaced her phone. 'She's on her way.'

A short while later, a door to the left opened and a tall woman wearing navy cargo trousers and a matching tunic top headed towards them.

'I'm Kate Simons. You must be from the police.'

'Yes,' Whitney said, showing her ID and then returning it to her pocket.

'If you'd like to come with me, we can talk in my treatment room which is out of the way.'

They followed her into a square room that had a chrome bed covered with a paper sheet along one of the walls, a skeleton in one corner, some bands, balls, and weights in the other corner, and a large mirror on the wall. There was an office desk under the window with three chairs beside it.

'I was stunned when the news about Gill and the rest of the family was announced on the TV,' Kate said, as they all sat.

'Did you inform the rest of the staff?'

'Yes, I phoned them all individually. I didn't want to leave it to any of the more junior staff. Most of them already knew when I called.'

'We'd like to ask you a few questions about Gillian, if we may.'

'Yes, of course. Whatever I can do to help, although I'm not sure that I know anything.'

'You'll be able to assist us in putting together a complete picture of the family. How long did Gillian work for you?' Whitney held a pen in her hand, poised to write.

'She joined us part-time three years ago. Her hours were flexible, depending on the children.'

'Did she apply for an advertised position, or did you already know her?' Brian asked.

Whitney shot a glance in his direction. He knew that she liked to ask all the questions. Then again, she had been letting him do more in interviews. Unlike her previous sergeant, Matt, Brian was intent on advancing his career, and took every opportunity he could to push himself forward.

'We advertised for a part-time physio and she applied. It helped that I'd trained with the woman she used for her referee.'

'Did Gillian tell you anything about her home life?' Whitney asked.

'We spoke generally, but not in any great depth. I know that David was often away on business and that did put pressure on her because she had full responsibility for the family. She didn't let that interfere with her work here, though.'

'What do you know about her relationship with David?'

'I didn't ever hear her complain about him, so I assumed it was fine.'

'Did Gillian have regular clients?'

'A few, but most of the time we see people for a while until their issue is solved. Some of them will come back, but not a high percentage.'

'Did she have any clients who caused her problems, or that she was concerned about?'

Kate shook her head. 'None that she reported to me. We had regular one-on-one supervision meetings to discuss her work, and I'm sure she would have said then if there were any issues. Gillian was very good at her job, and recently we'd been discussing her doing more hours now the children were less dependent on her.'

'Was Gillian friends with anyone in particular at work? Anyone she might have confided in regarding personal matters?'

'If there was to be anyone, it would be me. We'd sometimes go out for lunch together. I never got the impression that she was having problems. There are only six of us here. Five physios and Zoe on reception, and we all get on well together.'

'Do you socialise out of work?'

'Occasionally we'll all go out for a meal or a drink, but not often. We have families to get back to.'

'Did you ever see Gillian and David together socially?'

'At the office Christmas party. That's when we all brought our partners.'

'When they were together, did you detect any tension between them?'

'None. Do you think something happened between them and it resulted in all their deaths?' Kate asked, her brow furrowed.

'We don't know but have to look into every aspect of their lives. Do you know Gillian and David's history? How they met?'

'They met at university when Gill was training to be a physio. I'm not sure what David was studying.'

'Did you notice whether Gillian appeared distracted at all recently?' Whitney pushed. They were getting nowhere fast here.

'Gill was always on an even keel, and I'd have noticed if that changed. But it didn't. She was the same as always right up to … when it happened. I'm sorry I can't be of more use. I wish I did know something to help you catch the person who did this. Do you think it was directed at her or one of the family? Or were the killings random?'

'This is what we're investigating. Can you tell me what

you were doing on Saturday night between the hours of ten and midnight? We ask this of everyone we interview, to exclude them from our enquiries,' Whitney added, pre-empting the woman asking why.

'I went to London for the weekend with my partner to go shopping and catch a show. We stayed overnight and came back on Sunday afternoon. My partner can vouch for me if you'd like his number.'

'What show did you see?'

'*Pretty Woman*. It was excellent.'

There were a host of shows Whitney wanted to see, that being one of them. She'd mentioned to Martin about booking tickets for something, but they hadn't got around to it. There was no chance of a weekend away, now. Not until the murders were solved.

'Please will you write down your partner's contact details,' Whitney said, handing over her notebook.

'You can reach him on this number for most of the day. Is there anything else you need me for? My next client is due any minute now.' Kate passed back the notebook.

'That's all for now. Thank you for your time,' Whitney said.

'I'm sorry I couldn't be of more help.'

'You've given us more information to work with. Like I said, we want to get as full a picture as possible of the family. Please contact me if anything else comes to mind.' Whitney gave her a card.

They left the room and headed back outside.

'Do you want to speak to anyone else who works here, guv?' Brian asked.

'Not at the moment. We've got enough to work with.'

'Back to the station?'

'Yes.'

## Chapter 18

'Guv,' Ellie called out as Whitney and Brian walked into the incident room.

Whitney stopped in her tracks and turned to face her.

'What is it?'

'We've got a break in the case,' the officer said, a smile playing at the corners of her mouth.

'That's fantastic.'

Whitney took several steps in her direction. A break? That was the best news possible. Was it going to add to what she'd found out about David Barker?

'It's more than fantastic,' Doug said.

He was sitting next to Ellie, and since Matt had left, they'd struck up a good relationship. For all of Ellie's exceptional research skills, she still lacked in confidence sometimes, despite there being no reason for it.

'Why does he know and I don't?' Frank asked.

'Ellie didn't want you getting in first and taking the credit for all her hard work,' Doug said.

'Don't be stupid, the guv knows—'

'That you're not clever enough?' Doug interrupted.

'You two will be the death of me. Go ahead, Ellie. Ignore these Neanderthals.'

'You sure know how to hurt,' Doug said, pulling a face. Whitney glared at him. 'Sorry, guv,' he said, holding up both hands in mock surrender.

'Ellie?' Whitney asked, desperate to know what the officer had discovered.

'Corey Hudson was right about David Barker being with another woman.'

Whitney's heart dipped. They already had confirmation of that.

'That's great,' she said, not wanting to dampen the officer's enthusiasm. 'Keira's friends told us about it, too. It turns out Keira had discovered incriminating texts on her dad's phone, and she was very upset by it, and—'

'Guv, give Ellie a chance. There's a lot more than that,' Doug said, interrupting her.

She glanced at Ellie, who was still smiling.

'Sorry, you go ahead.'

'David Barker wasn't just having an affair. He had a whole other life with a woman who lives in Coventry called Tracy Osman. They have a young child together, aged four.'

Whoa. Now that really was a lead.

'And he kept it secret this whole time,' Whitney muttered.

'His job took him away from home, so he probably made out he was away more often than he needed to be,' Brian said.

'This really is excellent. What else did you discover, Ellie?' Whitney asked, sensing that there would be more.

'They've got a joint bank account, and he puts money in there each month.'

'Where does the money come from? You said there was

nothing out of the ordinary coming from the account he shared with his wife which is the account his monthly salary was paid into.'

'I discovered he had another one, in his own name, into which his bimonthly commission was paid. It was from here that he made monthly payments into the joint account he had with Tracy Osman.'

'The crafty bastard,' Frank said.

'Do they rent a place together?"'

'No. They live in a house that she inherited from her parents who died five years ago.'

'So, no rent or mortgage to pay. Does she work?'

'If she does, it's on the side because there's no record of her being employed, or any wages going into the account. David Barker was the only one to put money in there. She withdrew from it regularly using her debit card.'

'Good work. You're a genius. We need to pay this woman a visit. Would you like to come with me, Ellie? We'll leave straight away.'

Whitney asking was a spur-of-the-moment decision. She was determined to push the officer forward.

'Me?' Ellie asked, her eyes wide.

'Yes, you. Do you want to? It's about time we got you away from your desk. I know you love the research, but it's good to do something else now and again.'

'Cool. Thanks, guv.'

'Before we go, has Mac got back to you about Corey Hudson's laptop?'

'Not yet. I'm hoping he will by first thing tomorrow. He knows it's urgent. They've got a lot of work on.'

'I don't suppose he mentioned all the devices belonging to the family.'

'No, guv.'

'I want them to send back David Barker's mobile so you can put it through the self-service kiosk tomorrow now we've got this latest information from Keira's friends. Brian, can you do that for me, while we're out this afternoon?'

'Yes, guv. I'll do it straight away before I meet Gillian Barker's sister.'

'Thanks. Ellie, grab your things and we'll go. What car do you drive?'

'I came by bus this morning.' The DC took her handbag from the back of her chair and slung it over her shoulder.

'It looks like we'll go in mine then.'

They stopped at the station canteen for a quick sandwich and coffee, because Whitney was both hungry and in need of a caffeine fix, and then went into the car park and over to Whitney's old Ford Focus. One day she'd get around to buying something newer and more comfortable. At the moment, she'd rather spend her money on Tiffany and the baby. She'd been planning on putting a conservatory on the back of her house which would be a lot more useful than a new car.

'Now we're on our own, tell me your plans for the future in the force,' Whitney said, once she'd begun driving.

'I don't know,' Ellie said, biting down on her bottom lip.

That wasn't what she'd expected. The young woman was hiding something, Whitney thought, channelling her inner George.

'Are you going to take the sergeant exam?'

'I'm not cut out to lead an investigation or be in charge of other officers. I much prefer doing the research.'

'Are you happy being part of my team?' she asked outright, no point in pussyfooting around.

'Yes, but …'

Here it comes.

'Please don't tell me you're thinking of leaving.'

Damn. She hadn't meant to put her on the spot like that.

'Not yet.'

'When?'

'When Dean finishes his training, he wants us to move to London.'

'Dean?'

'My boyfriend.'

Ellie rarely said anything about her personal life. She'd mentioned a boyfriend once, a few months ago, but Whitney had no idea it was this serious.

'What's so attractive about London?'

'Great Ormond Street Hospital. He's training to be a paediatric nurse and has his heart set on working there.'

'When do you think you'll be leaving?'

'Not for a year or so. He still has another twelve months of training to go, and he might look to get some work experience locally before he applies.'

Whitney breathed a sigh of relief. Another year at least. That was good to hear.

'Will you transfer to one of the London forces?'

'I'm not sure. It's too soon to think about it.'

'Whatever you decide, you'll have a glowing reference from me. You can count on it.'

'Thanks so much. I'll give you plenty of notice so you can find someone to replace me.'

'No one will ever replace you, Ellie. Your skills are way outside the curve. I've always known we wouldn't be able to hang on to you forever.'

'There are other people who can do what I can, just not in our team. Although Brian ... I mean Sergeant Chapman ... is good at research.'

'Let's not talk about it now or I might get upset,' Whitney said, choking back a tear.

## Chapter 19

They arrived at Denby Street, and Whitney parked outside the traditional 1930s brick and pebble-dashed semi-detached house, where Tracy Osman lived.

The woman who answered the door was wearing leggings and a baggy T-shirt. Her eyes were red-rimmed, and black mascara streaks stained her cheeks.

'Are you Tracy Osman?' Whitney asked.

'Yes.'

'I'm DCI Whitney Walker and this is DC Ellie Naylor from Lenchester CID, we'd like to talk to you.'

'Is it about David?'

At least the woman knew, and Whitney didn't have to break the news to her. That was a relief. Considering she'd had some time to process the news and come to terms with it a little, she might be able to answer their questions.

'Yes, it is. May we come inside?'

Tracy turned, and they followed her into an open-plan lounge/dining area where there was a child sitting on a chair, her thumb in her mouth and holding a teddy bear.

She faced the telly which had cartoons blaring out at full blast.

'How did you find out about me?' Tracy asked, as they stood together.

'Is there somewhere quiet we can speak?' Whitney nodded at the child, not knowing how much she might understand of their conversation, nor what Tracy had told her.

'We'll go into the kitchen. This is Verity's favourite cartoon and she's not going to move until it's over.'

'How old is she?'

'Four.'

'She's a cutie.'

'Thanks. She's well-behaved … mostly.'

'I remember those days,' Whitney said, smiling, wanting to put the woman at her ease.

'I'll leave the doors open so I can hear if she calls out for anything.'

They returned to the hall and walked into an untidy kitchen. Every surface was covered with crockery, toys, books, and other bits. In the centre was a small circular table, on which stood a pile of magazines.

Interesting that this house was so different from the Barkers'. This was as untidy as theirs was tidy. Was that one of the attractions to David? Especially if it was Gillian who was so obsessively house-proud.

'We discovered your relationship with David after researching into his finances and finding your joint bank account. When did you discover what had happened to the family?' Whitney asked.

'David wasn't answering his phone or responding to my texts, and I got worried. He'd never done that before. He was always so considerate. Then I saw the murders reported on the news. It …' Her voice cracked.

Was she being genuine? She seemed to be. But Whitney wasn't going to rule her out. Not yet.

'I'm sorry for your loss and how you learnt of the news. We'd like to talk to you about your relationship with David, if you're up to it.'

'Yes. If it helps find who did this.' Her hands were balled into tight fists on the table.

'How long have you been together?'

'We met six years ago when he spent several months at the company I was working at. He was advising on the implementation of a new IT system, and I was his liaison person.'

'What was your position at the company?'

'I was a development officer. We got on well, and when my parents died, he supported me. Our relationship progressed from there. I know he was married, and I shouldn't have done it, but he told me they only stayed together for the sake of the children. He said they lived separate lives and had an understanding that once the children were older they would part and we could then be together all of the time.'

If that was true, it was the first Whitney had heard of it.

'Did you have a specific date set for when he'd be moving in with you permanently?'

'No. I did ask him about it recently, but he said not yet. He wanted to wait a while longer until Tyler was older. I didn't mind.'

Whitney didn't believe that for one moment. She wished George could've been there to assess the woman's body language. She was being too accepting of the whole situation. There was no way she wouldn't feel at least some resentment at having to play second fiddle. But why murder the whole family and not leave him? Her daughter was left without a father, and her source of income had been cut off. Unless he'd left her something in his will. They hadn't looked at the family wills yet.

'How would you describe your relationship?'

'David was kind and considerate, and very good with our little girl, Verity.'

'What was his reaction when you became pregnant?'

'It wasn't planned, but we were both excited.' Tracy blushed, and her fingers grazed across the side of her nose.

Even Whitney realised that wasn't the truth.

'You say it wasn't planned, but your body language is telling me otherwise. Did you deliberately get pregnant hoping to force David's hand because you wanted him to live with you?'

'It wasn't like that.'

'How was it?'

'I wanted to have a baby and admit that I stopped taking the contraceptive pill. It wasn't to persuade David to move in with me. I'd accepted that he wasn't ready. But I didn't want to wait because the older you get the harder it is to fall pregnant. I was telling the truth about him being excited. I told him it was an accident and he believed me. He was with me during the birth and stayed with me for the first five days before having to leave and go home.'

'How often did you see David?'

'He stayed here two or three nights a week, if he could. It wasn't always possible, it depended on his workload.'

'Did he talk about his family?'

'Yes. Well, about his children. He rarely mentioned Gillian. I know he struggled sometimes for money. They lived in a lovely house, and he had lots of expenses. He said when we lived together full-time we'd buy somewhere bigger, but this was the house I grew up in and I'm happy here. I told him that, but I think he felt I deserved to live somewhere larger.'

'How was David with Verity?'

'Very good. He was a great dad. He loved her and was happy for me to stay at home taking care of her. I don't know what I'm going to do now because there'll be no money coming in. I'll have to get a job. Thank goodness I own my house, or it could be dire.'

'Do you think Gillian was aware of you and Verity?'

Tracy glanced away and didn't answer immediately.

'I don't know. He told me that even though they lived separate lives, she wouldn't have liked it, so I'd say no.'

'Did you encourage David to tell her about the two of you, to get it out in the open, in the hope he'd leave her sooner?'

'No. Why would I?'

'For him to move in with you.'

'Look, of course I wanted him here. We were in love. But I also knew that it couldn't be. I was content to be with him a few nights a week. We'd got into a good routine.'

'Where were you on Saturday night?'

'Here.'

'Can anyone vouch for you?'

'No, I was on my own. Surely you're not thinking that I could have done it?' she asked, her voice rising in pitch.

'We ask everyone their whereabouts, to eliminate them from our enquiries.'

'That's okay, because no way would it have been me. First of all, why? Because now I'm left with nothing. Second, how could I have gone all the way to Beech Avenue and killed them all when I have my daughter to look after?'

'You know where they live. Have you actually been there?'

Tracy bit down on her bottom lip. 'One time I did visit. I wanted to see his house and what the rest of the family was like.'

'What did you do exactly?'

'I drove down with Verity and parked across the road for a few hours.'

'Did you see any of the family when you were there?'

'Yes. I knew it was them because I'd seen their photos on David's social media.'

'How long ago was this?'

'When Verity was a few months old. It was a time when I was feeling lonely and missing the company of my colleagues at work.'

'Did David know what you'd done?'

'I told him, and he got angry in case anyone had spotted me. He said that even though he was going to leave them to be with me in the future, he didn't want his hand forced. I got it. It was a stupid thing to do and I never did it again.'

'Has David left you and Verity anything in his will?'

'I don't know, we didn't ever discuss it.'

'You would have a claim on his estate, even if he didn't,' Whitney continued.

'Well, yes … maybe … I don't know. Why are you asking about the will? Surely you don't think I could've done this to all the family to get some money. What sort of monster do you think I am?' Her face was red, and her hands shaking.

'I'm just asking the question, not accusing you of anything,' Whitney said, wanting to reassure her. The last thing they needed was for her to clam up and ask for a solicitor. They didn't have time for that.

'Good. Because it wasn't me.'

'Did David stay here on the same nights each week?' Whitney asked, anxious to move the interview on.

'It varied, depending on his work and family commitments. It made cooking a bit tricky. Sometimes he'd turn up without telling me, and others he'd phone at the last minute to say he couldn't make it.'

'How did you contact him, was it on his usual phone?'

'No, he kept a separate phone just for us. It was easier that way and prevented any mix-ups.'

That didn't make sense, bearing in mind what Keira had seen. Surely, she would've known immediately if it wasn't his regular phone by all the other messages in there.

'Did you ever contact him on his everyday phone?'

'No. He told me not to. I did have the number in case of emergencies, but never had to use it.'

'Do you know where he kept this second phone?'

'No, I don't. But we used to speak to each other all the time, so he would have had it on him.'

'Please write down the number for me,' Whitney passed over her notebook and Tracy jotted it down.

'On the news, they didn't say what actually happened to David and the others. Can you tell me? I just want to know.'

'I'm sorry, I can't. We're waiting for confirmation from the pathologist.'

'Will you tell me then?'

'We'll be in touch again. While we're here, may we have a look around to get an idea of how David lived when he was with you?'

'Don't you need a search warrant for that?'

She was far more on the ball than she was letting on.

'We do, and obviously I can get one, but it's easier if you let us take a quick look.'

'Okay. I suppose so.'

'You go back to Verity, we won't be long.'

Whitney and Ellie went upstairs. There were three bedrooms, one which was clearly the child's, a spare room filled with boxes, and then the largest, which overlooked the road and was Tracy and David's.

'What are you looking for?' Ellie asked, pulling on the disposable gloves Whitney had passed to her.

'To see what their relationship was really like. Leading a double life would have put pressure on him.'

She looked at the photos in frames of the three of them.

'It can't have been easy to keep it secret,' Ellie agreed.

'Surely someone at his workplace would have known what was happening. When he claimed expenses, would it show him often being in Coventry? It needs further investigating. And the fact she doesn't have an alibi, too. We'll look for CCTV footage to see if her car was in the vicinity at all.'

'We need to find the second phone David Barker had,' Ellie said.

'Yes. More to the point, who was he texting if Keira found incriminating texts on his normal, everyday phone? I want you onto that as soon as we're back at the station.'

## Chapter 20

George knocked on Whitney's office door, in case her friend was there and not in the incident room. She was glad of the distraction. Last night she'd spent hours online with Ross looking at potential properties for them to buy. It had taken her a long time to find her current house, and this search seemed to be heading in the same direction. If the property was right, the location wasn't. And vice versa. Ross kept reminding her that it was all about compromise, but she'd found the perfect place before, so why not now?

'Come in.'

'Good morning,' she said, opening the door and seeing Whitney seated behind her desk, frowning at the computer screen.

'I'm glad you're here. After I've had a run through with the team, we're going to Birmingham to Hutt Consulting, David Barker's workplace. I'm hoping someone there might know more about this double life of his, which my gut is telling me is at the heart of these murders.'

Whitney had texted her yesterday regarding David Barker's other life.

'Very scientific,' George said, shaking her head in frustration.

'Say what you like, it works.' Whitney smirked in her direction as she stood up and walked around to where she was standing.

'Show me some irrefutable evidence and I might consider it.'

George enjoyed these bantering sessions with Whitney, even though she wasn't prepared to go along with *gut instinct* or *jinxing* or whatever else Whitney came up with. George suspected that some of the time the officer only said it to wind her up. It might have done in the past, but it didn't now.

She followed Whitney into the incident room and over to the two whiteboards. One was electronic, which Whitney avoided using, instead choosing the ordinary board she'd brought with them when they'd moved into the new purpose-built station six months ago. According to Whitney, she liked to be able to write things herself, and pin up photos. It helped her think.

'Listen up, everyone. George and I are going to Birmingham to speak to David Barker's colleagues. Ellie, any joy yet on finding his second phone?'

'I'm waiting to hear back from forensics to see if they found it during their search.'

'If the answer's negative, which I suspect it might be or we would've heard by now, Doug and Meena, I want you to go over to the house and have a thorough look around. Go through everything, including pockets in clothes, under the bed, anywhere he could've hidden it. What about his main phone, is that coming back from Mac?'

'It's on the way, and once it's here I'll check it straight away,' Ellie said.

'Excellent. Brian, I want you to find out whether David

and Gillian left wills, and if so, who are the beneficiaries. Tracy Osman claims to know nothing about them, but if it turns out she, or her daughter Verity, are due to inherit, it could be a motive.'

'Yes, guv,' Brian said.

'By the way, how did it go with Gillian's sister?'

'She was very upset, obviously, but Dr Dexter was kind to her and explained everything in terms she could understand. It surprised me.'

'Claire is a multifaceted person. We might get the rough end of her manner but she's always very good with family. Did you question her after she viewed the bodies?'

'A little, guv, but she wasn't up to it. I did discover that she kept in semi-regular contact with her sister. They'd phone every few months. She couldn't help regarding anyone who had a grudge against the family. She's staying in Lenchester for a few days. I thought I'd speak to her again in a couple of days.'

'Good idea. Did you ask her about the marriage and whether Gillian confided in her?'

'I didn't ask outright, but she volunteered that the couple had a good relationship, so either Gillian genuinely believed it was okay, or she didn't tell Penny.'

'Okay. It's all adding to the picture. Frank, I want you to check CCTV footage on roads coming from Tracy Osman's house in Coventry to the Barker house. See if her car was in the vicinity at any time recently.'

'Okay, guv,' Frank said. 'By the way, Mrs Hudson's car came back clean. Can it be returned?'

'Yes. Sort that out, will you? We'll be back later.' She turned to George. 'Right, let's go.'

When they arrived at Hutt Consulting, the subdued atmosphere was almost palpable. After Whitney had explained who they were, they waited to the side of the reception desk for David Barker's immediate boss to be found.

After a few minutes, a man in his fifties, of medium height and build, approached them.

'Hello, I'm Robin Tavistock, Chief Operating Officer here. I understand you want to speak to me about David Barker.'

'Yes. I'm DCI Walker and this is Dr Cavendish from Lenchester CID. Is there somewhere we can speak in private?'

He led them to a meeting room which was along the corridor from the main reception area. It had a large light oak table, with chairs to seat twenty. They sat at one end.

'David was a valued member of the team and what happened to him, and his family, has deeply shocked the whole company. If there's anything I can do to help, please ask.' He leant forward with his fingers steepled.

He spoke the appropriate words, but George wasn't convinced they were genuine. He hardly blinked and stared directly at Whitney. She would need to watch for any other telltale signs.

'Thank you. To start, we'd like to know more about David's work here,' Whitney said.

'He was one of our senior technology consultants and would spend much of his time on site with new, or existing, customers advising on their IT systems and how they could be utilised for delivering their business goals.'

'When did he join the company?'

'Ten years ago. He was my first hire as COO.'

'Did he come into the office often?'

'It varied, depending on where the particular client was based. If he was working within a sixty-mile radius of here, we would see him most weeks. Any further afield, and it would be less often. He kept in contact with his PA on a daily basis, and he'd be here for our monthly meetings. Other than that, he was autonomous.'

'Had his work always been like this?' George asked.

'Before he was promoted to a senior position, he would work more locally and have more supervision.'

'When was he promoted?'

'About six years ago.'

'Was David well liked?' Whitney asked.

'I believe so but, to be honest, it wasn't something I paid attention to. His PA would be able to tell you more.'

Again, another lie. The man was clearly trying to distance himself. From what, remained to be seen.

'Is his PA in today? We'd like to speak to them.'

'Yes, she is. I saw her earlier. I'll arrange for her to come in.' He walked out of the room, leaving them alone.

'He's hiding something. He couldn't get out of here quick enough and he wasn't being completely honest with you,' George said.

'In what way?'

'When you asked about David Barker's popularity, he knew more than he told you. He most likely didn't want to disparage the man because of the situation. His body language was very easy to read.'

'That's useful to know. Let's see what his PA tells us.'

The door opened, and Robin Tavistock returned with a woman in her late twenties.

'This is Lauren Maxwell, who worked for David. I'll leave you to it, if that's okay. I'm expecting a phone call.'

'That's fine. Thank you for your help,' Whitney said.

'Wanda on reception will call me if you need to speak to me again.'

Whitney gestured for Lauren to be seated and she sat on the chair opposite, twisting the wedding band on her finger around and around.

She was nervous, but George didn't detect from her manner that she was upset by what had happened.

'Thank you for coming to speak to us. We'd like to ask you a few questions about David, if that's okay,' Whitney said, her voice soft.

'Yes, of course. I expected you would want to because I reported directly to him.'

'How long were you his personal assistant?'

'Four years. I joined the company after leaving university.'

'Was he a good boss?'

'He left me alone to get on with my work and wasn't constantly breathing down my neck, which I appreciated. He delegated a lot of the customer liaison work to me, and I would prepare draft quotes for him.'

'David Barker was living a double life. Were you aware of this?'

Lauren looked away and bit down on her bottom lip. 'I suspected but didn't ask. It wasn't my business.'

'Why were your suspicions alerted?'

'Conversations I overhead. The way he immediately went into his office when there was a certain ringtone. I think he had two phones, but I'm not one hundred per cent sure.'

'What was it that made you believe that?'

'There was one time when he took a call and put his phone into one pocket of his jacket, then a while later he received another call, and he took his phone out from the other one. I remember thinking it was odd, but then decided that I might have got it wrong. But thinking back, I don't think I did.'

'Can you remember any of the conversations you over-heard that alerted you to David's double life?'

'Yes. One day when he was in his office and his door

was slightly open, I overheard him on the phone telling someone he'd see them later. I knew it wasn't his wife, because he'd only just told me that she'd taken the children away on holiday as it was half-term.'

'Could it have been a friend?'

'No. He told this person that he loved them. It was definitely said in a way you would to a partner.'

'Do you have any idea who it was?'

'It could be Natalie McKay who works here in the accounts department. Either her or Leigh Dempster who used to work here as a junior consultant.'

Now she was discovering why Robin Tavistock wanted to distance himself. If this woman was to be believed, and George had no reason to doubt her, David Barker was a serial womaniser.

'There was more than one person he was seeing?' Whitney asked, scribbling in her notebook.

'I don't want you to think I'm gossiping, but according to the rumours going around here, he did see both of them. I'm not sure if it was at the same time but I can tell you that before Leigh left, she was quite open about her dislike of David and the way he operated.'

'How do you know that she had a relationship with him?'

'It was common knowledge among the admin staff.'

'What did she say about him?'

'That he was difficult to work for, and that he only liked you if you'd pandered to his whims.'

'Do you agree with her assessment?'

'David had his ways, but we always worked well together. He knew to leave me to my own devices.'

That spoke volumes.

'When did Leigh leave?'

'A couple of months ago.'

'You mentioned that Natalie works in the accounts department. Would you be able to fetch her for us?'

'Sorry, she hasn't been in this week. I'm not sure if it's because she's so upset or if there's a different reason.'

'Okay, thank you. Before we leave, what were you doing on Saturday between the hours of ten and midnight?'

'I was at home with my husband.'

'And he can vouch for that?'

'Yes, of course he can. Would you like his mobile number?'

Whitney passed over her notebook and Lauren wrote down the number and then left the room, closing the door behind her.

Whitney turned to George. 'We need to speak to Leigh Dempster and Natalie McKay. They could hold the key to this whole thing.'

## Chapter 21

'Stop what you're doing. I have stuff to tell you,' Whitney said to the team when she'd returned to the incident room, pleased to see they were all there. 'It turns out that not only did David Barker lead a double life with a girlfriend and child, but he was also having other affairs,'

'Bloody hell, how did he have the energy?' Frank said, letting out a long sigh.

'Don't compare everyone with you. We don't all have one foot in the grave,' Doug said, smirking.

'You can talk,'

'Yeah, I can—'

'Boys … focus. One of the women, Natalie McKay works at Hutt Consulting in the accounts department, but hasn't been seen since the murders. Another woman, Leigh Dempster, used to work there and before she left was extremely vocal about her dislike for him. Ellie, I need contact details for both women.'

'Yes, guv.'

'Before you start, where are we on Barker's phones?'

'We're still waiting for forensics to get back to us on whether they found his second phone,' Meena said.

'What's the hold-up?'

'They're short-staffed and everyone's out on a job.'

'Well, keep on top of it. Ellie, have you had his main phone back from Mac, yet?'

'No, guv. He's been in a meeting for most of the day.'

'What? This is ridiculous. We're working a murder investigation. Doesn't that count for anything around here?'

'Sorry, guv.'

'I'm not getting at you. Just keep on top of it. Brian, where are we on the wills?' She forced her tense muscles to relax. It wasn't the team's fault. She'd be speaking to the super about resourcing in forensics. They couldn't work like this.

'They both had them, and in the event of death, every-thing passed to the other partner, and then following their death it went to the children. No other provisions were made.'

'Verity would have a claim on the whole estate, in that case. Providing Tracy could prove David Barker was the father. It could be done through a DNA test,' George said.

'Yeah. And that could be one hell of a motive. Frank, did you see Tracy Osman's car on any of the CCTV footage?'

'I've checked all the roads coming into the city and heading in the direction of Beech Avenue and didn't see it around the time of the murders, and—'

'Guv?' Brian interrupted.

'Yes?'

'There's a woman at the front desk who claims to have information regarding Corey Hudson.'

'Do we know what it is?'

She glanced at her watch. They still had over twelve hours to charge or let him go. This might speed up the process.

'No. They asked to speak to whoever's in charge of the case. She's been put into interview room one.'

'Okay. Come on, Brian, we'll speak to her.'

'Shall I come with you to observe?' George asked.

'No, not this time.'

'In that case, if you don't mind, I'll leave. I've got items requiring my attention.'

Only George could put it like that. It was most likely the property search.

'Sure, you go. Thanks for today. Are you available tomorrow?'

'If I'm required.'

'You probably will be. I'll call and let you know.'

Whitney and Brian took the lift to the ground floor and turned into the corridor to the suite of interview rooms.

They went into the first one and seated behind the table was a woman in her sixties. She was smartly dressed in a button-through, short-sleeved navy dress, with a splattering of colour on the print.

'Good afternoon, I'm DCI Walker and this is DS Chapman. I understand you have information regarding the Barker family case,' Whitney said, sitting directly opposite her.

The woman cleared her throat. 'Yes, I have. I'm Stephanie Court. Like I told the police officer who was on the reception desk, I have something to tell you about Corey, who you've arrested for the murders. I wanted to make sure that the person in charge knew. Is that you?'

'I'm the senior investigating officer on the case. Corey isn't under arrest. Currently he's helping us with our enquiries.'

'Oh. I didn't know that. But he's not allowed to go home, is he?'

'That's correct. What is this information?' Whitney didn't have time to pussyfoot around. There was a lot to do.

'I live opposite the Hudsons and we're family friends. I've watched the children grow up. It's a lovely neighbourhood and we look out for each other. When Julian Hudson told me you thought his son had murdered that family, I came to see you straight away because I know he didn't and can prove it.'

Whitney held up her hand. 'I'll need to stop you for a moment. I'm going to record our conversation for the record.' She leant over and pressed the button on the equipment and went through the formalities. 'Please continue.'

'Last Saturday, Corey was home by nine-seventeen. I saw him arrive through the window. When I told Julian, he was so relieved. I said that I'd come to the station and tell you everything I knew.'

If this was true, then Corey would most definitely be out of the picture. He'd have been nowhere near the house during the time of death period.

'You said you can prove it?' Whitney leant forward slightly.

'We have a security camera on the front of our house, which clearly shows him. I can let you see the footage. It's here on my phone.'

The woman took out her mobile and pressed some keys before sliding it over the table for Whitney to examine. She held it out so Brian could also see. The woman was right. Corey drove into the drive, got out of the car, and went to the front door at the exact time she'd said.

'Please will you forward this to me?' She pulled out a card and gave it to the woman, along with her phone.

'Now?'

'Yes. Did you continue watching when he went into the house?'

'For a short while, maybe five minutes. Once Corey was inside, the front door closed and the lights came on.'

'Which lights?'

'First the ones in the hall, and then those in the lounge, which has a window overlooking the front.'

'What about upstairs? Did you see any lights turn on up there?'

'No, but that doesn't mean he didn't go there. All I can tell you for definite is I saw him go inside and the lights were turned on in the hall and lounge. Are you going to let him go now I've told you what I saw?'

'We're not at liberty to discuss that with you, but thank you for coming in. The information you've given us has been most useful.'

'It was my duty. And even if I hadn't seen Corey, I'd have bet my last pound that he hadn't done it. He's a lovely boy. He's not a monster. If you knew him like I do, then you'd agree with me.'

They escorted the woman out of the station and stood watching as she walked towards the car park.

'That gives Corey Hudson a cast-iron alibi,' Brian said, when they turned away from the front entrance.

'It certainly does. He would have left not long after nine to be home by nine-seventeen, which means he couldn't have been responsible. There's no point in keeping him here any longer. It's not a good place for a young man of his age.'

They went to see the custody sergeant and Whitney

asked him to draw up the paperwork for releasing Corey, and to inform his parents so they could collect him.

They returned to the incident room, and she called the team to attention.

'Okay everyone, we have a development. Corey Hudson has an alibi, and he's going to be released, so we're back to square one. Well, not quite square one. Where are we on these women David Barker was seeing, Ellie?'

'They both live in Birmingham, guv. I've got their addresses.'

'Thanks.' She looked at her watch. It was too late for another trip over there. 'I'll take George and we'll go first thing tomorrow morning. I'd better go see the super and update her on where we are.'

Her boss's office door was slightly open indicating she was in there. Whitney knocked and waited.

'Come in.'

'I'm here to give you a quick update, ma'am.' She remained standing, not wanting to stay any longer than necessary.

'Do I need to ask Chief Superintendent Douglas to join us?'

'Not this time, ma'am. I'll just tell you, because I've got to get back upstairs. I'm expecting a call,' she lied. Out of necessity, she justified to herself. Or should that be sanity? 'Corey Hudson has an alibi, which I've verified, and we're in the process of releasing him.'

'I'm not surprised. From what you've told us, it seemed unlikely that he would be our killer.'

'Yes, ma'am. We do have another development. In addition to the woman with whom David Barker had a daughter and was living with part-time, we've also discovered two other women he was involved with. They both live in Birmingham. One works at the company, and one left recently. We're not sure whether he was seeing them both at the same time. It's something we'll be investigating tomorrow when we interview them.'

'Goodness, what a complex life he led. I'm due to give a press conference, but all I'll tell the media is that we're pursuing several lines of enquiry and that the person we had in custody is no longer a suspect. That will have to suffice.'

'Am I required to attend?'

She sincerely hoped not. Unlike her old boss, the super was perfectly capable of running them herself and fielding any questions thrown at her.

'No, you're not. I might actually wait until you get back on Thursday and then arrange one for Friday in case there's more I can inform them. Either way, you don't need to be involved. You have more pressing matters to deal with.'

'Thanks, ma'am. Before I go, I'd like to mention issues we're having with forensics.'

The super frowned. 'Issues?'

'Not with the quality of their work,' she added hastily. 'We're having to wait too long for feedback because they're so understaffed. I was wondering what the situation is regarding expanding the department.'

'Is it always like this, or just currently? We do have an unprecedented number of cases, which is stretching all of our resources.'

'That might be the reason, but it's not helping us investigate this case.'

'I'll look into it, Whitney. There may be money available to take on some temporary staff to ease the pressure. I can't promise, though.'

'Thanks, ma'am. I appreciate it.' She left the super and marched down the corridor with a spring in her step, happy with the outcome. Additional forensic staff and no Dickhead to contend with. What more could she ask for? On the way, she pulled out her phone and gave George a quick call. 'Are you still okay for tomorrow?' she asked when the psychologist answered.

'Yes, I believe we've already had this discussion before I left for the day.'

Whitney smiled to herself. George could be so literal at times.

'I was double-checking. I take it you left to continue with your house-hunt?'

'Yes.'

'How's it going?'

'Tediously.'

'I can't believe you're not enjoying the search. I find going into people's homes fascinating … to use one of your words.'

'That's where we differ, because it's taking up an inordinate amount of time that could be better used on more pressing things, like my research.'

'Well, fingers crossed you'll find something soon.'

'I wish I could share your optimism. Do you have anything specific for us to do tomorrow?' George added, signalling to Whitney it was the end of their discussion.

'Yes, we're going back to Birmingham in the morning to interview Natalie McKay and Leigh Dempster. We'll visit their homes first and hope to find them there. If not, we'll go to Hutt Consulting to see Natalie and I'll get Ellie to find out if Leigh is currently working and, if so, where.'

'In which case, I will see you first thing.'

## Chapter 22

*I throw my phone on the other side of the sofa. I don't know why I looked at social media. They're parasites, waiting to pounce. Making accusations they can't substantiate. How dare they start interpreting why I acted the way I did when they have no idea? And as for me being some sort of deranged monster, that's total crap.*

*They don't know what I'm like, or why I did it.*

*No one knows why, except for me. And that's how it's going to stay. Or should I say, no one alive knows why.*

*It took me a long time to plan exactly what I was going to do, but after I had, absolutely everything fell into place.*

*Is that behaviour of a monster? No, of course it isn't.*

*I didn't want to do it, but they brought it on themselves.*

*All they had to do was listen. To understand how I was feeling. But no, that was clearly too much for them.*

*Well, if there is an afterlife and they're looking down on me, maybe they now understand that you can't discard someone's feelings and think that it's going to be okay.*

*It isn't.*

*There are repercussions.*

*It's the only fair thing. And everything should be fair. To me. To them. To everyone.*

*I lean back on the sofa, allowing my mind to drift back to the night I did it.*

*They were all seated at the table, having their ritual evening meal. The time when they could each discuss their day. What a quaint custom. And no, I'm not jealous, if that's what you're thinking.*

*I didn't care about their day. Why should I, they didn't care about mine.*

*But they should have.*

*There was no need for them to be so precious about their tight little family circle and exclude everyone else.*

*That's what I told them. I explained how I didn't want to do this to them, but that they'd brought it on themselves. I said to them: 'What gives you the right to have something I don't?'*

*After that, they said they wanted to include me. But I saw right through their empty words. I'm not an idiot.*

*I've never killed anyone before. It was weird. But by the time I got to number five, it wasn't so bad. Bearable, almost.*

*It didn't make me feel good,*

*I didn't get some burning excitement or adrenaline rush like you hear about from some killers. Again, proof that I'm not some crazy person.*

*You see, that wasn't the point of the exercise.*

*It wasn't about me being excited by what I was doing. Getting some perverse satisfaction from ending five lives. No. That wasn't it at all.*

*It was all about them having what I don't.*

*It's as simple as that.*

*And now they're all dead.*

*Do I care?*

*I don't know. Maybe a little.*

*I'm never going to have what I wanted now.*

*But, then again, nor will they.*

## Chapter 23

'According to Ellie, Leigh Dempster isn't working, so we'll visit her place first,' Whitney said as George drove them onto the M1, in the direction of Birmingham.

'We should be there by ten,' George replied, after using voice recognition to input the address into her satnav and taking a quick look at the screen. 'Providing there are no hold-ups on the motorway.'

'Great. Then we'll go to Natalie McKay's, and if she's not at home, we'll assume she's gone back to work and go there to see her. Hopefully we shouldn't be back any later than two.'

'Do you have another appointment?'

'No. But the sooner we get this sorted, the sooner we'll solve the case. This double life of David Barker's has got to be linked to the murders. How could it not?'

'I'm assuming that was a rhetorical question,' George checked, knowing that they were getting back into the *gut instinct* territory.

'You're dead right. Anyway, what's going on with your dad? Any more news?'

George let out a sigh. 'I haven't heard from my parents since returning home. I'm hoping that following me turning them down regarding living there, they're looking into other solutions.'

'Are you upset about not hearing from them?'

'No. Why should I be? You know what my family is like.'

'But you'll keep in contact with them, won't you? They'll still need your support, even if you can't be with them all the time.'

'Yes, I will. I'll contact them at the weekend to find out how everything is progressing.'

She hadn't intended to, but now Whitney had mentioned it, she could see it was the right thing to do.

'What about your house-hunting? I know you're not enjoying it but have you found anything suitable?'

'Not yet, but Ross has arranged for us to view two properties on Sunday afternoon.'

'That's exciting.'

'Unless you're going to need me.'

George half-hoped she would be needed, which was ridiculous. No one was twisting her arm to take this step. She wanted to be with Ross permanently, and their current arrangement was becoming tiresome. So why was she resisting?

'I'm sure we can manage without you. This is important. Where are the houses, and what are they like?'

'Both are in villages east of Lenchester. One is a modern barn conversion that's only five years old, and—'

'But you don't like modern?'

'No, but it's been sympathetically restored, and does have all the space we require.'

'Hmm. You don't sound convinced.'

It was like a light had turned on in her head. Whitney

had inadvertently put her finger on why George was feeling reticent. She didn't want anything modern, *sympathetically restored* or otherwise.

'The other is a Georgian property with stables which, once converted, would make an ideal studio.'

'That sounds more like you.'

'Yes, you're right. But the conversion might take a while, and that would leave Ross without anywhere to work in the interim.'

'Can't he rent a studio somewhere local while you're undertaking the renovations?'

'Yes, that is an option we can consider. I'll mention it to Ross.'

'Have you put both of your houses on the market yet?'

'Ross has had his valued, and it will be listed straight away. I thought we should sell his first and keep mine until we've found our joint home and the sale has been completed. In case of any complications.'

'Will you need to get a bridging loan until you sell yours?'

Whitney didn't know that George still had money left over from an inheritance, and she didn't need to sell her house to put in her half. It wasn't something she would ever share with her friend, who wasn't in such a fortunate position.

'We should be fine with only selling his initially. To be honest, I don't know whether I can bring myself to sell mine.'

'It's not like you to be emotionally attached to anything.'

Whitney was right, which made her feelings even more bewildering.

'You're correct, and it's perplexing me.'

'Are you sure it's not linked to Ross rather than your

house? You might be having reservations about living together permanently, especially after your experience with that tosspot Stephen.'

'It's a good question to ask, but I don't believe it's anything to do with that. Ross and I have been residing together for a while now, and it's been most satisfactory.'

And certainly nothing like her previous experience.

'I'll assume that *most satisfactory* is George parlance for being bloody good. In which case, what's the point of keeping your house if you're not going to live there? I'm sure we've had this conversation in the past.'

'We'll sort it out. How are Tiffany and the baby?' she asked, wanting to steer the conversation in a different direction.

'Both are doing very well, and nothing's changed in the three days since you saw them.'

'And your mother and brother?'

'Funnily enough, after work today, I'm going to take Tiffany, Ava, and Rob to see Mum.'

'Has your mother seen the baby yet?'

Whitney gave a little sigh. 'Yes, several times, but she doesn't always remember. Rob is totally different, thank goodness. He idolises Ava already, even though she's only a few weeks old. He's lovely with her, very gentle and caring. It's going to do him the world of good.'

Fleetingly, a pang of envy coursed through George. Whitney's family might not have been affluent like hers, but what they had was something money couldn't buy. Being with Ross had given George a taste of what close family life was like, but it still wasn't the same as Whitney had. That only came with having children. She hurriedly dismissed that thought and concentrated on driving to their destination.

Leigh Dempster lived in a modern block of flats, in an

established and well-kept area, a mile from the city centre. They took the lift to the second floor and Whitney rung the bell. It was answered by a tall, attractive woman, in her late twenties, with blonde curls hanging to her shoulders.

'Yes.'

Whitney held out her ID. 'I'm DCI Walker from Lenchester CID, and this is Dr Cavendish. Are you Leigh Dempster?'

'Yes, that's me. What is it? Has something happened to my family?' Panic shone from her eyes.

'No, that's not why we're here. We'd like to talk inside.'

The woman opened the door, and they walked into a small oblong-shaped entrance hall.

'So, what's this about?' Leigh said, her arms folded and staring directly at Whitney.

'Are you aware of what happened to David Barker and his family?' Whitney asked.

'Yes, I heard on the news, but why are you here? Don't tell me you think I've got anything to do with it.'

Already on the offensive? No sign of being concerned over what had happened. George found the reactions from the woman odd. Although if she was guilty, then wouldn't she have pretended to be concerned?

'We've been informed you were angry with him when you left the company, and that you made your feelings known.'

'Anyone would if they were out of work with no reference, thanks to that man. I'm sorry they're all dead. But you don't know what he was like.'

'Perhaps you could tell us your version of events. Shall we sit down?' Whitney asked gently.

George nodded her approval at Whitney's attempt to put the woman at ease.

'Okay, come through to the lounge.'

They followed her into a small room with a sofa and matching chair focused on the TV in the corner.

'Please tell us about your relationship with David Barker,' Whitney asked once they were all seated.

'I suppose you'd call it an affair. We saw each other for six months, up until a short while before I left, when it all blew up and we finished.'

'How often did you see him?'

'Not as often as I wanted because he was busy with his family at home, and work took him away to other places. I suppose on average we'd be together once a week. He'd come around here after work.'

'Would he stay overnight?'

'Not usually because he had to get home. We'd have a meal and … you know.' She blushed.

'When you said it all blew up, what exactly happened?'

'It was my fault. I stupidly told my so-called best friend about us and she mentioned it to someone she knew, who happened to know someone who worked at Hutts. It got back to David, and he totally lost it. I told him we should deny it. It wasn't like anyone could've seen us together because we never went anywhere. He didn't see it like that and ended the relationship. He then proceeded to make my life hell.'

'In what way?'

'He belittled me in front of others in our department, and constantly criticised my work. In the end I couldn't take it, so one day I walked out and didn't go back.'

'You would have grounds for constructive dismissal. Did you complain to anyone about this?' George asked.

'How could I? They wouldn't believe me. They'd take his side because he was a senior consultant, and I was a junior. He had all the important accounts. I was no loss. Unlike him. It doesn't matter now he's gone. But I still can't get a job in my field because I don't have a good reference.'

'I suggest you go to the firm and talk to them regarding the factors behind you leaving. They may offer you a position, or a reference at least,' George suggested.

'I'll think about it.'

'Where were you on Saturday between the hours of ten and midnight?' Whitney asked.

Leigh looked at her, frowning. 'I was here.'

'Can anyone vouch for you?'

'No. I was on my own watching the telly. I can't afford to go out all the time. My benefits barely cover the rent.'

'Do you know where David Barker lived?'

'With his family in Lenchester.'

'Have you ever been to his house?'

'No.' She looked away and fidgeted in the chair.

'Your body language is telling me otherwise, so perhaps you'd like to revisit your answer,' George said.

Leigh tutted. 'Okay, I did drive there once to see where it was. All right? I didn't want to tell you because I knew you'd accuse me of murdering them. Which is ridiculous. I didn't have anything against his wife and children. If anything, I felt sorry for them having to live with the bastard and all his lies.'

George believed her.

'Was David seeing anyone else at work during the time you were with him?' Whitney asked.

'I don't know about that, but I do know he was seeing someone up to when he died, because I saw them together. She works at Hutts and her name's Natalie McKay,' Leigh said.

'You saw them by accident, or because you were following him?' Whitney asked.

'A bit of both. I went to the takeaway we often used, to pick up my order, and he was there with Natalie.'

'Did he notice you?'

'No. I didn't go in. Instead, I went back to my car and when they came out, I followed them to a hotel not far from there and watched them go in together. I waited a few minutes and then went back to pick up my meal.'

'Could it have been going on while you were seeing him?' Whitney asked.

'I don't think so, but I could be wrong.'

'How did seeing them together make you feel?' George asked.

'Bloody annoyed … But not enough to kill him, if that's what you're thinking.'

'Do you know Tracy Osman?' Whitney asked.

'No. Should I?' Leigh asked, frowning.

'I just wanted to check. What car do you drive?' Whitney asked.

'I have a Honda Jazz.'

'Please write down the registration number.' Whitney handed over her notebook and pen.

Leigh wrote it down and passed it back. 'If you're trying to see if I was in the Lenchester area on Saturday, you'll see I wasn't. My car stayed in the car park here all night.'

'Thank you. That's all for now. We may wish to speak to you again. Please don't leave the area without first telling me. Here's my card.' Whitney handed it to her.

# Chapter 24

'I can't believe this man had four women on the go at one time. Gillian, Tracy, Leigh, and Natalie,' Whitney said, once they were back in the car and driving towards their next destination.

'We don't know if Leigh and Natalie overlapped. But obviously he was a serial philanderer, of that there's no doubt,' George said.

'You think? But was this the reason he was murdered? Was it Tracy, Leigh, or Natalie? And, if so, why the rest of the family? Surely, they weren't collateral damage. It would take one crazy, fucked-up person to do that.'

'Jealousy has long been a motive for murder. If it was one of these women, and I'm not assuming either way, it could have been because they weren't able to be with him full-time.'

'Neither Tracy nor Leigh have an alibi. Let's see Natalie McKay and find out what she's got to say for herself … hang on … no …' she said to herself, as a thought pushed its way to the front of her mind. 'It's possible, I suppose … but …'

'Would you care to share this with me?' George asked, frowning in Whitney's direction.

'I know this might sound far-fetched, but what if all three women were in it together? Maybe they found out about each other and decided to take matters into their own hands. Especially if Tracy thought she'd have a claim on the estate with Verity being the only living relative. She could have agreed to split it three ways. Or maybe two of them, say Tracy and Leigh, and then it would be an equal fifty-fifty split. It could have been one of your folie thingie situations, like we had with the twins.'

'You mean folie à deux. Madness of two. It's possible, but not likely. For that to apply they would have known about each other for a while and spent time together. Long enough for the leader out of the two to influence the other.'

'Okay, so even if it's not that. Could they have all been in it together?'

'Anything is possible, but we'd need more concrete evidence than a fleeting thought.'

'I realise that, but it's still worth considering. I'll get Ellie on it when we get back to the station. She'll find out if anything connects them.'

'Yes, that's a good idea.'

The small, Victorian terraced house where Natalie McKay lived was a twenty-five-minute drive from Leigh Dempster's flat. Whitney knocked at the door and an elderly woman in her late seventies, early eighties, answered.

'Hello, we're looking for Natalie McKay. I'm DCI Walker and this is Dr Cavendish.' Whitney held out her warrant card for the woman to see.

'Natalie is my granddaughter. Is it about the man from work who was murdered with all of his family?'

'Please may we come in?' Whitney asked not answering the question.

'If it is about David Barker, then she's been devastated ever since we heard the news on the telly.'

'You know about him?' Whitney asked, frowning.

'Of course. Natalie tells us all about her colleagues. Please come in and wait in the front room. I'll fetch her. May I be with her during your questions, for support?'

'We'd rather she was alone.'

'I understand,' the elderly woman said, nodding.

They were shown into a small room which had a wrought-iron fireplace with a tiled surround along one wall, and a floral three-piece suite. There were family photos on every conceivable space. It was a comfortable, well-lived in space and reminded Whitney of the home she'd grown up in.

After a few minutes, a young woman in her mid-twenties walked into the room. She was tall, slim, and blonde. The same as Tracy and Leigh. Did he have a type? It certainly appeared that way.

'Hello, I'm Natalie.' She sniffed, and her eyes, which were red from crying, filled with tears. 'It's about David, isn't it? I keep hoping it's a bad dream, and I'm going to wake up from it.'

'Yes, it is. Let's all sit down,' Whitney said, kindly.

'Okay.' Natalie sat on the easy chairs, and Whitney and George on the sofa.

'We've been informed that you and David were a lot closer than colleagues. Is that correct?' Whitney asked.

Natalie blushed, stood up, and closed the door. 'I don't want Nanna to hear because she doesn't know and she wouldn't approve, what with him being married.' She returned to her chair.

'How long were you seeing David?'

'We'd been close for over a year, since I started in the department, but we only recently got together. About eight weeks ago. I can't believe I'll never see him again.'

'How often would you go out together?'

'It depended on his work. We'd sometimes stay late at the office and then go for a drink afterwards and on for something to eat. Or on to a … we had a hotel we'd go to, sometimes.'

'Did you ever bring David back here?'

'No. My nanna and grandpa wouldn't have liked it.'

'Would you say the relationship was serious?'

'David talked about the possibility of us living together.'

Seriously? Another one.

'Did he tell you he was going to leave his wife?'

'Not exactly. He said I should get my own place and that he'd help me with the rent if I couldn't afford it. He didn't want me to carry on living with my grandparents.'

'And you interpreted that as you possibly living together?' George asked.

'Well, no. But he said when his children were a bit older we would.'

Not that line again?

'Did you start looking for a flat?'

'Last week I found one online, and asked him to come with me to view it because I knew he was going to be in the office that day, but he said no.' She bit down on her bottom lip. 'We had an argument.'

'What about?'

'Me moving into a flat. He said he had a lot on his mind and that we should cool it for a while. He said I was getting ahead of myself. I wasn't. He was the one to suggest the flat, not me.' She balled her hands into tight fists in her lap.

'Do you know what he was worrying about? Did he say?'

'No, and I didn't ask. He wasn't in the right mood to discuss it. I thought maybe there was something going on at home with his wife. I know she could be difficult sometimes. He only stayed there because of the children.'

Something else they'd heard more than once.

'Is that what David told you?'

'Yes.'

'Did he talk about his children, Keira, Harvey, and Tyler?'

'Sometimes. He was proud of them and their achievements. He hated when he had to miss anything at their school because of being away with work. He was such a good father.'

Whitney squeezed the pen in her hand so tightly that it almost snapped. How could so many intelligent women be taken in by the creep?

'Have you heard of a woman called Tracy Osman?' Whitney asked, scrutinising Natalie's face to see if she showed any recognition.

'No, I haven't heard that name before, sorry.' She shook her head.

It seemed genuine to Whitney, but George would confirm. She noticed the tiniest of tells, which most other people would miss.

'Do you remember when Leigh Dempster was working at the firm?'

'Y-yes,' Natalie replied, her eyes pensive.

'Do you know why she left?'

'Her work wasn't up to scratch.'

'Who did you hear that from?'

'Everyone knew.'

'Even though it always used to be fine. Didn't people wonder what happened for her work to suddenly become unacceptable?'

'Apparently, it hadn't been good for a long time but it was covered up.'

'By whom?' Whitney asked, though knowing the answer.

'David. It had finally got to the stage when he could no longer accept the quality of what she was producing.'

Bingo.

'Did you know David had an affair with Leigh?'

'That was just office gossip. You know how it can be sometimes.' She glanced away. Was she being honest with them?

'How do you know it wasn't true?'

'Because David told me.'

'And you believed him?'

'Well … I'm … I mean … Yes. I think he was telling me the truth.'

Only *think*. Interesting.

'What were you doing last Saturday between 10 p.m. and midnight?'

'I was here at home.'

'Can anyone vouch for you?'

'Yes, I was with my grandparents.'

'So, you didn't go out on a Saturday night with your friends?'

That didn't ring true. Most women of Natalie's age wouldn't stay in at the weekend.

'Not this Saturday night. I'd planned to go clubbing with my friend and had arranged to meet in a pub in the city, but she backed out at the last minute, and I decided to stay in and didn't contact any other friends.'

'Thank you for your cooperation. We're going to leave now but will check with your grandmother on the way out to confirm that you were here the entire time on Saturday night.'

'Don't you believe me?'

'We have to exclude everyone from our enquiries, that's all.'

'Okay, I get it.'

After receiving confirmation from Natalie's grand-mother that she was there, they returned to the car.

Whitney pulled over her seat belt and clicked it in place just as her phone rang. She glanced at the screen.

'It's Claire. I'll put her on speaker.' She pressed the speaker button and rested the phone on the dashboard. 'Hi, Claire. You're on speaker. George is here with me.'

'Hello, both of you. I've heard back from toxicology and thought you'd want the results straight away.'

Whitney looked at George, mouthed, 'Wow,' and grinned. 'Thanks, Claire, what have you got?'

'As I suspected, midazolam was used on each of the victims.'

'Is it possible to tell the order in which they were killed, after David Barker who was first?' George asked.

'Not in respect of the children, because they all had equal amounts of the sedative in their bloodstream. In the case of Gillian Barker, it was less concentrated.'

'Do you believe that was on purpose?' Whitney asked.

'I have many talents, but mind-reading isn't one of them,' Claire snapped.

'Now you tell me,' Whitney said, tutting.

'I'm fairly confident I've mentioned that to you in the past. Having said that, it's possible she was the last person to be injected and the killer used what little they had left.'

'But she still was given enough to kill her?' Whitney said.

'Obviously, as she's dead. Is there a reason for your somewhat inane questioning?'

'That's harsh, even for you, Claire,' George said.

'Thanks, George. Why are you being so snippy, Claire?'

'Try because I've had to do more post-mortems in a single week than I usually get to do in six months. Add that to the department being short-staffed and you have your reason.'

'Apology accepted,' Whitney said.

'I don't recall saying sorry.'

'You meant to. Anyway, we have David Barker killed first and Gillian last. Keira tied them up, and Gillian was the only person to have duct tape on her mouth. Why? And how significant is this?' Whitney said.

'That's your conundrum,' Claire said.

'I'm still of the opinion that it's linked in some way to her being the last person killed, but, as I've already pointed out, without the motive it can't be established,' George said.

'Is there anything else that came back?' Whitney asked.

'There was no alcohol or drugs, other than the midazolam, found in the blood any of them. The meal left in front of them was properly cooked. No shortcuts taken, and it was all fresh food. Leeks, lentils, lamb, and fish sauce.'

'Fish sauce with lamb? That's disgusting. Who would do that?'

'Again, it's up to you to find out.'

'What about the wine?'

'I was coming to that. It was aromatised red wine, flavoured with cinnamon.'

'That's it,' George said, sharply.

'What is?'

'When you said—'

'As interesting as I'm sure this is, I'm too busy to listen to your musings.' Claire ended the call.

'So …' Whitney said.

'I know the significance of the meal.'

## Chapter 25

George walked behind Whitney into the incident room. She'd explained her theory to Whitney and there was one more thing she'd like confirming before being confident that she was correct.

'Attention, everyone. Dr Cavendish has something she'd like to tell you all. And, like me, you're going to be blown away by it. Over to you, George.'

'Before I start, do we know what crockery the meal left in front of the victims was served on?'

'Doug, you investigated that. What did you discover?' Whitney asked.

'It was stoneware and from what I could tell, didn't belong to the Barker family. Sorry, I meant to tell you, but it had totally slipped my mind.'

'No problem,' Whitney said, waving her hand. 'Is the crockery important, George?'

'It's the last piece of the puzzle. I'm now confident in my interpretation of the meal's significance.'

It was moments like this that confirmed her decision to continue working with the police, utilising her skills, and assisting in the solving of cases. She didn't wish to cast aspersions on her colleagues at the university, but she doubted they'd be as effective as she had proved herself to be.

She scanned the room. Every member of the team was looking directly at her, eagerness in their eyes. Very different from how suspicious they were of her when she'd first joined them. Though that was also due to Whitney's reluctance to be assisted by an academic.

'Come on, don't keep us in suspense,' Frank said, interrupting her thoughts.

'The killer has replicated Jesus's last supper in exact detail, even down to the plates used.'

'How did they know what was on the menu?' Brian asked.

'Good question, because until recently, no one did. There was a study undertaken by two Italian archaeologists who used a variety of sources to discover what was most likely to be on the table, based on what was available at the time. It was a groundbreaking discovery, and the killer had obviously read up on it.'

'But why the Last Supper? What's the significance?' Brian asked.

'Betrayal. Judas, betrayed Jesus,' Frank said.

'Whoa, get you,' Doug said.

'What's that meant to mean? I went to Sunday school as a kid. Some things stick in the old memory banks.'

'You are correct, Frank. These murders are all about betrayal.'

'And if we uncover who the betrayer is, or who's been betrayed, then we're on the way to solving the case,' Whitney added.

'Great call, doc,' Frank said.

'And that's why she's on the team,' Whitney said. 'Now,

let's run through everything else we have. Let's start with David Barker. He's married but had another life … a woman who had his child and who he saw on a regular basis. We know now of two other women who he'd had affairs with during this time—'

'Dirty—'

'Not now, Frank. I know what you're going to say, but we're not here to discuss the morals or otherwise of this man. To maintain this double life, he used more than one phone. Doug, did you manage to find the second one that Tracy Osman told us about?'

'Yes, it was hidden in one of his jacket pockets.'

'And this was definitely the one she shared with her? Ellie?'

'Yes, guv. I've gone through it using the self-service kiosk and there's no doubt that it is.'

'Anything of interest on there?'

'There were general messages between them, more like you'd have with someone you live with. Things like *what time will you be home* and *what would you like for dinner?* It was as if they were a married couple.'

'Was there anything which stood out?'

'No, guv.'

'Did you get his main phone back from forensics?'

'Yes. I ran it through the kiosk because they hadn't had time, as you know. This one was a lot more interesting. When I went back into the history, there were messages between him and Leigh Dempster from several months ago and—'

'They must have been the ones that Keira found,' Whitney said, interrupting.

'Yes, guv. There were also some nasty texts from Natalie McKay.'

'Really? Read them out.'

'This is what she sent a week before the deaths: *you'll pay for what you've done.*'

'Did he respond?'

'Yes, he said: *leave me alone. We're over.*'

'And this is from the woman who took the time off work after he'd been killed because she was so devastated by it,' Whitney said, shaking her head.

'If she's the killer, it's a reaction she could have orchestrated to put us off the scent,' George said.

'Well, she was a bloody good actor then. You saw her. All teary, red-eyed and sniffing. Did you suspect her of lying?'

'No, I didn't,' George admitted.

'My money would've been on Leigh Dempster out of the two of them, after what had happened to her. We need to bring Natalie McKay in for a formal interview. Brian, contact Birmingham police and ask them to escort her here tomorrow morning.'

'Yes, guv.'

'Ellie, was there anything else on his phone? Were there any texts from Leigh Dempster, other than the ones from a few months ago that Keira found?'

'No, nothing. Unless they'd been deleted.'

'I want you to look at Natalie McKay in more detail. She's living with her grandparents, and they gave her an alibi for the night in question. Although if they'd gone to bed early, she could have sneaked out without them knowing. Frank, get her car registration details and check CCTV to see if the car was in Lenchester on Saturday.'

'Okay, guv.'

'Who's looking at Gillian Barker? I know the investigation is throwing up issues with David, but we mustn't discount someone having an issue with her.'

'I am, guv,' Ellie said. 'I've done standard checks on

her, but nothing has alerted me to any issues. She was on the school parent-teacher association, regularly attended yoga classes, and helped at various charity events.'

'Continue digging. We can't make this a one-sided investigation. No stone left unturned or Douglas might make us regret it,' Whitney said.

'Yes, guv.'

She turned to George. 'Let's grab a coffee in the canteen as it's been ages since my last one.'

'Guv,' Frank called out, as they were heading towards the door.

'Yes?'

'The super wants you in her office in half an hour for a briefing with her and the chief super.'

'Thanks, Frank.' They headed out of the incident room and into the corridor. 'That's all I need, a meeting with Dickhead. Even more reason for the coffee.'

# Chapter 26

Loaded up on caffeine, and prepared to face Douglas to discuss the investigation, Whitney made her way to the super's office. To be honest, because he was keeping a low profile he hadn't been in her face as much as she'd imagined he would be, but that didn't mean she was going to let her guard down. She knew from experience that he could turn without any warning. She didn't trust him one bit.

'Come in,' the super called out, after she'd knocked on the door.

'Good afternoon, ma'am. Sir.'

Douglas gave a sharp nod in her direction. That was probably all she should expect.

'Good afternoon, Whitney. Take a seat.' The super gestured to one of the empty chairs at the table, and she took the one furthest from Douglas.

'You wanted to see me, ma'am?'

'The chief superintendent would like a full rundown on how the investigation is progressing. I haven't yet had chance to update him with what you told me yesterday, so include that in your briefing.'

Tempting as it was to maintain eye contact with the super and explain everything to her, she reluctantly turned her head to look at Douglas.

'Our enquiries have taken a different turn and the young man we had in custody has now been released. We—'

'Are you sure it wasn't him?' Douglas interrupted.

No. That's why they'd let him out. Did he really think she was that stupid?

She unclenched her fists, and let her shoulders relax. 'Yes, sir. He has a cast-iron alibi from the woman who lives opposite him. He was seen arriving home at nine-seventeen, which means he is out of the equation.'

'And he definitely couldn't have committed the murders before he came home?'

'We don't believe so, sir. Not according to the pathologist findings.'

'So, you wasted valuable time when you could've been investigating other avenues.' He looked at the super and rolled his eyes.

She chose to ignore him. 'The victims were all given midazolam, which is used in anaesthesia. The pathologist believes the husband was killed first and the wife last, other than that she couldn't determine the order.'

'What was her assessment of what happened?'

'David was most likely injected first to disable him, being the strongest.'

'How do they know that Gillian was the last?'

'Because she had the least amount of the drug in her system, most likely because it was all the killer had left. She was also the only victim to have duct tape over her mouth.'

'Do you know why?'

'We believe it's linked to the motive, which we have yet to ascertain.'

'What are the team working on now?'

'We're investigating who would have had a grudge against the family or felt betrayed by them.'

'Betrayed?'

'Dr Cavendish believes that the meal left in front of the family was a representation of the Last Supper and indicates that the killer felt betrayed by them. You know, like Judas.'

'I do know my Bible, Walker.'

'Yes, sir.'

'Have you identified any potential suspects?'

'Not yet, but it's quite likely linked to David. I mentioned to you that we suspected him of having an affair, but we've discovered it's more than that. Not only was he married to Gillian, but he had another life with a woman and child living in Coventry. The child, a girl called Verity, is his.'

'Oh …'

That had to be the first time she'd seen him speechless.

'There's more. During this time, he was also seeing two other women that we know of. There could be more.'

'Are you sure? My wife could hardly believe that he was having an affair, but this is a lot more than that. Surely we'd have suspected.'

'His work enabled him to lead a double life. Do you know of any other relationships he had in the past, sir?'

Douglas glanced away. Hmm, what wasn't he telling her?

'Many years ago, when he first married Gillian, I saw him out with another woman. They were in a village pub and were close to each other, if you know what I mean. It wasn't long after Keira was born.'

She let out an exasperated sigh. 'And you didn't think to mention this to us, *sir*?'

He shot an angry look in her direction. 'It was many years ago, and I deemed it not to be relevant, Walker. It was a judgement call.' He paused. 'Perhaps I was hasty in dismissing it.'

You think?

She glanced at the super, whose eyes were wide, and not in a good way.

'Do you know the name of this woman?'

'No. I'd never seen her before or since.'

'Did you tell your wife?'

'I kept it to myself. Didn't want to rock the boat as they had a newborn baby.'

'Can you describe her to me?'

'She was about the same age as him, late twenties. Blonde hair, attractive.'

'All the women he's been with are like that. He certainly has a type.'

'Apart from Gillian, who was short with dark hair,' Douglas said.

'Yes. And that's interesting in itself, and Dr Cavendish would know if it's relevant. What we do know is that he had a history of cheating on his wife from way back. I doubt we'll be able to discover the full extent, though.'

'Do you believe one of these latest women might have been involved? It's more likely to be one or other of them, I'd have thought, than someone from his past,' Douglas said.

'It's what we're investigating. We've discovered some threatening texts on his phone from one of them. The woman is in Birmingham and works for the same firm David did. She's being brought in for questioning tomorrow.'

'Why not today?'

199

'She's already been interviewed and won't be on alert because she gave us an alibi, which was verified.'

'But you still think it's her?'

'She lives with her grandparents. She could've slipped out when they were in bed, or without them knowing. She's no flight risk, and I'd rather make sure we have as much background on her as possible so we can prepare the most effective interview for when she arrives.'

'Let's hope you're right. I don't want to hear that she's done a runner.'

'You won't, sir.'

'I also don't want this to be a wild goose chase, like the last person you had in custody. The media is constantly breathing down our necks, wanting to know where we are with the investigation and querying why we haven't yet solved the case. This isn't going to be knocked off the top news spot for a while yet. We don't need bad publicity.'

'With all due respect, sir, the media's response is not my top priority.'

He scowled at her, and she wished she'd kept her mouth shut.

'And that's why you'll never be more than a DCI,' Douglas growled.

'Thank you, Whitney. If there's nothing further you can go,' the super said.

'Yes, ma'am.' She left the office as quickly as she could without actually running.

She could swing for the arrogant bastard. She'd show him. They'd solve the case, and soon.

# Chapter 27

'Come on, Rob,' Whitney said to her brother as they got out of the car at Cumberland Court, the care home where their mother lived. Even after all this time, she still couldn't get used to having her older brother and mum in care. Her mum had dementia and Rob had a learning disability following a violet attack in his teens and he was unable to take care of himself. He was happy where he was, and the carers allowed him to be self-reliant, whenever possible.

She'd read about vulnerable people in care homes suffering and was grateful that both Rob and her mum were in excellent facilities.

They waited while Tiffany took Ava out of her car seat and then they headed into the large Edwardian building, towards the reception desk where Angela, a senior carer whom Whitney was particularly fond of, was stationed.

'Let me see the baby,' Angela said, hurrying around the desk and up to them.

'This is Ava.' Tiffany held out the baby.

'She's such a cutey and looks just like you. She has your shaped face.'

Whitney smiled to herself. Everyone who saw the baby had an opinion, but truth be told it was too early to say who Ava took after.

'She's my great niece,' Rob said proudly, puffing out his chest.

'And she's very lucky to have you as an uncle.'

'A *great* uncle,' Rob said.

'Sorry. *Great Uncle.*' Angela smiled at him.

'Where's Mum?' Whitney asked.

'She's in the day room, but she's not having a good day today.'

A lump caught in Whitney's throat. As time went on, there were more *bad* days than good.

'Thanks, it's good to be forewarned. Hopefully, seeing the baby might help. She hasn't seen her for a couple of weeks.'

The day room was a comfortable area with easy chairs and a telly in the corner. The furniture was worn, but homely. Rob walked a few paces ahead of Whitney. He loved the visits, and Whitney wished she could bring him more often, but it really depended on her workload. Their mum was sitting in her usual chair on one side of the room, staring at one of the daily quiz shows on the television.'

'Hello, Mum,' Rob said as they approached.

Their mum stared blankly at them.

'She's not looking good,' Tiffany said quietly, so only Whitney could hear.

'I know. We'll stay here a little while to see if she improves a bit.'

'How are you doing, Mum?' Rob asked, pulling over a chair and sitting beside her.

'Who are you?' she said, ignoring Rob and staring at up at Tiffany.

Tears formed in Tiffany's eyes. 'It's me, Granny. I've brought Ava, your great-granddaughter, to see you.'

'I have a great-granddaughter?' the old woman frowned.

'Yes, say hello to Ava. She's only four weeks old.' Tiffany pulled over another chair and sat on the other side of her grandmother. She held out the baby so she could see.

Whitney sat opposite, so they formed a circle.

'She's gorgeous. It's lovely to see you, Tiffany,' Whitney's mum said, suddenly coming back into normal consciousness. She grazed her fingers over the baby's cheek.

Thank goodness. It was amazing how Ava could do that to her.

'You, too, Granny.' Tiffany rested her hand over her grandmother's and gave it a squeeze.

'Is the baby sleeping at night or does she give you trouble?'

'She's not too bad.'

'Not like your mum then.' She chuckled, nodding in Whitney's direction.

Tiffany looked at Whitney. 'Were you a difficult baby?'

'I didn't think so. Mum, was I?'

'Oh, yes. Not like, Rob. He was perfect from day one.' She smiled at her son. 'I'll let you into a little secret, Tiffany. If your mum had been my first child, then I wouldn't have had a second. She was very demanding and would never sleep, whatever I tried. And as she got older, we had the questions. Non-stop questions. Her dad would call her *Why*tney.'

'Mum, you didn't tell me this,' Tiffany said, grinning.

'It's the first I've heard of it.'

Was her mum getting confused? Whitney didn't remember any of this.

'We didn't want to discourage you, but I can assure you at times it drove us crazy. But it was worth it. Look what you've done with your life. We were always so very proud of you, and now Tiffany.'

'Thanks, Mum,' Whitney said, warmth flooding through her.

'I didn't drive you crazy, did I, Mum? I was good, wasn't I?' Rob said.

'Always. You were my precious boy. Still are.'

'I knew it,' Rob said, beaming with pride at his mum and then Whitney.

'Why are you here?' Her mum stared, her eyes unfocused.

Was she drifting again?

'So, you could see baby Ava, Mum. Remember? Are you feeling okay?'

'I've been watching the telly.'

'What programme?'

'I'm not sure because that woman over there keeps turning it over.' She pointed to the grey-haired woman sitting a few feet away. 'I start watching and then suddenly there's something else on.'

'Why don't you tell one of the carers and ask them to sort it out for you?'

'I can't.' Her mum picked up the edge of her cardigan and fiddled with one of the buttons. 'Where's Rob? Is Rob coming? I want to see him.'

'I'm here, Mum,' Rob said.

'You're not my Rob. You're a grown man. My boy's only seventeen. What have you done with him?'

Seventeen was the age when Rob was attacked. It had

changed all their lives forever. Was that why her mum was stuck there?

She stared at her brother. His face was screwed up and there were tears in his eyes.

'Rob's here, Mum. We all are,' Whitney said.

'Is it time for breakfast?'

'You've only just had your dinner. Don't you remember?'

'Is it time for bed?'

Rob jumped up and ran off. 'Tiffany, stay here with Granny while I speak to Rob, he's upset.' Whitney hurried after him.

'Why is she like this?' Rob asked when she'd caught up with him beside the French doors which led out into the garden.

'Let's go outside for a walk and we'll talk about it,' she suggested.

'I want my mum back.'

'I know you do, sweetheart, but this is how she's going to be from now on. Do you remember I explained to you about this illness? Sometimes Mum is like she's always been and sometimes she isn't, and she forgets things.' She drew him into a tight hug, which wasn't easy as he was so much taller than she was.

'Why didn't she know I was there?' He pulled from her grasp, wiped his eyes with the back of his hand, and gave a loud sniff.

'It's part of her being ill. She might recognise you when we go back in. Her memory comes and goes.'

'Why can't the doctors give her some medicine to make her better?'

'There isn't anything. But the scientists are working hard to find a cure. And one day they might. For now, we must be strong and not let Mum see how much it upsets us because it's not her fault. We'll be there for her whenever she needs us. Can you do that? Can you be strong and not tell her how we feel?'

'Yes,' he said emphatically, giving a sharp nod of his head. 'I know how to be strong because I've done it before. And I didn't tell anyone. I promise.' He glanced from side to side, uncertainty flickering in his eyes.

'What haven't you told?' Whitney asked, intrigued by what it was.

'I can't, I was told not to.'

'You can tell me *when* it happened, that's not the same, is it?'

'It was when we were all living at home. Mum, Dad, you and me.'

Ah. Most likely their dad had broken something and had told Rob not to say anything. How come he'd remembered it for such a long time?

'That's ages ago. You can tell me now. I'm sure it won't matter.'

'No, I can't. I had to promise to never tell anyone, ever. Or you, Mum and Dad would be hurt really bad.'

Whitney frowned. What the hell had happened?

'Is this something to do with when you were attacked all those years ago? Do you remember it happening?' she asked, taking a punt that it could be something to do with it.

'I'm not allowed to say.' He clamped his lips together, but she could tell by the worried look in his eyes that it was.

She remembered vividly when the police came to the door to tell them what had happened to her brother. He'd been out with friends and had been viciously assaulted. The police were never able to track down who'd done it. She'd been convinced they hadn't looked hard enough, and that's what prompted her to join the force as soon as she was old enough.

She stepped in front of him and stared directly into his eyes. 'Rob, do you remember being attacked?'

'I don't know.' He looked away.

'Do you remember who did it?'

'Stop,' he said, slamming both hands over his ears. 'Stop.'

'It's okay, Rob,' Whitney said, gently pulling his arms down to by his side. 'We won't talk about this anymore.'

'Because we don't want anyone to be hurt,' he said.

'That's right. Let's go back inside to see how Mum and Tiffany are.'

'And baby Ava.'

## Chapter 28

*The television's blaring and on the screen there's a picture of them. It's still front-page news, mainly because they're getting nowhere in their hunt for the killer.*

*Well, I could've told them that. They'll never find me. Never make the connection. They might as well give up and focus on something else. Lots of murders don't get solved, and these are going to be some of them.*

*I pick up my half-drunk bottle of beer and take a swallow while staring at the photo of them up there.*

*Did I do the right thing?*

*Yeah. I did. I don't have any regrets.*

*What else could I do?*

*It's pointless even going down this path. They put themselves in that situation, end of story. And now there's nothing anyone can do to change it.*

*Now that I've had time to reflect. If I had my time again, would I have done it differently?*

*Should I have tried harder to see if we could all be friends? That's all I ever wanted. To feel part of the family. To feel like I belonged. Why was that so hard?*

*And why should it have been down to me to make the effort to put things right when it wasn't my fault?*

*I pick up the remote and turn the television over. I can't bear to look at their faces. There's no point because they're never going to be connected with me now. I have to get on with my life and pretend like they'd never existed. Like I never existed for them.*

*I've got plans for my future. Plans that I'd put on hold. But now there's no stopping me. I can live a normal life like everyone else. It's not like I'm going to do it again.*

*I'm not some mad, deranged serial killer.*

*Have I already said that? Well, it's true, and I don't want anyone to think otherwise.*

*This was something very specific to the situation.*

*So why does my mind keep wandering back to whether what I'd done was the right thing? It wasn't a rash decision; it took planning. Very careful planning. And I did try to get to know them, but it was rejected, other than superficially.*

*I'm not to blame. I don't regret it. And that's final.*

*I glug back the remainder of my beer and go into the kitchen and grab another bottle. I can't get drunk, though. I need to have my wits about me tomorrow at work in case I let something slip.*

*Actually, I'd better have something to eat to soak up the booze. Then I'll go out for a walk to take my mind off everything. I've got to stop dwelling on what happened in the past and concentrate on the future. Because I've got one, unlike the Barkers. But they didn't deserve one, and I do.*

## Chapter 29

'Guv, Natalie McKay has arrived, and she's been put in interview room six,' Meena called out, as they'd walked into the main incident room from Whitney's office.

George had stopped there when she'd first arrived, and they'd been discussing the case, in particular the staging of the meal and the deep betrayal it symbolised. Whitney had seemed a little distracted, but George hadn't liked to enquire what was amiss as they needed to concentrate, and it would have taken them off task. If her friend continued in this way, she'd ask her at a more opportune moment.

'Thanks, Meena. We'll go down straight away. George, you might as well come with me and observe close up, which might be helpful when assessing her for little microexpressions. McKay has already met you, so it shouldn't put her on her guard.'

When they entered the interview room, Natalie McKay was sitting ramrod straight, with tight lines around her eyes and her lips pressed together in a firm line.

'Why have I been brought here?' she demanded before they'd even sat down.

A very interesting change in demeanour from the previous day. She was most definitely wary and could be hiding something.

'We have further questions for you,' Whitney said.

'Why couldn't you have called, or come around like you did yesterday? My grandparents were extremely worried when a police officer turned up at the door and demanded that I went with them.'

'We needed to make this a more formal interview, which is why you were brought here.' Whitney pressed the recording equipment. 'Interview on Friday, June 11. Those present DCI Walker, Dr Cavendish, and please state your full name for the recording.'

'Natalie Josephine McKay,' the woman replied in an icy tone, her eyes focused on Whitney.

'Further to our informal discussion yesterday, I'd like to confirm that you were in a relationship with David Barker until just before his death, and that you believed he was going to leave his wife and move in with you because your relationship was becoming serious?'

'Yes. He wanted me to find a flat and he was going to help me with the rent so I could move into somewhere comfortable. He didn't want anything basic because that wasn't what he was used to. It was so we could spend more time together, and not use hotels all the time.'

'You had a disagreement shortly before he died, and he ended it.'

'Yes. That's what I've already told you.'

'Can you explain why we found some threatening texts from you on David's phone?'

Colour drained from her face. 'It wasn't like that.'

'Perhaps you can tell us what it was like.' Whitney leant forward slightly.

The woman tensed and sucked in a breath. 'I wasn't

totally honest about why we ended things. It happened after I thought I was pregnant. I was so excited and thought David would be, too. But he told me I had to get rid of it because the time wasn't right. I refused. No way would I do that. I asked why we couldn't have the baby and he move in with me like we'd planned.' She paused, a pained expression on her face. 'He said no and refused to discuss it further.'

'You must have been upset.'

'I was. I sort of understood because it wasn't like we'd planned it. It turned out to be a false alarm so it didn't matter in the end.'

'Did you see him after that?'

'Once I'd told him there wasn't a baby we'd see each other occasionally, but it was different. After a while, he said I was becoming too clingy, and he had enough on his plate without me adding to it. He said we should cool it for a while. I knew that meant for good.'

'So, you decided to threaten him?'

'It wasn't like that. I was upset and angry. I loved him.'

'But because he didn't reciprocate you decided to kill him?'

'No. That's crazy.'

There was a knock on the door, and Brian stuck his head in. 'Can I have a word, guv?'

'Interview suspended.' Whitney and George left the room. 'What is it?'

'I thought you'd want to know that Natalie McKay's alibi doesn't hold up. Her car was seen in Lenchester on Saturday night.'

'How close to Beech Avenue was she?'

'Well, obviously we can't tell because the cameras don't go that far, but she was certainly in the vicinity and could easily have driven there.'

'Good work. Trace what time she returned to Birmingham.'

'Frank's looking at the CCTV footage right now. I'll see how he's getting on.' Brian turned and headed back down the corridor.

'Interview resumed,' Whitney said, once they'd returned. 'We understand that you weren't home on Saturday night. Your car was seen in Lenchester. You lied to us.'

Natalie ran a shaky hand through her hair. 'Am I being arrested? Do I need a solicitor?'

'That's entirely up to you. If you think you do, you're welcome to have one. We can arrange for one of the duty solicitors unless you have your own. It may take a while.'

'I didn't kill them. I wasn't anywhere near their house. You have to believe me.'

George couldn't detect any outward signs that the woman was lying, but she'd remain vigilant. Some people were able to cover up their lies, especially if they were aware of what would give them away. Although it was hard to maintain, and that's where George would catch them out.

'In that case, what were you doing in Lenchester on Saturday night?' Whitney asked.

'David had asked to meet so we could sort things out. He couldn't get to Birmingham, so I agreed to drive to Lenchester. He was going to make an excuse to go out for an hour.'

'Where and when was this meeting to take place?'

'We arranged to meet at the Tavern pub at nine-thirty.'

George hadn't heard of the pub.

'That's a bit of a dive. Why there?' Whitney asked.

'To make sure he didn't bump into anyone he knew. He didn't have the time to drive somewhere further away.'

'We know he couldn't have turned up, so what did you do then?'

'I waited until ten, then left and went home.'

'Did you text him to find out where he was?'

'I was going to, and then decided to forget it and not waste my time on him.'

'That was a sudden change of heart,' Whitney said.

'I realised while sitting in the pub, which didn't feel particularly safe, that if he could put me in this situation without caring what happened to me, then he wasn't worth it. I want to be with someone who treats me better than that.'

'What time did you arrive home?'

'Eleven.'

'How do we know this is the truth? When we spoke to you yesterday, you informed us that you had an alibi and that your grandparents would verify it. Which they did. You've put them in a position where they could be charged with obstructing the course of justice.'

Natalie's hand shot to her mouth. 'I didn't mean to do that. They weren't lying. They believed that I was there. They'd no idea I'd gone out. They go to bed at eight-thirty, and both have hearing aids, so they wouldn't have heard a thing.

'Why so early?'

'My granddad used to sell fruit and veg on the markets. He went to bed early his whole life because of having to get up at four in the morning. He still carried on after retiring and my nanna did the same so they would always be together. You're not going to charge them, are you?'

'We'll be considering it and will make a decision later. Is there anyone at the pub who can vouch for you being there?'

'I ordered a glass of wine, so maybe the woman who

served me, or others who were sitting on bar stools at the bar.'

'We will investigate. In the meantime, you can wait here.'

'Am I being arrested?'

'No, but if you try to leave you will be.'

They left the room and headed back to the office.

'Thoughts?' Whitney asked.

'There wasn't anything in her body language that alerted me to her lying. Although the fact she'd kept all of this from us in her previous interview could be viewed as suspicious.'

'Could she have been involved with someone else in the murders? We know of two disgruntled women, there could be more. What if they all got together and committed the murders? I've mentioned this before, and still believe it's possible.'

'And kill the entire family? That's something different altogether. I'm not convinced. Plus, we know that the killer made Keira tie up her brothers and parents. If there was more than one killer, it wouldn't have been necessary.'

'Good point. We'll drive to the pub to check her alibi. It won't take long. I'll pop back into the incident room first, to see where they are on checking the CCTV footage, and to let them know where we're going.'

## Chapter 30

The moment Whitney and George entered the incident room, Ellie came rushing over.

'Guv, I've found something. I'm not sure if it's going to be relevant, but you need to know about it.'

'Okay. Let's share it with everyone. Eyes on me,' she called out. 'Ellie has something for us.'

They all looked up and focused on Ellie, whose cheeks were pink.

'I've been looking deeper into Gillian Barker's background. Her maiden name was Findlay and I discovered that she was raped as a teenager. The man responsible was never caught. This resulted in a pregnancy, and the baby boy was given up for adoption.'

Whitney looked over at George. Was this connected to the murders?

'How old was Gillian when this happened?'

'Fifteen.'

'Brian, do you know where Penny Burn, Gillian's sister, is staying? She might know more about it.'

'The Midland Hotel.'

'I know it. We'll go on the way to checking Natalie McKay's alibi. Call and let her know we'll be there in ten minutes.'

'Yes, guv.'

'Ellie, who adopted the child?'

'A Mr and Mrs Roberts took him when he was only a few weeks old. They live in Bedford, which is where Gillian came from before the family moved to Poole, shortly after the baby was born.'

'To make a new start, I suspect,' Whitney said. 'I'm assuming you know the child's name?'

'He's called Mark, and he's their only child.'

'What do you think, George?'

'It's certainly worth investigating.'

'Agreed. We'll visit them after we've checked Natalie McKay's alibi. What else do we know about this couple and their son, Ellie?'

'John Roberts is sixty-six, and a retired accountant. Iris Roberts is sixty-seven, and a retired florist. I have very little on Mark, other than the school he went to, and then onto Nottingham Trent University. I'll keep digging.'

'Thanks. Natalie McKay's in an interview room downstairs and will stay there while we check her alibi. She now admits to being in a local pub waiting for David, who didn't turn up. Frank, did you discover the time she headed back to Birmingham?'

'Yes, guv. She was on her way back there after ten.'

'Which confirms what she told us. Do we have a photo of her?'

'There's one on the company website. I'll download and forward it to you, guv,' Ellie said.

'Great. Okay, we'll see you later.'

While George was driving to the hotel, Whitney stared out of the window.

'Is everything all right?' George asked, causing her to start, as she'd been miles away, her mind full of competing thoughts. Not all of them to do with the case.

She turned to face her. 'Why do you ask?'

'The team might not have noticed, but I've witnessed you being restless and distracted today.'

Whitney sighed. Sharing it with George would help. She hadn't wanted to burden her before, as there was so much else she had to deal with, what with her dad and the move.

'You're right, there is something on my mind, and I've been finding it hard to set it aside. You know I can't compartmentalise like you can.'

'That's because you don't try hard enough. It's not easy, but—'

'I thought you wanted to know what's wrong? I don't need a lesson in how …' She paused. 'Sorry, I didn't mean to go off on one. I went to see Mum last night and took Tiffany, Rob, and the baby. She wasn't having a good day and it really upset Rob. We went outside to talk about it and out of the blue he mentioned that he'd kept a secret from all of us for a long time. I tried to get him to tell me, but he wouldn't. He was too scared, because it could lead to the family being harmed. I think it was related to the time he was attacked. In fact, I'm sure of it.'

'Have you discussed the incident with him in the past?'

'Not really. I was only fourteen when it happened. From my recollection, he couldn't remember a thing. The doctors diagnosed him as having irreparable brain damage and he turned into a totally different person. He went from being a lively, outgoing, fun-loving teen to being quiet and unresponsive, although he did improve a lot over time, thanks to my mum and dad spending so much time with him. Thinking back on it, he was one of those guys who could've ended up getting himself in trouble, especially if he was hanging around with the wrong crowd. We've no idea whether the attack was targeted or random.'

'Did you know the people he was friends with?'

'No. I was too young, and it was long ago. Mum might have done, but I doubt she'll be able to tell me anything now.'

'People with dementia often remember facts from the past. That aside, Rob must have been asked about the attack, at the time.'

'I imagine he was, by the police, or my mum and dad, or the doctors. I don't really know. All I do remember is that the police hardly pursued it and it made me angry. Looking back on it now, with my knowledge of how the force works, it could have been because they had nothing concrete to pursue. It's not like there was much CCTV footage, or the ability to track mobile phones back then. And they might have had other cases to be working on and their resources stretched. I'm not excusing them because I'm sure more could've been done if they had the right mindset, but I accept that it probably wasn't as clear-cut as I believed at the time. If I hadn't interpreted the police's behaviour like that, I might not have ended up in the force. So, I should be grateful. If you know what I mean.'

'Out of adversity often comes a benefit.'

'I'm wondering whether the case should be reopened.'

'Would you be allowed to do that?'

'I'm in charge of the department so, in theory, yes. Except the super would need to know, and if she then mentioned it to Dickhead, he'd no doubt say no it would be a waste of resources because there isn't any new evidence. Even if it was allowed, he'd say I was too invested and give the case to someone else, like Masters, and I couldn't stand for that to happen.'

'I can see their point about someone else taking the case,' George said.

'I know. Anyway, I can't think about it now. It's not going to go away, so let's get this case solved, and I'll think about it then. The hotel is the next road on the right.'

George parked outside the Midland Hotel and they went through the revolving doors to the reception.

'Good morning,' the receptionist said.

Whitney held out her ID. 'We're here to see Penny Burn. What's her room number?'

'Mrs Burn is waiting for you over there.' The receptionist pointed to the other side of the lobby where a woman was sitting on her own in an easy chair, flicking through a magazine.

'Penny Burn?' Whitney asked when they'd reached her.

The woman looked up at them. 'Yes.'

'I'm DCI Walker and this Dr Cavendish. We'd like to ask a few questions about Gillian.'

'Yes, okay. Please sit down.' She placed her magazine on the table in front of her and gestured to the two chairs opposite her.

'We're very sorry for your loss, it must be a very difficult time for you,' Whitney said.

'It still hasn't sunk in. Even when I saw the bodies it …' her voice broke.

'Can I get you something? A glass of water or a cup of tea?' Whitney asked.

'I'm fine. Thank you. What would you like to know?'

'I understand Gillian was older than you. What was the age difference?'

'Nine years.'

'Do you remember when your family moved from Bedford to Poole?'

'Not really, I was only six. It wasn't a happy time, though.'

'In what way?' Whitney asked.

'It's a bit vague, but I remember Gillian had gone to stay with my grandparents and wasn't at home for a while. My mum was crying a lot, and when I asked her what was wrong she said it was nothing and that people sometimes get sad.'

'And when you moved, did it change?'

'Yes. Gillian came back, and Mum seemed a bit better. I remember being happier once we were living in Poole.'

'Did you know why Gillian went to stay with your grandparents?'

'Mum and Dad told me it was to keep them company. Looking back on it now, that can't be the truth. Did something happen?'

'Yes. Gillian was raped at fifteen and found herself pregnant. The baby was given up for adoption just before the family move.'

'Oh my goodness,' Penny exclaimed, her eyes wide. 'Why didn't she ever tell me?'

'She might have suppressed the memory, to make it easier for her to deal with,' George said.

'Is it linked to the murders?'

'We don't know, but it's important to investigate all aspect of their lives. Do you think David would have known?' Whitney asked.

'I honestly couldn't tell you.'

'How was Gillian the last time you spoke?'

'She seemed her usual self. We talked about our children and what they were doing. It was just a normal conversation. I can't believe what Gillian went through, and then to carry it around with her.' She gave a loud sigh.

'Are there any more questions? I'd like to go back to my room.'

'No, that's all. We appreciate you talking to us at a time like this. It can't have been easy. If you do remember anything you think might be relevant, please let me know.'

'I will. Thank you.'

They left Penny Burn waiting for the lift and returned to the car.

'That poor woman, having to learn about the rape and pregnancy on top of everything else,' Whitney said as they were driving to the pub.

'It was certainly a shock.'

'Interesting that she didn't enquire about the child Gillian had.'

'She might, once she's processed what you've told her. Will you give her details of the child, if she asks?'

'That's not something we would be involved in. She'd have to go through the adoption agency. The pub is up here on the right.'

The Tavern was built in the 1960s, and in the middle of a dodgy housing estate. At the end of the street was a gang of teenagers staring at them.

'I'm not sure about leaving my car here unattended,' George said.

'Yeah. I agree. You stay here and I'll go into the pub. I won't be long.'

'Are you sure?'

'It's the middle of the day and hardly going to be full of drunks. I doubt there'll be many in there.'

'Okay. If you're not out in ten minutes, I'll come in.'

Whitney walked into a large bar area, with green plastic seating against the walls and some square tables dotted around in the middle. She'd been correct. There were only a few customers.

She headed over to the bar and held out her warrant card for the woman behind it to see. 'I'm DCI Walker from Lenchester CID. Is the manager around?'

'That's me. I'm Dee Marsh. I own the pub.'

'Were you working last Saturday night?'

'Yes, love, I work here seven days a week. I haven't had a day off in months.'

'Do you remember this woman?' Whitney held out her phone and showed her the photo of Natalie McKay.

The woman stared at it for several seconds. 'I'm not sure. Saturday is our busiest night of the week. What time was she here?'

'Around nine-thirty, give or take a few minutes. She ordered a glass of wine.'

The woman nodded. 'Oh, yes. Now, I remember. I always associate people with their drinks. She had a house red and I was the one to serve her. Sorry, I didn't remember straight away.'

'No need to apologise. What can you tell me about her?'

'She came up to the bar and ordered her drink, and was pleasant. She did stand out as being different from the usual riff-raff I get in here.'

'In what way different?'

'A bit posher, I suppose. She said she was meeting someone.'

'Did she say who?'

'No, she didn't. She was dressed up nice, so I thought she must be on a date. But I didn't see her with anyone.'

'What time did she leave?'

'I don't know the exact time. She sat at a table and I remember looking over a couple of times and thinking, oh, her date's late. Then we had a bit of a rush on, and the next time I looked, she'd gone. I'd say she wasn't here at ten-fifteen, but that's as close as I can go. That was the time I collected her glass from the table.'

'How can you be so sure of the time?'

'I looked at the clock before going out to collect the glasses, thinking that it had been over two hours since I'd last done it and that we were running out. That's the trouble with a Saturday night, it can get so busy.'

'Well, it turned out you remembered a lot after all.'

'At my age, I sometimes need help, even when remembering someone tall, slim, and pretty. My whole life I've dreamed of being like that, but it wasn't to be as I'm only five feet and a quarter of an inch.' She sighed.

'I can relate to wanting some extra height,' Whitney agreed with a smile. 'Thanks for your time.'

She left the pub and headed back to the car.

'It looks like she's got a genuine alibi,' she told George. 'I'll call the station and instruct someone to take her back home, and we'll head for Bedford. There might be some nice houses for you to see. There are some lovely villages out that way. We could take a look while we're there.'

'I need to go with Ross,' George said.

'I get that, but if we pass any *For Sale* signs, we can have a nosey, and then you can check online and take him out there.'

'Surely we don't have time. You'll be needed back at the station as soon as we've made this visit.'

'True. Come on. Let's see what we can find out about Gillian Barker's son.'

# Chapter 31

The Roberts lived in a detached bungalow in a quiet cul-de-sac in a leafy suburb of Bedford.

'Two cars in the drive, which looks promising. Let's hope they're in,' Whitney said, as they got out of the car and marched down the drive to the front door.

She rang the bell and an older man answered.

'Hello?' he said.

'I'm DCI Walker and this is Dr Cavendish from Lenchester CID. Are you Mr Roberts?' She held out her ID, and he leant forward, taking a good look at it, and then at her.

'Yes, that's me.'

'I wonder if we might have a word with you. It's nothing serious,' she added, wanting to put him at ease straight away because of the look of horror on his face when she'd announced where she was from.

'What's this about?' he asked, not moving.

'We'd rather talk inside, if we may,' she said, returning her warrant card to her pocket. 'Is Mrs Roberts here with you?'

'Yes, she is. We were getting ready to go do the weekly shop.'

'We'd like to talk to you both. We won't take too much of your time.'

'Okay, come on in.'

He stepped to the side and ushered them into the long hallway.

'Thank you.'

'We'll sit in the living room. I'll show you the way and then fetch my wife, she's in the bedroom.'

'Thank you,' Whitney said.

He led them in to an airy, oblong room with French doors overlooking the garden. There were two large traditional sofas, situated at a ninety-degree angle from each, which matched the floral curtains. Whitney and George stood in the centre, waiting. After a couple of minutes, Mr and Mrs Roberts appeared.

'This is Iris, my wife. Please, sit.' He gestured for them to sit on one of the sofas, which they did, and they sat on the other.

'We'd like to talk to you about your son, Mark.'

Mrs Roberts' hand flew up to her mouth. 'What's happened? Is he okay? I thought this wasn't serious.'

'As far as we know, he's fine. We have some questions about him. Please could you confirm that he's adopted?'

'Yes, that's right. Is he in trouble? We haven't seen or heard from him for months,' Mr Roberts said.

'Is there a reason for him not keeping in contact with you?'

The elderly couple exchanged glances. 'He's drifted away from us.'

'Why? Did something happen?' Whitney asked.

'Mark was a lovely boy until he got to about fourteen,

and then he became obsessed with trying to find out about his birth parents,' Iris Roberts said.

Whitney's senses went on full alert.

'When you say *obsessed*, could you give me some more detail?' she asked, scribbling down some notes.

'It was all he ever talked about, even though we explained that he'd have to wait until he was eighteen before he could apply to find out more. He asked us all the time what we knew about them, but we stuck to the same story.'

'The story being?'

'That we didn't know anything about his background. We couldn't bring ourselves to tell him the truth about what happened to his mother. Mark has always been a sensitive child. Well, he's not a child now, obviously. But he is to us. We didn't believe he could cope with knowing about the rape. We refused to let him see his birth certificate until he was eighteen. We kept it hidden. The day he was eighteen, armed with his birth certificate he started looking for her. Gillian Findlay. There was a blank where the father's name should've been.'

'Did you tell him then about the circumstances of his birth?'

Iris Roberts bowed her head. 'No, because we didn't think he'd find her.'

'But he did?'

'Yes. She refused to see him and said she didn't want anything to do with him. She wouldn't tell him why. We then explained about the rape and told him that was why she most likely didn't want to know him. He wouldn't accept it.'

'Do you know how many times he contacted her?'

'No, he wouldn't tell us. He said it was our fault for not telling him sooner. He believed that she'd have seen him when he was a small child. I don't think she would have. Mark was convinced of it and wouldn't listen to me.'

'Why do you want to know all this?' Mr Roberts asked.

'We're investigating the murder of the Barker family, in Lenchester.'

'Oh, yes, we've heard about that. It's been all over the news.'

'Gillian Barker was Mark's birth mother.'

'And you think he had something to do with it?' Mr Roberts asked, his face ashen.

'No. Not Mark. He wouldn't kill anyone. He isn't that sort of person.' Mrs Roberts took hold of her husband's hand and squeezed it so tight it went white.

'Our lines of enquiry are covering all aspects of the Barker family's life, and this is only one avenue. We're not accusing Mark of anything,' Whitney said, hoping to reassure them.

'Because we'd stake our lives on him having nothing to do with it, wouldn't we, John?' Mrs Roberts said.

'Yes. He definitely wouldn't have been involved.'

'You mentioned that you hadn't seen Mark for months, which wasn't unusual. How often do you see him?'

'Maybe twice a year, if that. Ever since he left for university, thirteen years ago, it's like we're not important to him,' Mrs Roberts said. 'Occasionally he'll call in. He'll be polite but act like we're acquaintances—'

'I don't think the officer needs to know all this,' John Roberts said, interrupting his wife.

'Do you have a recent photo of Mark we could look at?'

'The latest is from his graduation ten years ago, which he said we could attend. I'll fetch it for you.'

Mrs Roberts hurried over to the lightwood sideboard

and took a photo in a frame from the top. She brought it over and showed it to them.

Whitney stared at it. He was smiling, but it didn't reach his eyes. More than that. She'd seen his face before, but she couldn't think where. 'Do you mind if I take a photo of this with my phone? For our records?'

'Of course not,' Mrs Roberts said.

Whitney took out her phone and as she clicked, her breath caught in her throat. She'd remembered who he was.

'What job does Mark do?' she asked, forcing her voice to sound normal and not betray the pounding of her heart.

'He's a teacher.'

'Do you know where?'

'The last we knew he was teaching in Nottingham. That's where he went to university. We don't know if he's still there, do we, John?' Mrs Roberts said.

'No.' He glanced at his watch.

'What did Mark study?' George asked.

'English and theology.'

'Did he have a religious upbringing?'

'We go to church every week, and Mark would come with us when he was younger. But he stopped when he was a teenager.'

'Was it around the time when he first became obsessed with finding his birth mother?' George asked.

'Yes. It was about that time. Do you think it was connected?'

'I can't be certain, but it's a possibility.'

'If you were to describe Mark's personality, what would it be?' Whitney asked.

'Meticulous. He likes everything to be in a certain way,' Mr Roberts said.

'Is he a perfectionist?' George asked.

'Yes, that's exactly what he's like,' Mrs Roberts said, nodding.

They needed to leave and return to the station pronto.

'We won't keep you any longer as you want to go shopping. Thank you very much for your help.'

They left the house and walked down the drive towards the car.

'You know him, don't you? I could tell by the expression on your face when you looked at the photograph,' George said.

'Yes. He's a teacher at the school the Barker children attended, only using the name Robinson instead of Roberts. I can't remember his first name but I'm fairly certain it wasn't Mark. I know this photo was taken ten years ago, but he's still recognisable. He's our killer. I know he is. We need to get back and plan to bring him in for questioning.'

'I'm concerned about Mr and Mrs Roberts. They might feel duty-bound to contact him and tell him that we've been enquiring about him.'

'Good point. Do me a favour. Go back inside and wait with them while I arrange for an officer to come over and stay with them until this is over.'

## Chapter 32

Within the hour, Whitney and George had returned to the station after leaving an officer with Mr and Mrs Roberts.

'Stop what you're doing,' Whitney shouted as they entered the incident room. 'We have a suspect for the Barker murders. Mr Robinson, a teacher at the children's school. He changed his surname from Roberts. Ellie, check for his first name. I've forgotten what it is.'

'Yes, guv. It will be on the school website.' Whitney waited for her to look, tapping her foot on the floor. 'It's *Eric* Robinson.'

'Oh yes. Eric. Thanks, Ellie. He rarely contacts his adoptive parents, but there's an officer at their house to prevent them from warning him that he's on our radar. We need to plan his arrest. It's best if we go to the school and take him by surprise. It won't look odd for us to be visiting again, so he shouldn't be alerted. Before we go, George, what can you say about his psychological profile? What type of person are we dealing with?'

'After listening to what his adoptive parents had said, and knowing how the crime scene was left, it's my opinion he was obsessed with knowing his *real* family, and he took the rejection of his birth mother badly.'

'Why did he murder the whole family and not just Gillian?' Brian asked.

'To make Gillian suffer. She was the last person to be killed and had to witness the deaths of everyone she loved. In his mind, he equated it to how much he had suffered. The fact he used duct tape to prevent her from talking was also important. He took away her voice. Again, he would have compared it with his own treatment. His adoptive parents didn't tell him anything about his family until he reached the age of eighteen, when he could legally search for her. Until that time he had no voice.'

'I get it,' Brian said, nodding.

'He has a complex psyche. Basically, if *he* wasn't allowed to be a part of the Barker family, then no one would,' George said.

'I know you said the meal symbolised betrayal, but why the extra setting?' Whitney asked.

'So he could be part of the family. He may have cooked and set the table after they were all dead. We won't know until he's interviewed.'

'That's totally bonkers. He killed them, but still wanted to be part of the family, so he made them all a meal, himself included,' Frank said. 'Why didn't he commit suicide after, so he could be dead like the rest of them?'

'That's a good question, Frank.'

'Wonders will never cease,' Doug said.

'Shut it—'

'I don't have an answer, Frank. It's something to ask during his questioning.'

'Do you think he trained as a teacher with a view to getting a job at the children's school?' Whitney asked.

'That really would have been playing the long game,' Doug said.

'It's quite possible. We do know that he had a religious upbringing and that he studied theology as part of his degree. That would explain his use of religious symbolism when staging the scene.'

'He must have been stalking Gillian Barker for a long time,' Doug said.

'Yes, he was,' George said.

'Okay, now we have the rundown, let's plan his arrest. Remember, the evidence we currently have is circumstantial. We don't know for certain yet whether he's the one.'

'I'll bet my pension he is,' Frank said.

'We'll leave for the school now. Brian, you and I will visit the head teacher and ask to speak to Robinson. If he comes along to see us, then we'll arrest him on the spot. Doug, Meena and Frank, you will go to the school in two separate cars and position yourselves at each entrance in case he susses us and attempts to do a runner. Ellie, continue digging. We need as much information we can get on both of his names.'

'What about me?' George asked.

'You know the answer to that one. You stay here and wait for us to return with Robinson. While we're out, perhaps you could think about whether there's anything specific I should focus on to get him talking. I'm going to let the super know what's happening, and as soon as I'm back, we'll leave.'

Whitney ran all the way, and by the time she reached the super's office she could hardly breathe. She hadn't realised she was so unfit, and really needed to do more about it. She knocked and poked her head around the open door, without waiting to be called in.

'Ma'am, I'm here to let you know we're about to bring

233

someone in for questioning regarding the Barker murders. He's a teacher from the children's school. Eric Robinson, previously known as Mark Roberts. Gillian Barker was his birth mother and he was obsessed about meeting up and getting to know her, but she had wanted nothing to do with him.'

'That would have been tough on him.'

'Gillian was raped as a teenager and the pregnancy resulted. After the baby was given up for adoption, the family moved from Bedford to Poole in Dorset, where they made a fresh start.'

'Good work, Whitney.'

'We're going to arrest him now. We have no physical evidence yet, but I hope we'll elicit his confession during the interview. Please could you arrange a search warrant for his place as soon as possible?'

'I'll get onto it now. If we can get this wrapped up within a week, that will certainly go in our favour and stop the media from hounding us.'

'Yes, ma'am. It will also get the chief super off our backs, which is a massive plus,' she said, grinning.

'I can neither confirm nor deny my agreement with that,' the super said, her lips turned up into a slight smile.

'I'll report back once we have Robinson in custody.'

Whitney left the office, smiling to herself. Beneath her seriousness, the super had a sense of humour. It was nice to be able to say that about a boss. But she didn't have time to dwell on that. They needed to get to the school before lessons finished and Robinson left for the day.

# Chapter 33

Brian parked his car outside the front of the school, and once Whitney had ascertained that the two other cars were in place, they walked through the entrance into the main building and headed for the administration area where the head teacher was situated.

'You're back again,' the school secretary said.

'We've got a few more things to go through. Is Dr Johnson available?' Whitney nodded at the closed door of the head teacher's office.

'Yes, I'll get her for you.'

The woman knocked and went straight in. After a few seconds, she returned with the head.

'Hello, Dr Johnson. We wanted to confirm some further details with one of the children's teachers. Mr Robinson. Do you know if he's available?'

'Trudy, please will you check the timetable to see where Eric is.'

The secretary went behind her desk and looked at her computer screen. 'He's been teaching year eight. Shall I fetch him?'

'If you wouldn't mind. I'm expecting a call from one of the governors any moment now.'

'We'll wait in the corridor for him, and let you get on,' Whitney said.

'Are you sure? You can wait here if you wish.'

'We're fine, thanks. This won't take long. We only want a quick chat.'

The last thing Whitney wanted to do was to cause alarm because it would alert Robinson. Her plan was to ask him to come outside with them so they could talk privately and not be overheard by any of the students. She was well aware that the situation had to be handled carefully, or it could get nasty. Hence the reason for having backup outside from the rest of the team.

They stood looking at the photos on the wall and a couple of minutes later their suspect was heading towards them, walking with the school secretary, appearing to be chatting amiably. He clearly wasn't aware of why they wanted to speak to him.

'Here he comes,' Brian muttered stepping towards him. 'Thanks for coming to see us, Mr Roberts …'

Robinson's jaw dropped. He turned, pushed Trudy out of the way, and ran.

Crap. Brian had called him by his old name.

'Quick, after him,' she said to her sergeant.

They ran down the corridor, trying to navigate the kids who were now swarming about as lessons had ended. She pulled out her radio.

'Suspect escaping. We're in pursuit heading towards the back entrance. See if you can stop him on the other side.'

They chased after him but didn't make up any ground. Through the corridors and out of a door onto the school playing fields. As he was running across he passed three young students standing in a huddle. He grabbed one by the arm.

'Right, you come with me,' Robinson said.

'But, sir,' the boy shouted as he was dragged away while being forced to run alongside his teacher.

'Do as you're told,' Robinson snapped.

'Suspect has taken a hostage. Call backup,' Whitney radioed. She slowed her pace, keeping the suspect in sight. She didn't want him to do anything rash and harm the child.

'We're coming from the other direction,' Doug said.

They followed Robinson to a large wooden shed. He opened the door and pushed the child inside.

'Don't come any closer, or the boy will be hurt,' he shouted, before going inside the shed and shutting the door.

Whitney and Brian came to a halt about ten yards away and waited for the others to join them.

'He's got a student in there. We've got to play this carefully. Brian, find the head and ask her to come out here straight away. I need to know what's in that shed.'

'Guv, I'm sorry about calling him by the wrong name, it—'

'Not now. We'll talk later.'

'Yes, guv.' He turned and ran back towards the school.

Through the window, Whitney could make out two moving shadows. It didn't look like the boy was being harmed. After a few minutes, Brian and Dr Johnson came back.

'What's happening? Your officer wouldn't tell me anything other than there's an emergency.'

'We believe that Mr Robinson is involved in the murders of the Barker family. When he realised why we were here, he ran.'

'Are you sure? Eric's one of our best teachers.'

'It's a long and involved story, which obviously we can't tell you about now. More importantly, he has taken a boy hostage. Can you tell me what's in the shed?'

'It's full of equipment the students use on the field.'

'What exactly do you have in there? Any potential weapons?'

'Yes, plenty. There are rounders bats, javelins, discus, cricket bats, balls and bails, football nets …'

Exactly what Whitney didn't want to hear. This was getting worse by the second.

'And how come it was open, don't you keep it locked to stop students from getting in there and stealing stuff?'

'It's always kept locked. All I think of is that it was opened earlier by the PE teacher getting ready for a training session after school.'

'Is the PE teacher in there as well?'

'No, I saw Mrs Nelson on my way out here to see you.'

'Okay. Now we know what we're dealing with, it's important to keep everybody away from this location. The area will be cordoned off and I'll contact Robinson. Do you have his mobile number?'

'I can get it. It'll be on the system.'

'Meena will go with you and bring back the number. I also need to know the name of the boy he has with him.'

'Yes, I can do that. Do you need me back here?' Dr Johnson asked.

'No. I need you to stay inside the school and ensure no one tries to sneak out. You'll need the help of other teachers. Don't tell them what's happening.'

'I can make something up. Are the children allowed to go home? The bell has gone but there are still plenty around.'

'Keep whoever's still there inside until it's all over. Doug, sort out the cordon and ensure no one enters or leaves the premises. Brian, you go with him.'

'Yes, guv,' they said in unison before running off towards the main entrance.

'Parents will be worried if they can't collect their children,' Dr Johnson said.

'In that case, it might be better if you wait outside the cordon on the street to answer any queries the parents may have. Remember, don't mention Robinson at all.'

'I understand,' Dr Johnson said before heading back to the school with Meena.

After a couple of minutes, Doug returned. 'The cordon's in place, guv.'

'Yes, thanks, I can see. Look over there, there are several students and a couple of adults watching on.' She pointed to the east of the school building.

'I'll move back them into the school.' Doug ran in their direction.

Whitney turned to look at the shed. She could no longer see shadows moving. What was going on in there? She glanced at the school and saw Meena hurrying towards her.

'The boy's name is Joshua Smith. He's only twelve. And this is Robinson's number, guv,' Meena said handing her a piece of paper.

'Thanks.'

She could see Doug and Brian in the distance and she waited for them to reach her. 'I'm going to phone Robinson now. I'll put it on speaker so we can all hear what he has to say.' She keyed in the number Meena gave and waited while it rang.

'Yes,' Robinson said, finally answering.

'This is DCI Walker. We know you're involved in what happened to the Barker family. Come out now so we can talk about it.'

'No.'

'Let Joshua go, he's done nothing.'

'No.'

Whitney sucked in a breath, grateful that only recently she'd renewed her hostage situation training. The man was giving away nothing. His voice was cold and emotionless. Not a good sign. 'Think logically, Eric. You can't stay in there forever, so why don't you tell me what you want, and we can work this out? We don't want any harm to come to you or Joshua.'

He was silent for what seemed like ages. If it wasn't for his breathing, she'd have thought he'd disconnected the call.

'I want a taxi to take us to a destination that I'll direct the driver to once I'm in there. Providing we're not followed, I'll release the boy.'

'Why don't you come with us now, and we can talk it through. I want to hear your side of the story.'

'No. You'll do it my way, or the boy will suffer. And then you'll have blood on your hands.'

'Okay, we'll call you a taxi.'

'It's got to be from the firm I use regularly. I know all the drivers, so don't think you can substitute one for a police officer.'

Of course he'd think of that. He wasn't going to let anything happen by chance.

'I understand. What's the name of the taxi company?'

'Combined Cabs. And remember, if anyone follows, the boy gets hurt. He won't be released until I'm safe.'

'All right. You'll have to give me a moment. I'll let you know when the taxi has arrived.'

'Make sure it's not too long.' He ended the call.

'He's been watching too many movies on television. I suppose we're lucky he didn't ask for a helicopter. Right, let's get in touch with this company and sort something out.'

## Chapter 34

'Stop snivelling,' I say to the boy, who's standing in the corner crying.

I can't believe they discovered my identity. It wasn't meant to happen like this.

But I'll get away from here and they won't find me.

I can blend in. I've done it before, and I'll do it again. It's easy when you know what to do.

'I want my mum.'

I wasn't thinking straight when I grabbed him. Of all the students I could've taken, I had to pick a pathetic weakling. Then again, at least he won't try to escape. One thing's for sure, I'm not going to feel sorry for him and let him go.

'Shut up.'

Except I do feel sorry for the kid. I enjoy my job and especially working with the younger kids. I don't want them to feel like I did at that age. Like I was second-rate and not worth anything.

If only Gillian had agreed to see me, none of this would've happened. All I ever wanted was to be part of a big family. My adoptive parents are okay, but they're old and boring. And even when they try, it's not enough. Why didn't they adopt another kid so I had a brother or sister? Was it because I was too much trouble? I never *asked. Not that they'd tell me. They think it's okay to keep secrets from me. I learnt that to my cost.*

*I couldn't believe it when the job for this school was advertised. I knew it was a sign for me to be close to my real family. And when I found out I'd be teaching my brothers and sister. That nearly blew my mind. It was almost enough for me. Until I saw the way Gillian was with them. Always putting her arms around them, caring for them. Why couldn't she have been like that with me? That's when I knew it wasn't right and I should do something about it.*

*'It was so unfair. And now they've all paid for it,' I say out loud.*

*'What is, sir?' Joshua says.*

*I'd forgotten he was there.*

*'Nothing to do with you, so shut up and we'll be out of here soon. Remember, if you try anything stupid, like running away, you won't be going home.'*

*The boy cried.*

*'Don't start that, again. Where the hell are they? Why is it taking so long?'*

*I'd lied about knowing all the drivers working for the taxi firm. I said it so they didn't think they could have a police officer driving me. I do know the firm. I've used them a few times in the past.*

*'I need the loo, Mr Robinson,' Joshua says.*

*'Well, you'll have to wait until we're out of here.'*

*'What if I can't?'*

*'Then you'll have to piss yourself and have wet clothes. Your choice. Understand?'*

*'Yes, sir.'*

# Chapter 35

'Okay, it's all arranged with the taxi company. They're going to use one of their regular drivers and he'll have his phone patched into mine, as well as his link with the head office, so we can listen and discover where they're heading. The phone is an extra precaution in case Robinson tells him to turn off his link thing to the company. We've also fitted a tracker to the taxi. We can't be too careful, not while there's a child with him. The driver has been instructed to use the phrase *do you mind if I open the window for some fresh air* if he sees that Robinson has a weapon.'

'I doubt he'll tell the driver his destination. He'll probably do it in stages,' Brian said.

'I agree, but it's imperative that we maintain contact. I've arranged for the driver to come on to the field and up to the shed.'

'Guv, the taxi's here,' Doug's voice came through the radio.

He'd been coordinating proceedings in the vicinity of the school. Uniformed officers had arrived, and the entire street was cordoned off with police positioned at every exit dealing with parents and other passers-by who wanted to enter.

'Send him down. Everyone else scatter,' she said to the rest of the team. 'I don't want him feeling pressured because there are so many of us.' She pulled out her phone and phoned Robinson. 'The taxi is driving up to the shed. Why don't you get in and let the boy go?'

'No. He'll be released when I'm ready. Tell your officers to keep well away or he'll get hurt.'

'No one is close to you. You'll be able to see from the window when the car is there.'

'Remember what I said, and the boy won't get hurt.'

The taxi drove up and Robinson came out, holding the boy's wrist and using him as a shield. Did he think they were going to shoot him?

The boy's face had lost all colour, but other than that he appeared unharmed.

They got into the waiting taxi and drove off. Whitney and the team ran across the field and watched as the car turned left out of the school grounds.

'Okay, everyone back to your cars. Follow Brian and me. We'll keep him in our sight but at a distance.'

Whitney and Brian ran to his car and she placed her phone on mute to prevent them from being heard in the taxi. She put it on the dash so they could hear what was going on. The driver had been instructed to drive at a steady pace.

'Where are we going?' the driver asked.

'Continue down Durham Road, and I'll tell you when to turn.'

'Right, we know where they are, so let's go.'

Brian drove quickly and soon the taxi was in eyesight.

'Now where?' the driver asked.

'Turn right at the next junction.'

'Sounds like we're heading towards the motorway,' Brian said.

'Yeah, but is he going north or south, both are accessible from there? Let's hope he says something soon.'

There was silence for a few minutes.

'Turn right here,' Robinson said.

'Which lane shall I take?' the driver asked.

'The inside.'

'So, you want me to head towards the motorway and keep left.'

'Why are you repeating everything I said?'

'Damn. Has he sussed what we're doing?' Whitney said.

'Because there's a roundabout coming up and one lane leads to the north entry and one to the south. I want to make sure I go the right way. I'm not repeating everything you said.'

'Nice save,' Brian said.

'I'm sorry,' Robinson said.

Whitney frowned. 'Why is he apologising? We could do with George to tell us what's going on inside the man's head.'

'I want you to go north,' Robinson said.

'Okay, this makes it easier. He doesn't know any of our cars which means we can all get on the M1.'

She radioed to the other cars, and they followed the taxi in convoy for thirty miles.

'I hope he's not going to Scotland, guv,' Brian said.

'They'll have to stop for petrol at one of the service stations if that's the case, and we'll arrest him then.'

'Pull in at the next service station,' Robinson said.

'I didn't know you practiced mind-reading in your spare time,' Brian said, flashing a grin in her direction.

'You'd be surprised what I can do. I—'

'I said the next service station,' Robinson said, interrupting her.

'This one?' the driver replied.

'Yes, turn now.'

'But there are cars in the way.'

'I don't care. Do it.'

'All units, vehicle turning left into the service station,' Whitney said.

The driver turned, narrowly missing a car coming up behind him.

'Now where?' the driver asked.

'Park at the top. The boy is getting out and then I want you to drive straight out and back onto the motorway.'

'We'll follow the taxi, Doug go to the left and Frank take the right. Be ready to block him in.'

The taxi drove through the car park and stopped at the back beside the fast-food restaurant.

'Get out,' Robinson said.

'How am I going to get home?' the boy said.

'Get out before I change my mind.'

'But …'

'I said get—'

Three unmarked cars screeched to a halt and surrounded the taxi.

Brian jumped out and ran to the front passenger door. He dragged Robinson from the car and threw him on the ground in front of Whitney.

She grabbed hold of Robinson's arm and pulled him up while Brian handcuffed him.

'Mark Roberts, I'm arresting you—'

'It's Eric Robinson. I changed it by deed poll.'

'Okay. *Eric Robinson*, I'm arresting you on suspicion of the murders of David, Gillian, Keira, Harvey, and Tyler Barker, and the kidnapping of Joshua Smith. You do not have to say anything, but it may harm your defence if you do not mention when questioned something which you later rely on in court. Anything you do say may be given in evidence. Do you understand?'

'Yes,' he muttered.

Two police cars, closely followed by an ambulance, sped into the car park. Four uniformed officers ran over to them.

'Take him away,' Whitney said.

## Chapter 36

George was seated at one of the spare desks in the incident room, checking online property sites. Her current Victorian house only had a single garage at the rear of the property. If they could find something with a set of garages, then she'd start a classic car collection. Whitney called her a petrolhead because she loved cars. She was right. George would love to own a Jaguar XK120 to start her collection.

Also, Ross's studio needed additional space for where people could come and discuss their requirements when they commissioned him. He'd recently been turning down work because he was so busy after he'd had some prestigious exhibitions. His work was becoming highly sought after. Even her mother had mentioned acquiring a piece from him.

They needed a good-sized garden. Gardening was one of her hobbies and she intended to grow her own vegetables and herbs.

She was making notes about a potential property when the door opened and the team came rushing in, all talking at once. The operation must have been a success. She headed over to Whitney, who was standing by the board, a beaming smile on her face.

'We've got him, but not until after he kidnapped a boy from the school and we had to pursue him up the motorway,' Whitney said, the words rushing out of her mouth.

'How is the child?'

'The medics checked him out at the scene, and he was unharmed. He's home with his parents and a family liaison officer.'

'Are you going to interview Robinson now?'

'Not until his solicitor arrives.'

'First of all, providing the warrants have arrived, we're going to search Robinson's house and then I want to visit Joshua Smith, the kidnapped child, at home. I'll get the address details from Ellie.'

'Would you like me to come with you?'

'Of course. I've just got to speak to the super and tell her what went down. You can wait here. What have you been doing while we've been away?'

'Thinking about the questioning as you requested, and then looking at properties.'

'Were any of them suitable?'

'There are some possibilities.'

'Why don't you wait for me in my office. I won't be long.'

'Okay.'

Whitney returned ten minutes later.

'Search warrants have come through, so let's go.'

Robinson was renting a small semi-detached property, not far from the Barker's house. Whitney handed George some disposable gloves, which she pulled on, and they entered using the key he'd handed over.

The front door led immediately into an open-plan lounge, dining, and kitchen area. It was minimally furnished with modern furniture and nothing was out of place. They headed to the kitchen.

'He's obviously a cook, judging by the selection of spices and herbs growing on the windowsill,' George said.

'And very healthy. Nothing pre-packaged in the fridge or pantry.'

'Look for cinnamon, lentils, sea salt, anchovies, and leeks. Those are ingredients needed for the meal he cooked for the family.'

'Why anchovies, they weren't there?'

'Traditional fish sauce is made from them, with sea salt. The fish is covered in salt and then left to ferment.'

'How do you know that? Don't tell me, you've made it in the past.'

'No, I haven't but I researched it after Claire told us fish sauce was part of the meal.'

'Well, you're spot on because all those ingredients are here. There's also a container in the fridge with something in it. I'll open it.' She put the container on the side. 'Eww. It stinks. Is this it?'

George walked over and sniffed the liquid. 'Yes.'

'Right, this all needs to come with us.' Whitney pulled out some evidence bags and placed the food inside. 'Let's go upstairs to see what else we can find.'

'We'll need to get the sauce into a fridge once we're back at the station or it will smell dreadfully.'

'We'll leave that for forensics. I'll put it back in the fridge until we're ready to leave. It should be okay from here until we get back.'

'Yes, that will be fine.'

The first bedroom they came to was obviously Robinson's. Again, very tidy, nothing out of place. Whitney opened the wardrobe door.

'Look at this. All colour-coded. I wish someone would do that to my wardrobe.'

'I'd give it a week before it would be back to its usual mess. You couldn't maintain it.'

'I could be offended, except I know you're right. I haven't seen his laptop, have you?'

'He might be using the other bedroom as a study. I'll take a look.'

George went next door and when she pushed open the door her eyes widened.

The walls were covered from floor to ceiling with photos and newspaper cuttings of the Barker family.

'Wow,' Whitney said, coming up behind George. 'He was seriously obsessed with this family. We need to get forensics around here.' She pulled out her phone and took photos of all the walls.

'This material isn't randomly placed. Each of the children has their own section, and there are very few photos of the family together. I believe this is all related to him being adopted. He wanted to be part of the family and because Gillian excluded him, he refused to show them as a whole. By having only the constituent parts up there, he could pretend he was a part of it. It's complex.'

'You're telling me. I think we've seen enough here. I want to speak to Joshua Smith. We won't stay long, in case you're worried about the fish sauce.'

George frowned. 'I'm not.'

'And I'm kidding.'

'Oh.'

They drove out to the Smith house, and the door was opened by the family liaison officer.

'Hello, Caroline. We've come to have a chat with Joshua and his parents. How is he holding up?'

'Shaken, but unharmed. I've been instructed to stay with them until this evening.'

The officer took them into the lounge where Joshua was sitting next to his mother.

'I'm DCI Walker and this is Dr Cavendish. Do you mind if we have a quick chat with you about what happened earlier?'

'Yes, that's okay,' Joshua said, glancing up at his mother who nodded.

'You've been very brave. When Mr Robinson took you, did he tell you why he did it?'

'No. But he did say something.'

'Can you remember what it was?'

'Yes. He said, it was so unfair. And now they've all paid for it.'

'Did he threaten to harm you?'

'He told me to shut up when I spoke and wouldn't let me go to the toilet. He said as long as I behaved myself I'd be all right. But if I didn't, he would do something to hurt me.'

'He didn't actually harm you, did he?'

'No.' Joshua shook his head.

'What was Mr Robinson like at school?'

'He was my favourite teacher. Everybody liked him. He wouldn't shout all the time, you know, not like some teachers. He was strict, but hardly anyone messed around in his lessons.'

'Thank you for your help. If you do remember anything else, tell Caroline and she'll let me know. Is there anything you'd like to ask us, before we leave?'

'Can I go to school tomorrow?'

'I don't think he should,' his mother said.

'I want to be with my friends. I don't want to be here on my own.'

'What do you think?' his mother asked.

'Why don't you play it by ear and see how you feel in the morning. Joshua, if you don't mind I'd like a quick chat with your mum outside.'

'Okay.'

They went into the hall, and Whitney closed the door so the boy couldn't hear.

'I wanted to let you know that Mr Robinson has been arrested for the murders of the Barker family. It's going to be on the news, so you might want to prepare Joshua.'

'Oh my goodness. I definitely should keep him off school, then.'

'He might be better with his friends,' George said. 'I do suggest that you take him to see a counsellor. The school will have details of one they recommend. The shock of it might hit him hard at a later date.'

'Yes, of course, I'll do that, thank you. How could Mr Robinson have done such a thing? He was such a nice man.'

'His anger was directed solely at the Barker family, which I believe is why he didn't harm Joshua physically.'

# Chapter 37

'Brian, you and I will interview Robinson while George watches. His solicitor is here,' Whitney said. 'What suggestions did you come up with regarding questioning?' she asked George.

'He believes that he's been betrayed by people for his entire life. In his mind he was justified in taking the action he did and it's unlikely that the act of murdering the family caused him any fulfilment. It would have been a means to an end. With this in mind, I suggest that you take a more softly-softly approach. If he believes that you understand the reasoning behind what he did, he might open up.'

'Even if he is totally crazy,' Brian said.

'If the aim is to elicit a confession, then yes,' George said.

Whitney and Brian walked into the room and sat opposite the suspect.

'Interview on Friday, June 11, those present DCI Walker, DS Chapman and, please state your names for the recording.'

'Lance Critchell, solicitor for Eric Robinson.'

'Eric Robinson.'

'Mr Robinson, you are still under caution. Do you admit to the Barker family murders?'

'You don't have to answer that,' the solicitor said.

'I wouldn't have done it if Gillian Barker hadn't rejected me. All I wanted was a family.'

Wow. They didn't even have to try George's approach. He'd told them straight away.

'Mr Robinson,' the solicitor said.

Robinson turned to him. 'I don't care. They know I did it. What's the point in pretending I didn't?'

'That's your decision, but you're not acting on my advice.'

Whitney shook her head. Nothing like covering your back.

'You already have a family,' she said.

'That's not the same. They're not my *real* family. I wanted to know my birth mother and be part of her family.'

'She didn't want that.'

'I was her son. Surely that should stand for something.'

'Do you know the circumstances surrounding her pregnancy?'

'Yes. She was raped at fifteen and found herself pregnant. That's not my fault. I'm still her son.'

'She was very young at the time and the victim of a terrible crime which would've haunted her. She wanted to try to forget about it. How could you hold that against her?' Whitney drew in a breath, she had to remain calm. But it was hard.

'She could've told me that instead of refusing to see me,' Robinson snapped, his eyes flashing.

'Don't continue with this line of questioning, Whitney, or he'll close up,' George said in her ear.

'Eric, tell us all about what happened the evening when you went to the house. Did you go with the intention of killing the family?'

'No.'

'Yet you had sufficient anaesthetic on your person to do so.'

'I hadn't decided exactly how it was going to play out.'

*Play out.* Was it all a game to him?

'He's lying. He's virtually stopped blinking,' George said, cutting into her thoughts.

'I don't agree, I think you went in there with the sole purpose of ending the lives of all the family because they didn't want you in their lives.'

'It wasn't like that. You don't understand.'

'Then make me understand. Because from where I'm sitting it's clear-cut.'

'Look, I'd been observing the family for a while and when I went into the house last Saturday, all I wanted to do was speak to them. I wanted to explain how I felt. Let them know how lonely I was. I wanted to give them the chance of welcoming me into the family.'

'Yet you took with you some midazolam.'

'It was a precaution to stop them from trying anything stupid. I showed it to them and warned them I'd use it if necessary.'

'Which clearly you found it was. What happened during the evening? Run through everything.'

He sat back in his chair and drew in a breath. 'I went through the back door into the kitchen. I'd brought with me food to cook and left it on the island in the middle of the kitchen. I then went into the dining room and found them sitting at the table. They'd just eaten dinner. Harvey noticed me first and called out. I had a gun in my hand to make sure they did as they were told. David Barker shouted at me to leave and I pointed the gun directly at him. I said *move and you're all dead.*'

'Did that work?'

'Initially. I had some rope with me and instructed Keira to tie everyone up so they couldn't move. I then tied her.' He paused, a glazed expression crossing his face.

'Then what happened?'

Robinson jumped and stared at Whitney. 'I told them who I was, but they didn't believe me. Not until I made Gillian admit it was the truth. She hadn't told anyone about me. I wanted them to like me, but they didn't. They were mean.' His voice rose in pitch.

'So you decided to kill them?'

'No. It wasn't like that. David Barker tried to come at me, even though he was restrained and I pulled out the syringe from my pocket. I injected him in the neck.'

'And after that?'

'Gillian swore at me and I taped her mouth shut. None of this would've happened if she'd welcomed me into the family.'

'After David, why did you kill the rest of them?'

'I had no choice. They'd incriminate me, and I'd end up in prison for the rest of my life.'

'Were they all dead when you cooked the meal?'

'Yes.'

'So why cook for them?'

'They were my family.'

'But they betrayed you, didn't they? That's why you cooked their *Last Supper*. You were never going to let them go. You went to the house determined to kill them all.'

He ran his hands through his hair, rocking backwards and forwards in his chair. 'That's not true. It's not. They didn't have to die. It was their fault. Their fault …'

'My client's had enough questioning. He needs medical attention,' Critchell said.

'He's right, Whitney,' George said.

'Interview suspended. I'll arrange for Mr Robinson to be escorted back to his cell and for him to see a doctor.'

Whitney and Brian left the room and met George in the corridor.

'It looks like he's having some sort of breakdown. Is it real? Or is he trying to fool us? I wouldn't put it past him,' Whitney asked.

'A psychiatric assessment will be made regarding his fitness to stand trial,' George said.

'And if they say he isn't, it means he can enter a plea of diminished responsibility and get away with it. Bloody typical,' Brian said, shaking his head.

'Don't remind me,' Whitney said. Her phone rang. 'Walker.'

'It's Melissa from PR. You're required at a press conference immediately.'

'I'm on my way.' She ended the call. 'I've got to go. There's a press conference. I'm not sure why they want me there. Drinks are on me. Get the team together, Brian, and I'll meet you in the pub. I want a quick chat with the super after we've spoken to the media. Are you staying for drinks, George?'

'Yes.'

'Great. You go over with the team and I'll see you there.'

## Chapter 38

Whitney stood behind the super and *Dickhead* who was preening and acting like he'd solved the entire case himself. Would it make a good story for the press if she told them he'd done nothing other than be a pain in the arse the entire time? Not only that, was it okay that he was there, considering the conflict of interest even if it wasn't public knowledge? The conference room was packed with reporters all holding out their phones to capture what was being said. Cameras were at the back.

'Thank you for coming in,' Melissa said. 'I'd like to hand over to Chief Superintendent Douglas for an update.' She stepped down from the podium and Douglas took her place.

'We've called you in today to announce that we have arrested someone for the Barker family murders.'

'What's their name?' a reporter in the front called out.

'We're not able to discuss that at the moment, as you know, but we're not seeking anyone else in relation to our enquires.'

'What *can* you tell us?' the reporter asked.

'The suspect is male, and connected to the family through the children's school,' Douglas said.

Whitney glanced across at the super, whose face was set hard. Why had he said that? The school would now be swamped. They needed time to work out a strategy for dealing with the fallout. Typical bloody *Dickhead*.

'Was it a teacher?'

'I have nothing more to add.'

'Chief Superintendent is it right that your wife was related to David Barker?' a reporter called out.

Douglas flashed an angry glare in Whitney's direction.

'I am not in a position to discuss anything further regarding the investigation. Thank you all for coming in.' Douglas stood down and they followed as he marched out of the room. 'Walker?'

'I have no idea how they found out, sir. It wasn't anyone from my team.'

'Well, it better not be.' He turned to the super. 'Good work in solving the case so quickly, Helen.'

'It was down to Whitney and her team.'

'Yes. Good work,' he said gruffly, before marching off down the corridor.

'Well, I suppose that's something. He doesn't normally praise anything I do,' Whitney said.

'I would like to echo his praise, Whitney. To solve the crime in under a week is excellent.'

'Thank you, ma'am.'

'There is something I'd like clearing up. I understand it was DS Chapman's error that caused Robinson to flee.'

'Yes, ma'am. I'll be making a formal report and discussing it with him, but not today. My team have worked hard and have earnt the right to celebrate.'

'Of course. That's the correction decision to make. Enjoy your celebration.'

'Before going, I'd like a quick word if you've got a minute.'

'Yes. Do we need to find somewhere quiet?'

'No, I'm happy to talk on the way back to our offices. I mentioned to you a while ago about my brother, Rob, who has a brain injury following an attack when he was in his teens.'

'Yes, a dreadful thing to have happened.'

'The attackers were never found, and at the time Rob wasn't able to assist. I now have some information and would like the case reopened.'

The super came to a halt and turned to Whitney. 'I'm not sure how appropriate it would be for you to lead an investigation like this. What information do you have?'

'Rob has remembered something which can be used. Yes, I agree that it's not appropriate for me to undertake. I had an idea that I'd like to run by you. Sebastian Clifford, the ex-DI from the Met who helped us with the Ryan Armstrong shooting, is still assisting the Met as a consultant, and I thought we could ask him to investigate. Not as part of his Met duties, but under a different contract.'

'We don't have an open-ended budget to employ consultants.'

'I understand that, but I was thinking we could employ him for say a two-week period to see what he uncovers. There is a national push for solving cold cases.'

'Yes, I'm fully aware of that. If you're convinced there's sufficient evidence for the case to be reopened, then I will sanction it. But only for two weeks. After that time, report to me.'

'Thanks, ma'am. That's great. I don't even know whether he's available, but I'll contact him to find out.'

Whitney walked on ahead and took the lift to her floor.

On the way back to her office to collect George she pulled out her phone and called Seb.

'Clifford,' he answered.

'It's Whitney Walker from Lenchester.'

'Hello, Whitney, how are you?'

'Fine, thanks. I've phoned for a favour. Well, not a favour exactly. I'd like to employ you as a consultant to look into a cold case.'

'I wasn't intending to act as a consultant for the force.'

'But you're working for the Met?'

'That's different. It's for an ex-colleague.'

'That's what I am. Look, it's only for two weeks.'

'What the case?'

'I'd rather explain in person. Can we meet up on Sunday for lunch? My treat.'

'Okay, but I'm not promising anything. I'll drive to Lenchester.'

'That's fantastic. Meet me at one o'clock at the Victoria Arms in Little Hampton.'

'Looking forward to it.'

'Me, too.' She ended the call and stared at her phone. Was she finally going to get justice for Rob?

## Chapter 39

George stood with the team beside a tall table in the Railway Tavern, the pub closest to the police station. As usual, the music had blared out from the moment they'd set foot inside. It was the epitome of the worst in modern pubs. But she couldn't leave and she'd told Whitney she'd be there for drinks. They'd already been there twenty minutes, and her friend had yet to arrive.

'Here's the guv,' Frank said.

She glanced up as Whitney approached them 'What are you all drinking?'

They gave their orders and George accompanied Whitney to the bar to help.

Once everyone had a drink, Whitney held up her glass. 'Here's to a case well solved. And no, I haven't forgotten that I owe you all a meal.'

'Except he might get away with it if he claims to be bonkers,' Frank said.

'If he's deemed unfit to be tried, then he will still be placed in a secure facility,' George said.

'It's not the same. And for the record, I think he's

perfectly sane. He managed to hold down a job as a teacher and live a perfectly normal life.'

'I'll let the psychiatrist know of your opinion,' Whitney said.

'Which they'll be holding their breath for,' Doug said.

'I'm just saying, that's all.'

'We've done our bit. The rest is up to the courts and the medical fraternity. We've done a good job … even the chief super said so.'

'Blimey, guv. That's got to be a first,' Frank said.

'My sentiments exactly. So, drink up and celebrate.' Whitney turned to George. 'I've got something to tell you.'

'Exactly what I suspected by your demeanour.'

Whitney stepped to the side and George followed.

'I've had permission from the super to ask Clifford if he'd like to look into my brother's attack.'

'Why Clifford?'

'Don't you think that's a good idea?'

'I didn't say that. I was curious.'

'No way would I be allowed to investigate myself, and so Clifford is the next best thing, and certainly better than the options at this station. It means he'll report directly to me. I can assist, even if I'm not directly involved.'

'And there's money for that? I thought budgets were stretched.'

'We're giving it two weeks. It's a cold case and solving them is flavour of the month.'

'I think it's an excellent idea. When will you ask him?'

'I already have, and we're meeting for lunch on Sunday to discuss it.'

'Has he agreed to accept the case?'

'Not yet. But I'm sure he will. I can't wait to meet him.' Whitney's eyes shone with excitement.

'Don't get your hopes up until he's made a firm decision.'

'Are you trying to ji—'

'No, I'm not,' George said, not giving Whitney time to finish.

'Good. Let's and join the others. I'm in the mood for some serious celebrating.'

∼

Whitney and George return in **Broken Screams,** book 12 in the series, when they investigate an attempted murder that's linked to a string of unsolved sexual assaults.

Tap here to buy

∼

Would you like to read about the case involving Whitney's brother Rob?

In the book **Never Too Late** Sebastian Clifford investigates. But the deeper he digs, the more secrets he uncovers, and soon he discovers that Rob's not the only one in danger. It's book 3 in the Detective Sebastian Clifford series, and can be read as a stand-alone.

Tap here to buy

# Read more about Cavendish & Walker

## DEADLY GAMES - Cavendish & Walker Book 1

### A killer is playing cat and mouse....... and winning.

DCI Whitney Walker wants to save her career. Forensic psychologist, Dr Georgina Cavendish, wants to avenge the death of her student.

Sparks fly when real world policing meets academic theory, and it's not a pretty sight.

When two more bodies are discovered, Walker and Cavendish form an uneasy alliance. But are they in time to save the next victim?

*Deadly Games* is the first book in the Cavendish and Walker crime fiction series. If you like serial killer thrillers and psychological intrigue, then you'll love Sally Rigby's page-turning book.

Pick up *Deadly Games* today to read Cavendish & Walker's first case.

## FATAL JUSTICE - Cavendish & Walker Book 2

### A vigilante's on the loose, dishing out their kind of justice...

A string of mutilated bodies sees Detective Chief Inspector Whitney Walker back in action. But when she discovers the victims have all been grooming young girls, she fears a vigilante is on the loose. And while she understands the motive, no one is above the law.

Once again, she turns to forensic psychologist, Dr Georgina Cavendish, to unravel the cryptic clues. But will they be able to save the next victim from a gruesome death?

*Fatal Justice* is the second book in the Cavendish & Walker crime fiction series. If you like your mysteries dark, and with a twist, pick up a copy of Sally Rigby's book today.

∾

**DEATH TRACK - Cavendish & Walker Book 3**

**Catch the train if you dare...**

After a teenage boy is found dead on a Lenchester train, Detective Chief Inspector Whitney Walker believes they're being targeted by the notorious Carriage Killer, who chooses a local rail network, commits four murders, and moves on.

Against her wishes, Walker's boss brings in officers from another force to help the investigation and prevent more deaths, but she's forced to defend her team against this outside interference.

Forensic psychologist, Dr Georgina Cavendish, is by her side in an attempt to bring to an end this killing spree. But how can they get into the mind of a killer who has already killed twelve times in two years without leaving a single clue behind?

For fans of Rachel Abbott, L J Ross and Angela Marsons, *Death Track* is the third in the Cavendish & Walker series. A gripping serial killer thriller that will have you hooked.

## LETHAL SECRET - Cavendish & Walker Book 4

### Someone has a secret. A secret worth killing for....

When a series of suicides, linked to the Wellness Spirit Centre, turn out to be murder, it brings together DCI Whitney Walker and forensic psychologist Dr Georgina Cavendish for another investigation. But as they delve deeper, they come across a tangle of secrets and the very real risk that the killer will strike again.

As the clock ticks down, the only way forward is to infiltrate the centre. But the outcome is disastrous, in more ways than one.

For fans of Angela Marsons, Rachel Abbott and M A Comley, *Lethal Secret* is the fourth book in the Cavendish & Walker crime fiction series.

~

## LAST BREATH - Cavendish & Walker Book 5

### Has the Lenchester Strangler returned?

When a murderer leaves a familiar pink scarf as his calling card, Detective Chief Inspector Whitney Walker is forced to dig into a cold case, not sure if she's looking for a killer or a copycat.

With a growing pile of bodies, and no clues, she turns to forensic psychologist, Dr Georgina Cavendish, despite their relationship being at an all-time low.

Can they overcome the bad blood between them to solve the

unsolvable?

For fans of Rachel Abbott, Angela Marsons and M A Comley, *Last Breath* is the fifth book in the Cavendish & Walker crime fiction series.

～

## FINAL VERDICT - Cavendish & Walker Book 6

### The judge has spoken......everyone must die.

When a killer starts murdering lawyers in a prestigious law firm, and every lead takes them to a dead end, DCI Whitney Walker finds herself grappling for a motive.

What links these deaths, and why use a lethal injection?

Alongside forensic psychologist, Dr Georgina Cavendish, they close in on the killer, while all the time trying to not let their personal lives get in the way of the investigation.

For fans of Rachel Abbott, Mark Dawson and M A Comley, Final Verdict is the sixth in the Cavendish & Walker series. A fast paced murder mystery which will keep you guessing.

～

## RITUAL DEMISE - Cavendish & Walker Book 7

### Someone is watching.... No one is safe

The once tranquil woods in a picturesque part of Lenchester have become the bloody stage to a series of ritualistic murders. With no suspects, Detective Chief Inspector Whitney Walker is once again forced to call on the services of forensic psychologist Dr Georgina Cavendish.

But this murderer isn't like any they've faced before. The murders are highly elaborate, but different in their own way and, with the clock ticking, they need to get inside the killer's head before it's too late.

For fans of Angela Marsons, Rachel Abbott and L J Ross. Ritual Demise is the seventh book in the Cavendish & Walker crime fiction series.

∾

## MORTAL REMAINS - Cavendish & Walker Book 8

### Someone's playing with fire…. There's no escape.

A serial arsonist is on the loose and as the death toll continues to mount DCI Whitney Walker calls on forensic psychologist Dr Georgina Cavendish for help.

But Lenchester isn't the only thing burning. There are monumental changes taking place within the police force and there's a chance Whitney might lose the job she loves. She has to find the killer before that happens. Before any more lives are lost.

Mortal Remains is the eighth book in the acclaimed Cavendish & Walker series. Perfect for fans of Angela Marsons, Rachel Abbott and L J Ross.

∾

## SILENT GRAVES - Cavendish & Walker Book 9

**Nothing remains buried forever...**

When the bodies of two teenage girls are discovered on a building site, DCI Whitney Walker knows she's on the hunt for a killer. The problem is the murders happened in 1980 and this is her first case with the new team. What makes it even tougher is that with budgetary restrictions in place, she only has two weeks to solve it.

Once again, she enlists the help of forensic psychologist Dr Georgina Cavendish, but as she digs deeper into the past, she uncovers hidden truths that reverberate through the decades and into the present.

Silent Graves is the ninth book in the acclaimed Cavendish & Walker series. Perfect for fans of L J Ross, J M Dalgleish and Rachel Abbott.

~

**KILL SHOT - Cavendish & Walker Book 10**

**The game is over.....there's nowhere to hide.**

When Lenchester's most famous sportsman is shot dead, DCI Whitney Walker and her team are thrown into the world of snooker.

She calls on forensic psychologist Dr Georgina Cavendish to assist, but the investigation takes them in a direction which has far-reaching, international ramifications.

Much to Whitney's annoyance, an officer from one of the Met's special squads is sent to assist.

But as everyone knows…three's a crowd.

Kill Shot is the tenth book in the acclaimed Cavendish & Walker series. Perfect for fans of Simon McCleave, J M Dalgleish, J R Ellis and Faith Martin.

~

## DARK SECRETS - Cavendish & Walker Book 11

**An uninvited guest...a deadly secret....and a terrible crime.**

When a well-loved family of five are found dead sitting around their dining table with an untouched meal in front of them, it sends shockwaves throughout the community.

Was it a murder suicide, or was someone else involved?

It's one of DCI Whitney Walker's most baffling cases, and even with the help of forensic psychologist Dr Georgina Cavendish, they struggle to find any clues or motives to help them catch the killer.

But with a community in mourning and growing pressure to get answers, Cavendish and Walker are forced to go deeper into a murderer's mind than they've ever gone before.

Dark Secrets is the eleventh book in the Cavendish & Walker series. Perfect for fans of Angela Marsons, Joy Ellis and Rachel McLean.

~

## BROKEN SCREAMS - Cavendish & Walker Book 12

**Scream all you want, no one can hear you....**

When an attempted murder is linked to a string of unsolved sexual attacks, Detective Chief Inspector Whitney Walker is incensed. All those women who still have sleepless nights because the man who terrorises their dreams is still on the loose.

Calling on forensic psychologist Dr Georgina Cavendish to help, they follow the clues and are alarmed to discover the victims all had one thing in common. Their birthdays were on the 29th February. The same date as a female officer on Whitney's team.

As the clock ticks down and they're no nearer to finding the truth, can they stop the villain before he makes sure his next victim will never scream again.

Broken Screams is the twelfth book in the acclaimed Cavendish & Walker series and is perfect for fans of Angela Marsons, Helen H Durrant and Rachel McClean.

## Other books by Sally Rigby

**WEB OF LIES: A Midlands Crime Thriller (Detective Sebastian Clifford - Book 1)**

**A trail of secrets. A dangerous discovery. A deadly turn.**

Police officer Sebastian Clifford never planned on becoming a private investigator. But when a scandal leads to the disbandment of his London based special squad, he finds himself out of a job. That is, until his cousin calls on him to investigate her husband's high-profile death, and prove that it wasn't a suicide.

Clifford's reluctant to get involved, but the more he digs, the more evidence he finds. With his ability to remember everything he's ever seen, he's the perfect person to untangle the layers of deceit.

He meets Detective Constable Bird, an underutilised detective at Market Harborough's police force, who refuses to give him access to the records he's requested unless he allows her to help with the investigation. Clifford isn't thrilled. The last time he worked as part of a team it ended his career.

But with time running out, Clifford is out of options. Together they must wade through the web of lies in the hope that they'll find the truth before it kills them.

Web of Lies is the first in the new Detective Sebastian Clifford series. Perfect for readers of Joy Ellis, Robert Galbraith and Mark Dawson.

~

**SPEAK NO EVIL: A Midlands Crime Thriller (Detective Sebastian Clifford - Book 2)**

**What happens when someone's too scared to speak?**

Ex-police officer Sebastian Clifford had decided to limit his work as a private investigator, until Detective Constable Bird, aka Birdie, asks for his help.

Twelve months ago a young girl was abandoned on the streets of Market Harborough in shocking circumstances. Since then the child has barely spoken and with the police unable to trace her identity, they've given up.

The social services team in charge of the case worry that the child has an intellectual disability but Birdie and her aunt, who's fostering the little girl, disagree and believe she's gifted and intelligent, but something bad happened and she's living in constant fear.

Clifford trusts Birdie's instinct and together they work to find out who the girl is, so she can be freed from the past. But as secrets are uncovered, the pair realise it's not just the child who's in danger.

Speak No Evil is the second in the Detective Sebastian Clifford series. Perfect for readers of Faith Martin, Matt Brolly and Joy Ellis.

~

**NEVER TOO LATE: A Midlands Crime Thriller (Detective Sebastian Clifford - Book 3)**

**A vicious attack. A dirty secret. And a chance for justice**

Ex-police officer Sebastian Clifford is quickly finding that life as a private investigator is never quiet. His doors have only been open a few weeks when DCI Whitney Walker approaches him to investigate the brutal attack that left her older brother, Rob, with irreversible brain damage.

For twenty years Rob had no memory of that night, but lately things are coming back to him, and Whitney's worried that her brother might, once again, be in danger.

Clifford knows only too well what it's like be haunted by the past, and so he agrees to help. But the deeper he digs, the more secrets he uncovers, and soon he discovers that Rob's not the only one in danger.

***Never Too Late*** is the third in the Detective Sebastian Clifford series, perfect for readers who love gripping crime fiction.

# Writing as Amanda Rigby

Sally also writes psychological thrillers as **Amanda Rigby**, in collaboration with another author.

**REMEMBER ME?: A brand new addictive psychological thriller that you won't be able to put down in 2021**

**A perfect life…**

Paul Henderson leads a normal life. A deputy headteacher at a good school, a loving relationship with girlfriend Jenna, and a baby on the way. Everything *seems* perfect.

**A shocking message…**

Until Paul receives a message from his ex-fiance Nicole. Beautiful, ambitious and fierce, Nicole is everything Jenna is not. And now it seems Nicole is back, and she has a score to settle with Paul…

**A deadly secret.**

But Paul can't understand how Nicole is back. Because he's pretty sure he killed her with his own bare hands….

Which means, someone else knows the truth about what happened that night. And they'll stop at nothing to make Paul pay…

**A brand new psychological thriller that will keep you guessing till the end! Perfect for fans of Sue Watson, Nina Manning, Shalini Boland**

## Acknowledgments

I'd like to acknowledge all those who have helped me produce this book. Thanks Emma Mitchell and Kate Noble for being fabulous editors. Thanks to both of my advanced reader teams for your continued help and support. There are too many of you to name individually, but please know that this is as much your effort as it is mine.

Thanks to Stuart Bache for another fantastic cover, you really are the best.

No acknowledgements is complete without mentioning Amanda Ashby and Christina Phillips, the best writing friends a person could ever have.

I'd like to mention my brother David, who wanted a character name after him, which is why we have David Barker.

To the rest of my family, especially Garry, Alicia, and Marcus, thanks for your continued support.

## About the Author

Sally Rigby was born in Northampton, in the UK. She has always had the travel bug, and after living in both Manchester and London, eventually moved overseas. From 2001 she has lived with her family in New Zealand, which she considers to be the most beautiful place in the world. During this time she also lived for five years in Australia.

Sally has always loved crime fiction books, films and TV programmes, and has a particular fascination with the psychology of serial killers.

Sally loves to hear from her readers, so do feel free to get in touch via her website www.sallyrigby.com